BOOK ONE OF THE RIM CONFEDERACY

Pirates

By Jim Rudnick

RUDNICK PRESS
www.jimrudnick.ca

This is purely a work of fiction. Names, characters, places and incidents are the product of the author's imagination or are used fictitiously.

Any resemblance to actual persons, living or dead, is purely coincidental.

This book may not be re-sold or given away without permission in writing from the author.

No part of this book may be reproduced, copied, or distributed in any form or by any electronic or mechanical means past, present or future.

ISBN-13: 978-0-9939410-6-1

The RIM Confederacy: Pirates

"*Tanner Scott, a RIM Confederacy Naval officer, has fought many battles against both humans and aliens. Years ago, he proved victorious against a band of aliens. His ongoing fight with his own alcoholism however remains a stalemate.*

And suddenly, Pirates have appeared out on the RIM. They have kidnapped the passengers of many craft and sold them into slavery and Scott is ordered to find them and rescue them.

But the pirates aren't acting alone. They are sponsored by a powerful Royal with ambitious plans, and she isn't about to let some Navy captain stand in the way of her mining empire. Scott must rescue the slaves while simultaneously navigating the treacherous space of interstellar politics.

If he fails, a Royal will gain more power, the entire Confederacy may unravel, and Scott's alcohol addiction will be the least of his worries..."

Pirates-CreateSpace

For my Susan...

Prologue...

From deep space, the Pirates came, each of them boarding with what could only be called glee. They had come up behind the merchant passenger ship from due aft, on the way back from the ringed planet of Eons to Juno, about four light-years off DenKoss. They had matched TachyonDrive speed with the quarry, and had used the newest weapon in their arsenal, to slow and then stop the merchant passenger ship dead in space. When they came aboard using the aft boarding port, they blasted it open with magnetic mines and stuck a force-field in the hole once they were in.

The two boarding teams split up upon entry, with one heading directly to the cargo holds on this deck. Pushing thru the corridors with sleds for hauling away their spoils, the team burned off the locks on the cargo hold and entered quickly. Inside, they took an aisle each and searched for cargo chests with the correct bills of lading, and finding the right nine containers, they began to load up the containers to move them back to their ship. One Pirate said, "Nine, right?" and got a nod in reply from the team leader who made a notation on his wrist-mounted PDA as they began to manhandle the sleds out of the bay.

The other larger team had made their

way up one deck and was moving from passenger room to room, where the passengers simply cowered and accepted the stunners that were applied to each of them and then lay like cord-wood, ready for a fire. Not a one of these Issians had bowed or called on their own God to help; the devastating depressurization made them imagine they had only seconds until they imploded. As lambs to the slaughterhouse, they fell where they trembled. Even those among them that were Adepts—humans who had the power of reading another human's mind— shrunk as they were approached and answered none of the questions that their families left unasked.

Within one passenger's quarters, a small girl hid in the cabinet in her cabin's bathroom, burrowing under the collection of personal care products and towels. As an Adept, she knew why the boarders were there; she knew they would take all on board and that her Aunt had already been stunned and lay paralyzed out on the sofa, and she knew that she too would be found and cried into the towels with anguish. Where she was going, she had never even heard of, but judging by the feel of the name in the boarder's minds, it was a place that many went and none ever left. Her cries went unanswered until the boarders entered her cabin, and then in her mind, she heard a voice snap, "Bathroom cabinet, bottom shelf." She turned to stone at the image of that mind so close to hers. She tried to inch around it in her consciousness and watched in fear as the mind turned toward her. This too was an Adept, but she quaked at the power within that mind and tried to fight it, to push back, but she was losing ground. She knew power-wise her mind was not as strong. She felt the power of the Adept Pirate, and then had to shy away, trying to burrow back and into the shelf itself. Moments later as she was dragged out into the deck hallway, she looked up at a tall woman who stood watching her, a woman dressed all in black, her robe clinging to her slim frame. This was the mind that had scared her so much, and she watched as the woman crossed off the name Roison on a list grunted in agreement, and stunned her onto the floor. In a low voice, she said, "Powerful little one ... too bad ..." and moved out into the corridor again.

In the Bridge, the captain still shouted at the comm officer to get around the jamming and let Juno know that they had been attacked. The lieutenant shouted back that he couldn't and asked if he could send out a probe ahead to Juno to let them know and was rewarded with a huge yes from the captain. Pressing the launch sequence to start, he quickly typed in the message about the attack and the facts that the Pirates had come up from due astern, had been able at a distance to somehow cause their FTL TachyonDrive to slow and then quit unexpectedly, and that they were now taking all the passengers and crew off-ship to no one knew where.

As he typed, around him the other ship's officers were passing out their meager projectile weapons and awaiting the assault on the Bridge doors. As he flipped the final switch, he knew the probe would be launched, take word back to Juno about the attack, and get the Rim Navy out and on search and rescue.

He considered the Issians for a moment; most likely as the Rim religious sect that advocated non-violence, all their passengers were giving up below without a fuss. But we're not Issians, he thought, grabbed an extra clip for his weapon, and turned to face the captain as he barked tactical orders about defending the Bridge. The cargo bay alarm still rang, and he wondered what that was all about. As he glanced over the ship deck LCD, he saw the boarders were now only two decks below the crew deck ... soon, he thought, they would be here soon.

Outside the merchant ship, some of the Pirates moved a weightless gangway between the two ships to link them via their aft boarding ports. Once linked, they killed the force-field and began to push each passenger through the walkway and into their own ship where they were all put in a cargo hold. None of the stunned passengers was able to speak or move, though they were aware of the new ship and each had to content themselves with awaiting freedom in a few hours. The black-clad Pirates worked quickly as they'd done this before and ensured that the cargo sleds moved all nine of the containers into their ship at the end of the passenger movement. They slapped up the force-field again, took back the gangway, used their Inertial Drive to move off, and then went to faster-than-light and disappeared. Gone.

On the Bridge, the captain and his small crew still wondered about the sudden departure of the Pirates and were busy buddying-up and starting out to search the ship for any passengers left behind. Everyone had their doubts that any had been missed, but still the search must go on, and they went armed in case there were any other surprises awaiting them. Only the captain and two ensigns stayed behind to re-start the TachyonDrive and to again take the heading to Juno, still six days away at full-speed FTL through the blackness to the very edge of the galaxy, returning to the Rim Confederacy.

A loose confederation of more than forty planets was the place where the detritus of the galaxy ended up ... where the inhabitants were for the most part lonely, iconoclasts or mavericks or hermits. Stellar worlds and republics, Duchies, Baronies, feudal planets and systems, and more made up the Rim Confederacy. Aliens and humans combined into one large left-out slice of the galaxy that was more than 25,000 light-years from Earth, from where man had come centuries earlier. And now at the edge of the galaxy, the Confederacy looked outward ... at nothing within reach. Deep space ... and the Rim.

Pirates-CreateSpace

Chapter One

In the XO's cabin, Tanner Scott slipped a bit on a wet spot and spilled more Scotch to join what was already on the floor. He sneered down at the smeary floor.

"You piss me off, Mr. Scotch. You're hard to hold onto and hard to come by this trip. Yessir, six days out and seventeen to go, and there's not more'n a case left. Now that's a serious problem, what?" he said to no one and swayed as he held onto the light fixture beside the bunk.

"And it was our old XO, Commander Lyons who wouldn't get me the okay for that other case either ... hope he enjoys himself in UrPoPo land." He lifted his plas-glass to drink, downed the Scotch, and toppled into the bunk. He quickly grinned at his lumbering drunken clumsiness, and he slammed the glass against the bulkhead as revenge. Bits rained down on him and stuck in his hair as he continued to slump further on the bed.

"Stupid Scotch, stupid bloody stupid ..." he swore. "And those lieutenants of mine, all five of them, bloody awful the way that they scurry out of the cabin soon's as I walk in after duty and that Lieutenant Torres, always with the scowl. I'll fix them ... I will ..." IIis eyes closed as he raised a hand to wave gloriously about the room.

As he slept it off, the frigate *Kerry* moved at regular TachyonDrive speed of approximately one light-year per day and ate up the distance between Roor and Juno, the Confederacy capital world. As he was the only lieutenant commander on board, he'd grabbed the private cabin and left his own bunk back in the lieutenants' shared quarters. At least this way, he could drink to his fill each and every hour he was off duty.

The more than eighty crew and twenty-two officers who manned this class of ship carried out the duties of a regular Navy frigate around him. The next morning, they approached the boundaries of the Barony of Neres, and the bridge duty officer, one Lieutenant Garrison looked to his comm officer.

"Anything yet, Simpson?" he said, turning to again glance at the Sensor display to his left. There, an astrophysical display showed that the *RN Kerry* moved quite close to the outer boundary of the Barony, and as yet, they'd not been challenged by the Baroness's own Navy. He looked forward again to see the main forward display that showed their motion within the fringe of the Rim and the wispy Tachyonic-affected stars and noted that as yet, even though close, they were not quite encroaching on the Baroness's domain.

"Attention: Frigate class ship, this is the *Barony Cruiser Mephisto*; please heave to," the voice said over the Ansible speaker as the ensign held out his hands.

"They found us, Lieutenant. Looks like they were here all the time," the ensign said as he nodded toward the Sensor display that now clearly showed the Barony ship dead ahead.

"Helm, heave to," Garrison said, and watched as the helm ensign, slowed the TachyonDrive and the stars jumped back out in the main forward display.

"Notify Shuttle Three that they are free to deliver." They watched the screens as the shuttle moved out and away from the frigate towards the much bigger Barony Cruiser. It hovered for a moment or two as it negotiated with the Landing Control AI and then moved into the shuttle bay on the Barony ship.

"This shouldn't take long," he said, and they all waited while Confederacy cargo and Council documents were being delivered. This was the standard method of handling the business of the Confederacy and all RIM Navy ships used the same procedures. Moments later, they watched as the shuttle reappeared, coming out of the Cruiser shuttle bay, and made its way back to their own ship. And shortly after that, the Ansible squawked again.

"Attention: RIM Navy frigate class ship,

please follow us through the Barony, and please allow synchronization of TachyonDrive speeds and headings. As the voice spoke, the comm officer nodded and sent the vectors and speeds over to the Helm, and soon after they were underway again.

Following the Barony Cruiser, the Kerry moved through the Barony in quick order, and in just three more days, they left Barony space and moved again through free space towards Juno.

To their left side, though not see able on the main forward display, lay the galaxy. A glowing mass of stars more than two billion strong with the Confederacy perched out here at the Rim. From here, you couldn't see the core, nor for that matter much of the Perseus Arm or any of the normal landmarks that humans had once had in their night sky. Here, more than 25,000 light-years from Earth, the stars were ultra-thin in number, and while still fairly close grouped, they ended just past the Confederacy in a line running from UrPoPo on the easternmost flank to Randi on the western side. A grouping of no more than a hundred stars, forty of which were members of the RIM Confederacy, jutted out like an isthmus into a black ocean. It was the final spot for humankind to come and to await whatever lay out there, and for that, the waiting would continue.

#####

In the XO's quarters, a few days later, Tanner stirred, rolling to his right, and had to catch himself from falling out of his bunk. The mere effort required to hold his weight off the floor with one shaking arm unleashed the contents of his stomach, and he retched on the floor. As a dribble dripped from his lips and then hung there not letting go. A wry smile appeared on his face, as his eyes crinkled at the corners. He knew not to shake off the spit icicle; to do so would again make his temples pound, and he didn't want to do that. He wiped the yellowish spittle with his free 'sleeve, and the grin faded as his temples throbbed anyways when he let himself go and dropped into the puddle of vomit at the side of the bunk. He waited for breath, ignoring the ugly smell and even the taste of last night's dinner again and wondered if he could drop off and back to sleep again. With a sigh, he pushed himself to his knees as he realized that he had duty in less than an hour and crawled to the head for a quick shower and shave. He hoped that his almost forty-year-old body wouldn't rebel again.

On the Bridge, he reported as always by saluting the bridge duty officer, Lieutenant Garrison and requesting takeover of command.

"Lieutenant Commander Scott requesting the Conn, Lieutenant" he said as he pushed the last of his wrinkled shirttail into his uniform pants. His eyes were about the only thing on his face that was up to par; sunken cheeks with a razor cut on the left were offset by the dripping still-wet hair that badly needed a trim. His collar insignias of rank, the gold oak leaf, were twisted, and one was in danger of falling out while his shoulder epaulet on the right side was bent almost in two. He was here to assume command of the Bridge, but as some on board had guessed already, he really wasn't capable of much more at this point in his life.

Lieutenant Garrison frowned and saluted back.

"Aye, Sir, you have the Conn. Update, Sir?" he questioned.

"Aye, Lieutenant. Go ahead," said Tanner as he poured a coffee for himself, a big double-double from the Bridge's supply brought up by stewards every so often. Turning his back to the rest of the Bridge, he popped two hangover pills into his mouth and swallowed them as he added a third sugar for luck. In a few minutes, he thought as he stirred the brown liquid, he'd pop down to quarters and have a shot or maybe two to help start his day.

"We rendezvoused with the *Barony Cruiser Mephisto* three days ago and passed over our Confederacy cargo and such. Normal it was though a bit unusual, that meeting itself ... it was like they weren't there, and then they were, Sir. Neither on the long-range sensors nor even short-range Mass sensors either. Then they just popped into view, sorta like a ghost." He nodded at Tanner, his superior, and looked around at the rest of the Bridge crew for support and they all nodded.

"Thing was, LC," piped up Thompson, the bull ensign, "we really did a quick all frequency search as we hit the coordinates, and they suddenly 'popped' up even though we had scanned that sector dead ahead and it was empty." As the bull, he was in charge of all the ensigns, and it had fallen to him often to walk Tanner back to his quarters after a night in the Officers' Mess had given them all a load. He considered himself a friend as well as a subordinate though he never let his perceived friendship interfere with neither his duties nor his respect for the rank. He shook his head once more.

"Fact is, we've got the logs here too that we printed off earlier in the shift to take a better look at too, LC. And we're still stumped—more so in that once we'd cleared Barony space, that cruiser the *Mephisto* again just disappeared. We couldn't find her at all again on either sensor at all. Again, they weren't there."

Tanner sat in the captain's chair at the center of the Bridge and sipped his coffee, savoring the extra sugar that would keep him going until the next one, food the farthest thing from his mind.

"Okay, Bull, I'll look at them later. Dismissed if there's nothing else?" he said.

"Aye, Sir." The new Bridge crew took over from those ending their shift and got squared away.

As he sipped, Tanner noted the sensor logs and listened to reports on their current position and the ETA for Juno. He handled minor problems with Engineering and asked for a diagnostic to be run on the long-range sensor array first, figuring that perhaps the missing Barony *Mephisto* might be a product of an equipment malfunction. He awaited word back from Engineering on that set of tests and got himself another coffee. And another sugar too.

The regular Ansible reports came every two hours from headquarters at Juno, and the next one came in with the URGENT bell ringing loudly. Ensign Matthews scanned the screen, jabbed the off-bell switch, and hustled the hard copy over to the Comm. He stood at attention after saluting and passing over the sheet of paper and awaited the pleasure of his superior officer.

"We don't stand on all regs, Ensign,"

Tanner said dryly as he took the proffered sheet of paper. "Dismissed and whatever you do, don't salute again." He forgot and shook his head, suddenly hating ensigns as the pulsing began again in his temples...

As he read the transmission from the Navy Comm, he was a bit perturbed. Seems a merchant class passenger ship had been attacked by Pirates about six light-years off DenKoss, en route from Eons to Juno. The Pirates had successfully boarded the ship and had kidnapped every passenger they found, as well as taking only some of the cargo. The crew had not been touched, and while a few had been stunned only, the attackers had taken their captives and left the ship before the crew could even mount a defense to the boarders. Also it was reported that the ship had not even seen the Pirates coming and that somehow the attackers were able to stop their TachyonDrive from even working.

Finishing up reading, he purposely spilled a slop of coffee down the front of his uniform shirt.

"Lieutenant," he said to the Helm, "you have the Comm while I pop down to my quarters—appears that I need a clean shirt." He sighed.

Three minutes later he was in a fresh shirt and back on the Bridge, again sitting in his chair with his now spiked coffee in hand. Two shots and then a triple added to the thermos cup and he'd be fine. For a while at least, he thought as he carefully searched the faces of the on-duty Bridge crew for any notice or raised eyebrow.

My morning coffees always include a shot or three. He grinned to himself. This is the way that a shift should always start. And always would as long as I'm on the Comm. He sipped his coffee again, swirled the sweet intoxicating brew, and then the Pirates came back to the front of his focus.

They had attacked using some new method, and he pondered this for a moment or two, thinking that the FTL TachyonDrive had been the one single scientific invention that had let man come out to the Rim. In addition, as far as he knew, no one could "make" a TachyonDrive do anything if you were not at the controls for same. This "puppeting" of another ship's controls may be a function of some other type of newest tactic by the Pirates, but he couldn't as yet determine how this was done. And as far as the Pirates not being seen before the attack, well, he knew that the merchant-class ships out here on the Rim had the worst of all possible officers available ... out here on the Rim, you took what you could find.

I should 'a joined them myself, he

thought, they'd a hired me surely, where I could even drink on the Bridge. Most likely, their own potted captain could not read their sensors was more like it. For a moment, the nagging thought that the Pirates might have suddenly popped into view just like the Barony cruiser last night zipped through his brain, but he shrugged and took a final big gulp of coffee and tossed the bulletin as he went to get more sustenance. More coffee, sweet, sugary, and edgy.

Ensign Pruitt, the helm officer announced, "Sir, we're nearing Genie; no traffic to report. Do we add on a stop on Bottle?" His tone implied he'd love to do just that.

Bottle was the fourth planet in that system and had a reputation for being a welcome spot for Navy men. The planet itself was an alien world, still only as advanced as the Bronze Age had been back on earth three millennia ago. But that didn't matter out here on the Rim. Every world was fair game for trade, and while there were only so many items that could be used from such a society, the natives here were willing to do anything to achieve superiority among their peers. Their women were tall, tanned, and all had the long-haired look of a warrior with their blue eyes, hawkish noses, ample breasts, and long, long legs. Pruitt turned towards the Comm and looked for permission.

"Not this time, Lieutenant," Tanner said, sipping his fourth coffee of the shift. "We're heading back to Juno straightaway. This is just a milk run, boys." He drained the double-double in his hand. "No reason for us to stop either. Bathroom visit, lads," he said and made to get up to refresh his liquid lunch back in quarters.

"Aye, Comm," Pruitt said, and as he turned back toward the Helm, the ship rocked violently to the left. Klaxons came on from the Mass Sensor, and the sounds of straining deck plates could be heard all in an instant.

"Status," Tanner roared as he grabbed the stanchion beside the coffee station that was now on the floor. "Captain to the Bridge— Tactical online," he shouted to the crew. His head was being split open, but he remembered his duties from long ago.

"Unknown aggressor, off port beam," Pruitt screamed back.

"Decks Four and Five took a direct energy pulse hit and now under force-field stasis—we've lost life support on those decks completely," the Ansible officer, Lieutenant Smith added.

"Sir, the captain and Lieutenant Darnell were in the gym." He didn't have to add that the gym had also been on Deck Five.

"So it's you," Lieutenant Smith added, "Sir, and the TachyonDrive is off ..." He turned back to his display.

Ahead of Tanner and to his left at Tactical, Lieutenant Price scanned his sensor displays and thumbed buttons and toggles as he spoke up.

"Shields up, at 100 percent, and we're online with all armaments, Comm. Plasma cannons are fully charged and ready, and the men are all at ready stations. Um ... looks like we've lost nine crewmen that were on four and five—their stations are unattended ..." His quiet voice gave notice of their added loss.

"Right, where'd they come from will have to wait," Tanner spoke as he dropped into the captain's chair. "Helm, spin us ninety degrees to port and put the IntertialDrive online but at rest —let's face those bastards." His voice was quiet under the strain of the moment.

"Comm, they're not showing at all in the RIM ship dBase, these guys are Pirates for sure," Lieutenant JG Anders at the Science station reported. "Their Ansible is not registered and they're jamming our own. Permission to kill klaxons, Sir?"

With the ship's Ansible jammed, the automatic sending of the URGENT bulletin back to Juno would not get through, and no one would know of the attack, Tanner thought as he nodded to the Ansible officer. Jamming their Ansible frequency can be done quite easily, he knew, but the un-jamming of it had never been done. They were without the ability to report this attack, and as such, no one would know if the Pirates won the day.

"Science, send a probe now. Fill in the spatial co-ords and let them know about the fact we didn't see 'em coming either. Send it soonest," he stated matter-of-factly, not bothering to wait the outcome of the battle.

"Tactical, add your battle display to the main forwards and let's see what we've got here, boys." In the big display on the forward bulkhead, their ship and the attacker were outlined, and beside each, a list of stats appeared. It was a frigate-class ship the same as the Kerry, and it had the same armament of two pulse cannons, one forward and one aft, and a single particle cannon as well as the forward and rear facing lasers. It looked like the Pirate ship had just recharged their forward pulse cannon and would bring down their shields to fire again soon. Tanner had awaited that chance knowing his head would not explode but knowing any single pulse cannon blast could be fatal.

"Tactical, lock onto their engines, and let's see if we can't kill her ability to move away from us for now. Await their shields down—and Helm, move us past them by at least a kilometer at their shields down instant. Let's jump and fire the aft cannon at the same time, Tactical," he commanded. It was an old navy trick that required nano-second timing but could often mean a less experienced opponent fired where you'd been and not where you were. The Tactical computer could do exactly that if handled by a Tactical Officer who knew the trick. His didn't, but Tanner did.

In a second or two, the display ahead jumped ever so slightly as the *Kerry* now appeared behind the Pirates and faced them stern to stern. The display registered the pulse cannon of the Pirate ship behind them. They had missed the *Kerry*.

"Got 'em, Sir. Their InertialDrive is offline, and they won't go to TachyonDrive without it, now will they?" he said. "Damn fine trick!" he offered up a moment later.

On the display ahead of them, the flashing red print of updated stats on the Pirate frigate showed their InertialDrive was offline and they were using thrusters to now swing to again face the *Kerry*. Their pulse cannon was again recharging, and they were targeting the Kerry's aft cannon array and moving swiftly to attack again.

"Spin her to beam, Helm, and let's see if

we can—"

The shock of the Pirates' particle cannon as it hit the *Kerry's* aft quarter shields was sudden, and the quick maneuvering by the helm officer moved them out of the particle stream as best he could. The *Kerry* took on no damage but still vibrated from their shields and the assault they had taken. Shields will hold up for a few seconds under particle assault but not for long. As the *Kerry* swung to starboard, Tanner considered his options and wondered if he could command the ship and be successful in his defense of the men. He knew in his past that he could have done so, but that was four long years ago and more than 1200 light-years distant in another man's Navy. He had known how to win tactically then, but now had him much worried. He straightened his shoulders and shook his head regardless of the hangover and got to work.

"Right, Tactical, target their Ansible array, and see if you can't cut it off with our forward laser. Ansible, try to hail them, that is, make their Ansible respond to our attempt to contact them even though their jamming us. That may get the job done," he said with some conviction, his mouth now dry and wishing for a shot, regardless of how he felt about this ploy.

As the forward display showed the laser flashing out toward the Pirate ship, the shields around her responded and glowed, but then as the Ansible called out to the Pirates, their shields flashed and the laser cut through to sheer off the Ansible array itself.

"Bingo, Comm ... we got them," Smith said, as they all watched the array drift off after being severed from the Pirates' ship.

"Good, now, Tactical, see if you can—"

Again, the *Kerry* shook as a pulse of plasma shook their shields and spun them back to port. The shields would hold against a direct hit of plasma, Tanner knew, but they declined in their strength at each pulse. Too many hits meant you lost shields and the pulses then destroyed hull plating and the decks below.

"Shields?" he inquired.

"Sixty percent still and holding," Tactical replied.

"Right, now we back up," said Tanner as the crew turned to face him. "Take us back to the initial starting point, Helm." He watched as they obeyed. No time to explain and they still had InertialDrive so they could move about the Pirates who were only on thrusters. The screen display jumped again, and they were again behind the Pirates, whose aft shields showed at forty percent. Their pulse of plasma rocked hard against the Pirates and took their shields out completely. Tanner felt the tremors starting as he winced at the display.

"Recharge and then let's take out their—"

In the display ahead, the Pirate ship suddenly disappeared, like it had suddenly gone to TachyonDrive, and they were alone again in space. They watched the screen for a moment, each of them alone in their thoughts as the sudden end to the battle meant the crisis was over. They turned to look at Tanner, their faces open and wondering.

He cleared his throat, tried to freeze out the tremors, and looked to Lieutenant Smith.

"Our Ansible back up and running," Lieutenant Smith said, and Tanner rewarded him with a nod.

"Fine, then send HQ a copy of the logs and our spatial co-ords again. We lived through this one, gentlemen, but I think that the Rim now has Pirates we can't see coming. They seemed to leave in a hurry so I suspect that they were just testing us though it cost us dearly. Tactical, stand down, and Helm, set course for Juno and engage."

"Price, you're with me," he said, got up, and went to the Bridge turbo-lift door. "I'm making you Repair Officer for now, so let's get down to Deck Five." They moved onto the turbo-lift and went down five decks, and when the door slid open, they saw the damage the opening Pirate shot had made as they floated up

29

in the weightlessness.

The plasma pulse had come from just off the beam, punching its way through the hull plating, and had eaten up almost twenty-five feet of deck. The hull was now sealed with the radiant blue glow of the force field as it kept the vacuum at bay, while around them emergency lighting showed the floating debris of the plasma hit. Pieces of decking, rivets, and bulkhead trim drifted by, and clouds of water vapor rose to the ceiling, which was the floor of Deck Six above them. No body parts at least, Tanner thought, as he carefully dragged his way through the piecemeal debris that milled about the corridor. Occasionally he gave a little push to a piece or two that got in his way as he made his way toward the torn-up floor and what was left of the port Deck Four beneath him.

"Gym was about here," Price said, noting that in fact it was gone as he pointed at where the walls had stood and the machines inside had been. Each ship in the line carried a complete gym that allowed all men, both officers and enlisted, to work out and to stay in shape.

"Gone. All gone," Tanner said, and they moved together past and as close to the edge of the hull as they could get. Careful not to touch the force-field, they peered out at the edges of the hull that were now blackened and twisted in their melted state.

"Full plasma hit, it seems," Tanner noted, and Price made more notes in his log PDA. He moved to the side to peer down at the remains of the hull below on Deck Four and nodded.

"These guys were pulling no punches," he said. "Full plasma hit and it was lucky for us it didn't go right through," he said as he turned to look down the torn-up corridor.

"So, Price ... let's get some men up here. I want immediate work done on the replacement of the hull plates—weld in what you got and seal off what you can't replace right now. Forget the life support on Four and Five, but get gravity back up and running if you can. See what kind of extra gym equipment we can find in storage, and set up a temporary gym up on Deck Seven in Cargo Bay Two. Let's get rid of that force-field soon as we can and get back underway ASAP. Now hop to it," he said, and he noted Price was copying down his orders and already beaming them to various CPOs throughout the ship. Repairs would be underway in mere minutes, and they'd be back underway soon after.

Tanner returned to the Bridge's ready room—he actually acknowledged that it belonged to the captain but he was just using it for now as he stepped over the sill.

"First things first," he said to himself as he coded in his entry to open up his own stanchion cupboard and pulled out his reserved thermos that he kept for special purposes. "And yes, this is surely one of same," he said as he pulled the lid wide open with one hand, took a swig, then another, and then still another. He swallowed the Scotch gratefully and rubbed the cool plas-bottle against his sweaty neck.

There were dead and as the current superior ranking officer, he knew it fell to him to carry on. Another pull. And then one more and he sat at the console and opened up the ship's logs. As he began to dictate in his own reports of what had happened with the Pirates, he accepted, read, and then thumb-print signed off on reports from Price as they came in.

He thought about returning to his quarters for that last full bottle of Scotch and then paused as he remembered what was still in front of him. He was now the acting captain, and for that he decided he would need to stay at least semi-sober until he saw his admiral. He closed off the logs and then realized that he would now have to write letters of condolence to each of the lost crew member's families and a special note to his captain's wife who he had met at a backyard party almost six months previously. He had gotten drunk at that social, had fallen asleep on their couch, and had crawled away early in the dawn's light to avoid embarrassment, but had always thought she would have made him feel at ease had he stayed for breakfast. He knew she would take this hard and that she should; the captain had been a good man, and his loss was truly a tragedy for her and for the Navy.

Pirates, he shook his head as he turned back to the console and began dictating his letters, his thermos at hand. Maybe later he'd go to quarters and quietly get drunk. Maybe later this might not hurt as much with a layer of Scotch over top. Maybe, he thought, as he sighed and returned to the keyboard.

Chapter Two

A block away from Navy Hall, in a bar that was quiet and dark and usually populated with silent, solitary drinkers, Tanner sat quietly too. Around him on the walls were vid screens of a home world. Obviously a Randi owned this place, Tanner thought, as the huge waterfalls that made the planet famous for tourists were everywhere. Some, he noted, were of water that was opaque and yellow while others were normal water colored. Still more were even higher, and it was no wonder that the Randi race, though humanoid, loved their views.

The nice thing about Juno, Tanner thought, was that as the RIM capital world, it was populated with many races and nationalities and that meant there was an overabundance of places to unwind. To calm ones nerves or to steel them for what was to come.

"Yes, that's it," Tanner said, "it's to make me impervious to what is to come. It's to help me face the admiral." He downed the shot and chased it with a big gulp of beer. Randi beer was beer that had a tang that he'd had nowhere else; perhaps because it was made with grown-only-on-Randi hops, the bartender had said a few visits ago.

Now, he looked at Tanner and raised an eyebrow.

Tanner nodded, held up a single finger, and watched as the free-poured double shot appeared with the chestnut-colored Randi beer. He nursed them until it was almost time to go. Downing them quickly, he slapped his card against the pay terminal built into the bar in front of him and left, swaying only once as the auto-door closed behind him and he strode off toward Navy Hall.

His boots rang out on the terrazzo floor as he marched into Navy Hall on Juno. They'd set down less than three hours ago and the *Kerry* was still swarming with repair droids doing their measuring and figuring as they worked on sending out requests for needed parts over at the Navy dry-dock. Once they were done, the Comm would move the ship over to the dock to begin repairs and that was how it should be. Most of the crew meanwhile would be debriefed and then receive shore leave while the officers would oversee repairs and take their own leaves as needed.

Tanner knew those repairs would be speedy and welcomed being back aboard the *Kerry* when she was refitted. The Navy funerals would be next, and he shook his head at that sad thought, and instead he tried to smile as he strode along, trying to ignore his sore left knee from the punishment he'd received falling in the mess hall over a table, a bit tipsy he knew, just a couple of days ago. Either that or the Scotch was getting stronger and better, he grinned to himself ruefully. Better for what though was still the question.

He moved through the soaring arched lobby and up to the elevators that would take him up to the next-to-the-top floor. Awaiting the floor, he barely noticed the other occupants except to see that their everyday uniforms made his dress grays look shoddy, and that made him a bit uncomfortable too. Adding to my problems today, he thought, as he marched out of the turbo-lift and over to the chief petty officer who was the admiral's adjutant.

"Lieutenant Commander Scott, reporting, CPO. Here to see Admiral McQueen," he reeled off quickly as she looked up at him.

Flashing him a quick smile as she studied him, she looked down then at the appointment book and ran a finger down a column.

"Right, Lieutenant Commander, here you are. You made it back okay, we see?" she said as she checked off his presence in the book.

"Took a bit of effort to get us space-worthy, Chief, but yes, we made good time all the same," he said as she pointed to the chairs opposite her desk and he sat down in front of her. She picked up the comm phone and made a quiet comment that he didn't catch and then hung up. "You can go right in, Lieutenant Commander," she said and watched as he turned and first knocked at the admiral's office door then entered.

The admiral had a large office on the corner of the building, and Tanner had to walk a bit to stand at attention before the desk and his superior officer.

"Lieutenant Commander Scott reporting, Sir," he said as he stood at attention and saluted the man seated behind the desk. The admiral stopped his reading of papers on his desk and gave a close inspection of him, Tanner noticed, before saluting back and saying, "sit and relax, Commander—and report."

Tanner did and as he spoke, the admiral's face was like it was carved out of stone as he didn't show one sign of emotion as he heard the complete story. More than eighty years old, McQueen was the model of a man in his prime, his waist narrow, his shoulders square, and his face cleanly shaved and devoid of lines or wrinkles. Nor did he ask any questions at the telling and waited until Tanner was done. He did, however, make a few notes on a desk pad and turned to them as Tanner finished with the items of repairs and that they were currently being moved to dry-dock to start repairs.

"Right, Commander. So, the old 'where are we' trick worked again, did it?" he said, as he leaned back and smiled at him. He'd been Tanner's superior for almost a dozen years or so, long before they'd both come to the Rim, and they had been together since they'd met in the Earl of Kinross' Navy. It was he that had invented this tactic, and Tanner had taken it for his own against the Pirates. And it was he who had brought Tanner to the Rim as part of repayment for saving his life. But that was more than four years ago.

"Yes, Admiral, it still worked fine. Course, they'll be ready for that next time," he cautioned and eased his left knee by sliding his foot forward a bit and tilting his body slightly to the right, mentally still cursing at the mess hall table.

"Um ... okay, Commander. I take it that the shock of this loss is something you're 'working' on overcoming. Would I be correct there, Commander?" McQueen said quietly, his eyes narrowing as he spoke.

Tanner didn't know what to say. He'd not made a slip up at all, so there was no way that the admiral would know he'd just "steeled his nerves" and that's for sure.

So Tanner just nodded at the question and said nothing.

The admiral looked at Tanner and looked at him hard, his left eyebrow askew as he often did when he studied something.

"I see that you've fulfilled all the requirements that a captain himself would have had to fulfill," he said.

"You've undertaken repairs and gotten the crew and officers organized. You've made the proper paperwork out for the new equipment, and we've already gotten ETAs on the replacement shipping and installations have been scheduled over at the port." McQueen nodded and checked the list in front of him once again.

"Moreover, as I've noted, you've also written all the letters of condolence that you should have—and you've also been good enough to be kind to Captain Richard's wife, Ramona, via your letters to her over the past days. That says a lot, Commander—quite a bit in fact," he noted and waited for Tanner to speak.

And he didn't know what to say. The admiral expected a reply but what could he say. He'd done what any Navy man would have done. But the loss of a captain was as serious as it came for any Navy man. He hung his head and shrugged ... wishing for just another Randi beer right this very minute.

"Don't know what to say, Admiral—just doing my duty, I suppose," he said and looked him straight in the eye. Which was mostly true, he thought, and he waited for whatever came next.

The admiral shrugged and nodded too.

"Me too, Commander. And a part of that duty will be to find a new captain for the *Kerry*, when she's due out of dry-dock in some weeks. However, the Cruiser Marwick comes out in only three days, and she needs a captain now. And that's you, Captain Scott. Consider this your promotion," he said as he opened up his desk drawer and tossed over the silver collar eagles.

Tanner stared at the eagles in front of him and gulped.

"But ... well that's a double-jump, Sir. Surely there must be more deserving commanders already that are due for promotion. I'm ... I'm not sure that I'm the best choice for this, I guess—"

"Nonsense, Captain. I've been banging the hatches trying to find a captain for the Marwick and you're it. Council's been leaning on me for a name, and now I need two as I've still got to find one for the *Kerry* within three weeks when she's out of dock and that's another chore that's worrisome. But you're on your way. Report to the *Marwick* in dock and take over. Here's your orders, Captain, dismissed," he said as he passed over a sealed envelope and turned back to the pile of paperwork on his desk.

As Tanner was leaving and only a few feet from the door, the admiral called out to him.

"Tanner ... nice to see you back, my boy ... continue ... and you take care." Tanner nodded at the admiral and left the office and Navy Hall on his way to dry-dock across the port.

The Baroness was furious and threw the tablet against the wall as she motioned for her EliteGuard bodyguard to leave the room.

"You idiot," she yelled at the man slouched in front of her, "do you not know that you're NOT supposed to take on the damn RIM Navy as yet?" She was vicious in her tantrum and slammed her fist down on the table between them. As the door to the ante-room closed, the bodyguard now gone, she added, "Who gave you that order? It wasn't me—and you work for me!

The man on the couch in the all black un-insigniaed uniform facing her shrugged.

"Um, no one, of course. But I thought it time to try out our latest gadget on the real powers that be out here on the Rim. Besides, we got back safe and the gadget's fine. Only our Inertials were knocked out for a time," he said and shrugged once again.

The Baroness looked at him with open disgust. He was her man, no doubt about that, but that he'd taken on the new responsibility of making tactical choices infuriated her, especially since he'd failed at destroying a Navy frigate.

"You must understand, Rhys, that it's not your job to decide what to do—that's up to me, and my money and title say so. Do you agree?" she said, staring straight at him and awaiting his answer.

He nodded.

She looked at him even more deeply and said as slowly as possible "Then you will realize that you must then await orders and not take matters into your own hands. You know what my cause is and why you must support me, not to mention that I hold your family as ransom should you ever try to betray me, Rhys. The consequences of your little action a bit ago have awaited your return. Now see what will happen if you ever try something like this again," she said as she made a few button stabs on her PDA bracelet and a video comm screen against the far wall came to life.

On the screen was a small girl, Rhys' nine-year-old daughter, who filled the screen. As the picture pulled out to take a wider view, Rhys could see that someone was holding her high above the street below; should that person let go, his daughter would fall to her death. It was a simple but sickening example of what his family would endure; he had no idea on whether this was live or recorded, and he wouldn't ask either. He nodded violently to her as if he wanted to ensure his voice would not fail him.

"I understand completely, Baroness. This will not happen again and on that you have my word." He noticed that her poised finger over another of those bracelet PDA buttons never wavered, but at least it did not stab his daughter's life out of existence.

"Yes, the word of a man who thinks he knows better, there's a comforting thought," she said as she pressed instead a different button and his daughter was brought back to safety on the roof of the building they were watching, and then the picture faded to black.

"Rhys, I believe you, but remind you that your family is your word. Now don't disappoint me again. No more attacks against the Navy until I say so."

She clasped the file from beside her on her couch and looked down at it as she read the contents of the file carefully.

"I see you were successful in getting those nine cargo containers which is important to us for sure ... would you care to know what was in them?" she asked quietly.

Rhys nodded in response ... knowing what he risked his life for might come in handy one day, he thought.

"They were the first ever of those new chemically made diamonds from Eons, via Ttseen ... seems they test almost double the natural kind on the Mohr's scale I'm told ..." She looked down at her wrist PDA and made a few pushes.

"Here, let me beam over the latest revised merchant and freighter passenger lines routes and itineraries for you. We have made our choices and they're highlighted for you. Ensure that the cargo containers off the big freighter moving to Merilda are successful for sure. No mistakes, understood?"

She looked straight at Rhys, her stare never wavering.

She beamed the information over, and moments later, Rhys stared down at his own display of various changes to normal passenger routes and times for the next few weeks on the Rim.

"I will follow orders, Baroness. And all other things the same, I take it?" His voice was quieter and his head a bit bowed as he looked over at her.

She could tell that the daughter threat had worked fine and was glad that she'd had many different scenarios recorded for both his wife and daughter before they'd been shipped off to the colony mines on ITO. Could already be dead, she thought, but that's really no consequence to me. And as long as he thinks he can save them, he'll stay in line from now on.. She raised her head to look down at him. She was the Baroness; he was merely a paid mercenary.

"Yes, Rhys ... get us at least 100 more hostages to work the mines. Get us another shipload for next week; they die far too fast mining what we need. Far too fast ..." She dismissed her head of the Pirates and leaned back against her chair.

Mining on ITO was such a chore, but now much easier as she was able to do away with much of the safety equipment that her late husband, the Baron, had to put in to mine the rare earth ores that were so lucrative for the Barony treasury.

Add in the recent seizure of those chemical diamonds which should enrich the treasury nicely and if Rhys was successful in weeks to come once again, the treasury would grow.

It's just that the damn mines on ITO were so costly.

If only Duke D'Avigdor hadn't pushed them to appease their colonists, they could have left out such onerous and costly tasks and found the new Argosenium ore that much quicker. Of course, that would have maybe meant the Duke would have courted the colony himself and tried to bring them into his own Duchy and away from the Baron who had died trying to save his precious colony, she thought, the brainless old man.

He'd begun the colony even before she'd met him and while it took a back seat to his courtship of her—which she'd really had to work at to get him interested—eventually after their marriage a few years ago, he began to pay attention again to the ITO colony and how the Duke was trying to woo them away. He knew that the then-upcoming vote at the colony's registration date would be close and had moved in the safety equipment, the sprayers and the detoxifiers, the new insulated materials for their housing, and the purifiers for their water supply as soon as he was able.

That had most likely helped win the registration and the colony's allegiance to the Barony rather than the Duchy but had proved in the long run to be not worthwhile to the colonists once the new ore had been discovered. While originally mining for Lawrencium, a vein of strange new Argosenium ore had been discovered, and even being near it proved deadly to the miners. It's location and the number two tunnel in which it lay were put off-limits to the non-hostage miners, but after some testing had been done, it was shipped back to Neres, the Barony's home world, and there undergone much more rigorous testing.

She remembered that only a dozen or so scientists had died during that period until it was discovered that the new element, named Argosenium by some mid-level scientist of hers, could be made to "adapt" the TachyonDrive magnetic candle that powered the ships all across the galaxy. By pushing her white-coated idiots, she had eventually learned that a drive unit with a special mechanical modifier made of the new material could somehow be made "invisible" as it moved along under the drive's power. And further, recently they'd been able to learn they could also control other candles that got within a light-year but only if both candles were on the same axis. Even being off by less than a degree and the Pirates who now used the newly adapted TachyonDrive units couldn't control their quarry.

Enough, she thought. Now who else to aid her in her larger quest today? She turned on her wrist PDA again.

#####

As he moved across the tarmac toward the dock, Tanner realized he'd have to see the quartermaster and stopped by quickly to order new uniforms and even an extra set of dress grays. No sense in looking like a country cousin, he thought and signed the order form and was back out in the Jeep in a few minutes. The seaman at the wheel cleared his throat and said nicely, "I hear you beat back the Pirates, Captain, well done, Sir!"

Tanner let that sit for a moment, and then puzzled, he looked at his driver. The lad was about twenty-five or so, rake-thin, and judging by the folds in his uniform shirt had seen little of space by the lack of any ribbons above his chest badging.

"Seaman, my rank is on my uniform. So how'd you know that I just made captain? Aren't I still a lieutenant commander?"

The seaman grinned. "You're the talk of the yard, Sir. You pulled some kind of trick on the Pirates and they were beat so they took off. We all heard about it, Sir, and we're all happy that they got theirs—and hopefully, they'll get lots more, Sir."

Tanner nodded. It made sense that they'd heard, looked at his exploits, and figured out his reward for same. Wouldn't have been the way I planned it, he reasoned, seeing as this is the second time I've been a captain in a Navy. As he rode along, he looked at the still uncompleted ships in the dry-dock in their partial skeletal form. There were the frigates *Henderson* and *Davies* and over there the cruiser *Carpenter*. And beside it the almost finished *Marwick*, now standing tall, her hull burnished silver. As he watched, he saw the droids who were linking up the just attached various arrays and saw the sparkle of the welder's torch from afar. Moving ever closer, he saw the flaring fins and their rippled vents and beneath them the massive landing vanes that kept her upright when on the ground. As they pulled up to the entrance boarding escalator, he motioned for the seaman to pull up short and got out to look at his new command from below.

Above him for almost 600 feet straight up she soared, and at 23,000 tons, she was as massive as she looked. Carrying 290 crew and almost sixty-five officers, she was the tenth cruiser that the Navy had commissioned, and she was almost ready to go. They had bigger, he knew—the destroyer Nugent was a full 1100 feet and had two of the immense Perseus engines. And while like Navy men everywhere, he wanted the biggest and fastest, today he just smiled as he strode now toward the boarding officer on duty at the base of the escalator. He saluted as he arrived.

"Permission to come aboard, Lieutenant," he said as his presence was noticed by the busy lieutenant who suddenly was flustered and almost dropped his PDA tablet. He threw it to his left hand and snapped a salute back as he came to attention.

"Uh, permission granted, Lieutenant Commander—er—are you the new CO, Sir?" He really was a bit at odds with the fact that while he thought the officer before him was his new captain, the man was still wearing the rank of a lieutenant commander. He couldn't seem to process that quick enough and remained rigid.

"At ease, Lieutenant. Yup, it's me, your new CO ... but I'm without uniforms yet from the quartermaster and no need to make a fuss," he said as he moved to get on the escalator's moving bottom stair. He was surprised that the lieutenant put an arm in front of him and turned back to him with a question on his face.

"Tradition, Sir, requires that we pipe the new CO on board, and that means, Sir, that we await the CPO who is on bosun duty right now ... Sir, if you please, may I ask that you await same. It's a big deal to us, Sir, and your XO demands it be done from all of us." He lowered his arm slowly, and Tanner pulled back a few steps from the moving stairs.

"Thank you, Sir, please bear with us," he said as he madly tapped on his tablet. The stair's movement ceased within a few moments as they waited and then began to move downward and toward them. Tanner looked up and saw a few men in khakis moving down toward them and moved back to allow them to get off at the bottom.

His new XO called them into line and then moved to the front rank himself while the CPO bosun stood off at a tangent.

"Sir, we welcome you aboard the cruiser *Marwick*. You can spit on the mat and call the cat a bastard!" the XO said.

"Sir, yes, Sir!" was echoed by all present except Tanner, and he grinned at the old Navy custom as the bosun piped him on board. He stepped on the lowest step as the lieutenant, who remained behind, started up the escalator again and the others paraded behind him up and into the boarding port at the base of the ship.

When inside the port, the XO pushed to the front, saluted, and then held out his hand.

"Sir, Commander Craig Templeton, your XO. Welcome aboard, Captain," he said with respect in his voice. He too had heard about the Pirate attack it seemed to Tanner and was as impressed as the admiral had been.

There were choruses of yes Sirs and way-to-go from the rest of the now crowded boarding port. The men surely would have patted him on the back if he didn't outrank them, Tanner thought. He nodded and let them quiet down.

"Thanks, Commander and the rest of you too. Just been jumped to your CO and it's still a bit new for me too. But mostly, what I want to do is to survey the ship and see how she stacks up. XO, if you could show me to my quarters and someone can arrange to move my personals over from the *Kerry*, I'd like to get to it."

The XO grinned at him.

"We're a bit ahead of you, Sir," he said. "We got word this morning about the appointment and have already moved your items to your quarters. Your steward would've most likely already stowed same, and we've received word that your new uniforms are on their way over right now. Um ... Lieutenant Greeley, take charge here, and the rest of you, as you were. If you'd follow me, Sir," he said politely and moved off and down the corridor to the left of the boarding port.

As he followed, Tanner was pleased to note the much larger size of the cruiser as compared to a frigate. He listened as the XO explained the numbering system that appeared over every hatchway or doorway and showed him how to use those digits to find his way anywhere on-board. As they moved toward the elevators at the center of the ship in its axis, they passed other crew members, seamen mostly, who kept working as the XO instructed rather than coming to attention as their new CO passed by. Once in a while, a CPO boomed it out before the XO could excuse them, and Tanner had to salute them all in return, but for the most part, they made good progress toward the elevators. Though it was only about eighty feet away, it took a good five minutes to get to the elevators with work parties, droids, and tech housings strewn in their path. But eventually they were there, and the XO called for the elevator and turned to Tanner.

"Sir, your quarters are up on Deck Twenty-nine, one below the top deck which houses the Bridge and your ready room. As well, some of the officers are located on Twenty-nine with you while others are down on Twenty-four. Crews on Twenty-eight down to Twenty-four, and mess, gym, library, and theater are all on Twenty-three. Engineering takes up the bottom ten and between Ten and Twenty are the normal cargo bays, hydroponics, life support, shuttle bays, and most of the utility areas we have. The armory takes up most of Twenty-one while armament still runs through the axis of the ship as per usual for Navy cruisers, being protected and all."

As he spoke, the XO moved within the turbo-lift and pressed twenty-nine, and as they moved up somewhat slowly, Tanner noticed the XO seemed to be waiting for questions. No need to keep him in suspense, Tanner thought.

"So, XO, is she on time to leave the docks in three days? Or are we looking at a changed ETA at this point?"

The XO fidgeted as they flew upward, seeming to pick his answers from a few he carried around inside his head.

"Don't rightly know, Sir. I believe we'll be dang close, but the Tachyon technicians are the ones who're slow—or slowest maybe. They seem to be doing a lot of testing, and while I'd love to interfere, you know you just can't do that while she's in dock. We have little that we can do 'til she's fully commissioned and that's not yet. Course, for the way they seem to be moving on their problem lists, it seems like they're slow Sir." He held his hand before the now opened door and escorted his captain out of the turbo-lift door. He pointed down to his left again, and they moved clockwise around the much shorter length corridor and stopped at a closed doorway.

"This one's yours, Captain," he said and pushed the door-pad. It opened for him by sliding back into the frame of the bulkhead. Ahead of them lay a rather large cabin, complete with at first glance a large double bunk and a complete console at a desk that had a view-port that currently showed the gray skies of Juno. As he moved within, Tanner noted there was a wall safe for documents and a few stanchion cupboards a few feet away from the desk. Against the far wall was the open doorway to the bathroom, and he crossed the space to peer inside. He saw a full shower and sink, nice full-length mirror, and a healthy selection of bath towels and toiletries.

Moving back to the center of the room, he observed that the inside bulkhead across from the view-port had a full schematic of the ship and that it flickered occasionally. He pointed and looked questioningly at his XO.

"Sir, that display is dependent on the computer AI updates that are being installed today and as such may flicker occasionally. All I know is that it's supposed to harden once they're done ... which I understand will be tomorrow. 'Til then," he said as he shrugged.

Dry-dock was certainly a daunting process, Tanner thought, and he nodded as he grinned at his XO.

"Right ... and Garnuthian pigs will fly tomorrow too. We'll see, XO, we'll see. Now I'm going to take a quick shower and await my new uniforms, and then I'll move up to the Bridge. We got stairs up one deck, XO?"

"Yes, Sir, just a few feet down the corridor. Takes you right up to the entrance to the Bridge and most likely will always be faster than the turbo-lift, Sir." He nodded as he spoke and Tanner knew that the man had been around the block a few times. Stairs were usually quicker and especially on board a cruiser, no doubt about it.

The XO excused himself after promising to see that the captain's steward would get those uniforms up and into his cabin as soon as possible as Tanner closed the door behind him.

Searching his hard-shelled case, he pulled out a bottle of Scotch and popped into the bathroom to grab a glass, and a moment later, he stared out the view window. He looked down at the dry-dock yards around him. Over there the *Carpenter* lay, her interior decks being welded as he watched from above, each droid moving along so very slowly as the seams glowed behind them still red-hot. He could also see down at ground level as there was a steady stream of materials moving out to her and empty handlers moving back for more. She still had at least three weeks left of production he'd learned, before she'd be ready to move while he only had three days to enjoy the same. The knock from his steward delivering his new uniforms was only a moment's break; he noted the freshly pressed khakis and dress grays each with the four stripes on both boards and sleeves where needed. He shooed out the steward and put them away himself and left out one pair of new khakis to change into, but before he did, he sat on his bed and got out the new silver eagles to put into the collars.

It wasn't the first time he'd done the same thing he remembered as he sat and thought back four years and 1200 light-years inward as he fingered the silver eagles...

Chapter Three

The cruiser *Gillmarten* stood to, and like the rest of the fleet under Admiral McQueen, Captain Tanner Scott awaited his orders. On the admiral's flagship, the destroyer *Keenan*, he too awaited word of the battle going on between another of the Earl's fleets led by Admiral Canton and the Franauts, the alien race that had conquered most of the Earldom's surrounding territory.

They had come from no one knew where and had moved with speed at picking off many of the smaller less technological planets. As they advanced with success after success, the Earl himself had tried to contact them to work at finding a solution that was other than full war but had been rebuffed at every turn. His ambassadors were sent back dead, his Ansible messages were ignored, and his fleets now stood ground over their furthest border, the aliens just a few light-years away. With more than forty of his own planets, the Earl knew that many would fall to these aliens if they chose to attack, but his Navy with over fifty ships of the line, including three full battleships and a host of destroyers and cruisers now faced the coming enemy, their line drawn in the sand. Or rather space.

There was no movement for almost a month, as the enemy seemed to feed on their latest conquests, three smaller worlds that had been independent at the southern borders of the Earldom. Had they accepted the offer to join the rest of the Earl's empire, they would have at this point been safe, but that was not to be. Instead, sensors showed that their planets were being razed for primary resources, water, timber, ores, and chemicals while still others showed the populations were shrinking and one could only assume they were being taken onto the almost mile-long and unknown alien mother ships, of a class that had not been seen before.

Tanner, sitting in his captain's chair, wondered even more about what kind of technology they would have that the rest of the galaxy didn't. He shrugged and pondered on that even more.

It was not even supposed that they used the same TachyonDrive that the rest of the galaxy in this quadrant used as one could not assume anything about them. Their ships were all large and moved via some other kind of IntertialDrive that made them a bit clumsy, and when they went to FTL, they just disappeared; then word was received that they had appeared somewhere else. No known FTL drive could do that, and as they seemed to want nothing to do with either humans or other races already there in the reaches of the Perseus arm, it seemed that this mystery would always be unknown.

But in the past few days, they'd moved within the boundaries of the Earldom. They'd moved right past the boundary buoys, and while for the most part all six of the ships stayed together, they did split off one ship which moved to sit above the planet Koo, a small and highly technical world that prided itself on its export of technology. The alien ship just sat there; it made no movement and just waited, as did the fifteen ships in the admiral's fleet.

As Tanner turned toward his Ansible officer, he saw the man's face contorted slowly as his hands tried to move up and toward the headphones that were cupped on his ears. He turned red so quickly that Tanner, who had gotten up and was moving toward him to help the man, almost didn't get there—and then he was there and tore the headphones off as he saw blood pouring from those ears.

"Lieutenant Morgan, flash the admiral's flagship, the Ansible frequency is under attack," he said as the lieutenant lay coughing in his arms. Morgan jumped to the Ansible console and quickly punched out the message that would now travel over light pulses instead of the subspace Ansible band that was under attack.

Around them all, they could see the effects of such a thrust as the display flickered and then went out, as it too was Ansible driven.

"Henry," he called out to the Science officer, "put up the video display from the forward cameras, and heighten the gain." This put an actual photographic display on the main forward display that they could use to orient themselves.

"Sir, incoming. The admiral gives us all 'at-wills' and only ordered us to use the flash system for all future comm activity."

Figuring that the aliens must now control the sub-space and the Ansible channels, McQueen had now undone the tether that kept all fifteen ships at bay and moved against the enemy himself. As the battleship *Keenan* moved toward the alien ship now parked in high orbit above Koo, its shields went up as Tanner could see the slight purplish glow along its edges on the display screen. He shouted at the Helm to move the *Gillmarten* off the battleship's left flank and ordered for top speed, as the distance between the battleship and them grew because of the much larger battleship's engines; Tanner knew that he'd be able to watch the admiral's six. He urged the Science officer to split their display and waited while aft pictures came online to see as well as abeam ones too.

As the fleet advanced toward the high

orbit, the alien ship began to also glow, a dull brown emanating off its shiny blue hull and the glow expanding to be a full shield around the ship.

As Tanner watched, the fleet's lead destroyer sent out its pulse cannon plasma balls, and he and everyone held their breath. He snapped his fingers over at his Tactical officer.

"Tactical, see if you can read their shields when those hit."

But the Tactical officer shook his head immediately. "Sorry, CO, but without the Ansible feeding in its stats, I'm blind except for what I see just like you."

On the front display, the arcing plasma balls moved like roman candles down, down and then simply disappeared against those dull brown screens. Nothing happened, and the shields looked as solid as ever. Tanner groaned to himself. With shields that could withstand a plasma cannon off one of their destroyers, these guys looked invincible at present. But perhaps when they opened fire, those shields would have to come down and that might offer up an opportunity for the fleet to make its mark.

As each of the smaller cruisers took up a vantage point to ring the alien ship, Tanner could see something that surprised him. From the side of the alien ship closest to him, the brown shield grew, enlarging as it did, and it wasn't until almost a full minute later that he realized the glow was just a part of the whole side of the ship that was opening up, revealing bay after bay after bay. And suddenly, there were hundreds and hundreds of smaller ships, each flying out of the fighter bays, and each looked capable of doing some damage too. Strangely shaped was his first thought and the odd looking arrays meant that they were never meant for atmospheric flight, but deep space alone.

Tanner quickly ordered his Tactical officer to turn on the automatic lasers and watched as occasionally they did cut one down, but for the most part, it was apparent that each time his cruiser dropped shields for a millisecond or two to fire, the smaller fighters were using that time to strafe his arrays and to cause as much damage as they could. They're faster, he realized.

"Tactical, is there anything we can do to prevent them from getting in and firing when our shields are down?" he queried. He knew the answer but wanted confirmation and got it with a shake of the head as the lieutenant continued to change the frequency of the timing randomly so that the fighters wouldn't be able to lock on logarithmically.

"Seems the big dog doesn't fight, so never puts down its shields, but carries in fighters to do their dirty work, knowing we too have to drop our shields to fire at them. It's a strange way to fight a battle by our standards, but if we don't fight, then it's a stalemate, and if we do, then they get through some of them," he said as the port beam camera suddenly blazed with pure blue light. Something had happened to the *Jefferson* on the admiral's other side and Tanner was sick because he then knew that the alien fighters had gotten through her shields enough to destroy the ship completely, as the blue flare slowly died off.

The admiral sent word then to retreat, and they moved back to reform the fleet 100,000 miles away. Ansibles went back on at this distance from the aliens, and Tanner had wasted no time in jumping into a shuttle and getting to the meeting the admiral had called on board the fleet's flagship destroyer. Somehow they had taken one of the alien fighters into their keeping after it flamed out over one of the destroyer's massive shuttle bay doors, and they had to move fast to tractor it when its shields were down. Now it laid before them, in the bay, a lighter blue copy of its larger mother ship.

The admiral's techies were already going over the guts of the ship, while near it the alien was sitting in a force-field cage on the deck, quite calm it appeared. As they went over to look at him, it appeared to Tanner that he looked humanoid except for the slightly myopic much angled eyes and the indented nose with three nostrils. He looked back at them and said or did nothing, as if they and he weren't even there, though his head did swivel as they walked around him. The green of the field colored what would be his skin color, but even so it looked slightly pink to them, not at all unlike the color of their own human skin though much more uniform in color. He wore simple garb, a one-piece jumpsuit that had some markings on the collar and cuffs, but it didn't seem to be a uniform, though it most probably was just that, his keepers, the marine guards had to say.

"Right," Admiral McQueen said, "this will keep, but we will get to debrief this fellow later. 'Til then, the techies are looking into their technology which does at first blush look a bit more advanced than our own—though not that far ahead. We've been able to identify so far, drive controls and mechanisms and their own Ansible controls, which as yet, we can't determine how it works, but we will. Let's meet," he said and led the way to a meeting room just off the bay. They sat around the table and fidgeted while he brought up the view-screen on the wall.

As they poured over the past battle and tendered reports about losses and gains, it appeared that they were at a stalemate that seemed to have no avenue to success. The aliens had better technology that both canceled out their Navy Ansibles and killed their operators— and not being able to be in touch with each other meant there would be no unified actions under the admiral's orders.

On top of that, as the mother ship did not lower her shields, she was never in danger of taking any hits as well. What they had been able to record, using high-speed pulse technology, was that the shields had dipped ever so slightly at each pulse. The effect of the plasma on those brown shields had looked like it was futile, but there had been a slight drain. Enough though, said the admiral, that they'd immediately sent out for two battleships, and they would be here in only three more hours. Figuring that they would co-ordinate an attack using the battleships as the wedge to drive into the alien mother ship, they listened to each of the actions as planned by the admiral and left with their own agenda and orders.

Back on board the *Gillmarten*, Tanner had outlined those orders to the Bridge crew and made sure each man knew his part and the roles the others would play too, as a contingency backup. He felt their role just might be pivotal in the attack on the mother ship, and if the Admiral had figured out what was needed, that they'd all know and be able to help.

He drank his favorite double sweet coffees and called for stewards to bring more and then more again. He fidgeted with his chair adjusting the rake and the height a few times and even barked at the crew when they didn't respond quickly enough, though he was quick to praise them when needed as well.

And then the Ansible squawked, and the battleships *Griffon* and *Hillman* arrived, and the admiral quickly got on to all of them with final battle orders. They went to meet the alien mother ship off Koo again.

While still in high-orbit, the alien mother ship had her shields on that glowed brownly in the evening sun as she lay near the terminator. Below, the alien freighters were coming and going to the planet. Empty when they went down, and filled when they came back up, Tanner thought. Wonder what they're doing on the planet, but that will have to wait.

He watched the display as the two Orion class battleships winked into existence about 100 miles away, and as they appeared, he saw that yes, they were firing their pulse plasma cannons in tandem. Bigger than the admiral's destroyer by a factor of five, and using the power of three Perseus engines, their plasma balls hit those brown shields, and even Tanner could see them dim considerably for an instant.

"Readings?" he shouted.

"Fell by twelve percent, on impact, but went back up ... only four percent. They will fail in ... eleven more dual impact hits, Sir," Lieutenant Neilson said as he leaned over his Science display. "We move in twenty-one seconds, Sir" he added as the twin plasma balls continued to arc down on the mother ship.

Tanner nodded as he watched the fighters come up from the mother ship in swarms. The battleships would be able to withstand the hits from same, he knew, due to their vast size and the relatively lower firepower that the alien fighters carried. He counted down the last few seconds and yelled "Engage" to the Helm when it was time.

Moving quickly under Inertial Drive, the *Gillmarten* drove down toward the mile-long mother ship and leveled off just as the brown shields disappeared. As they lined up for their pass at their target, automatic laser cannons on the mother ship began to fire at them, as Tanner gave the order to kill their shields. Like all the attacking forces, without their shields up, they were vulnerable, but as the admiral had surmised, once they were shield-less, the enemy couldn't find them. And he was right; as soon as the shields were down, the laser cannon turrets stopped their firing and spun hopelessly looking for a target.

Tanner grinned and congratulated the admiral under his breath. The mother ship was reacting though to her sudden loss of shields as she clumsily began to leave high-orbit and move away from the gravity well of the planet. To engage their star drive, Tanner thought.

"Stay with them, Helm," he ordered and was glad to see they lost no more than a few thousand yards of position as they clung to their target ahead.

Beside them and only a few hundred yards away, the admiral's destroyer Keenan was also shield-less and already pounding plasma at what appeared to be the Bridge of the ship, using her three forward cannons in sync. As she did, the *Gillmarten* on her port flank flew level, as the Tactical officer began to fire their own forward plasma cannon at their assigned array, the function of which they didn't understand. It took two full bombing passes, but they eventually took it down, as it exploded and twisted away into space. Tanner smiled, mission accomplished, and as they turned to starboard to look for more targets, it happened.

Unknown to them, an alien fighter had followed in their wake and had spun when they did and now surged to almost their aft port quarter. While it took a hit and it's shields dropped drastically from the admiral's destroyer *Keenan*, which was now just to starboard, the fighter immediately responded by trying to ram the *Gillmarten* from the side, to vector it into the *Keenan* herself. In an instant, they had become the missile that would pierce the admiral's flagship and destroy all on board as well as themselves.

Tanner swore as he screamed at the Helm, "Take her to port, take those bastards out!"

The Helm officer responded promptly, and the crash into the alien fighter was brief, but in space, deadly. Tanner knew the fighter was so much smaller than the *Gillmarten* so the major damage would not be as severe as they hit the smaller fighter and he heard their hull plating split.

"Kill Inertial," he barked at the Helm, as they tossed like a leaf in a storm and they glanced off the mother ship. The fighter had splintered into many pieces, with no sign of the alien pilot, and Tanner knew that might be true for them all. As they twisted over onto their back, the *Gillmarten* seemed to roll to port as well, which put them on a closing vector to the *Keenan* again, and Tanner gave the order quickly as he saw the flagship grow swiftly in the forward display.

"Blow her, Tactical. Captain's priority A-11A." He watched the officer's thumb slide down to jam the button on his console, as he already had pushed his own button on the captain's console beside him. For a moment, time seemed to stand still, and then the *Gillmarten* split apart, the forward bridge section spinning away as the decks from engineering on down went one way and the middle part of the cruiser vectored the other. As force-fields tried to spring into being, the Bridge power fluctuated and strobed for a few seconds as they twisted up and off the mother ship as it continued to move itself up and out of orbit.

Only seconds after they'd blown their ship, Tanner glanced at their life support and saw it was not operational though the force-fields would hold them out of the vacuum. As they spun, he suddenly got a view of the *Keenan* and saw his engineering section had indeed moved away from that collision, but the middle third of the *Gillmarten* must have crashed directly into the destroyer, and like a brick through a pumpkin, it damaged much as it crashed. As they spun again, Tanner and the rest of the Bridge crew saw the interior of the destroyer as it spewed out bodies and equipment; obviously it's automatic force-fields could not compensate quickly enough for this large of an impact wound, and as they turned again and the *Keenan* was more distant, they watched as she spun too, cartwheeling with the vented stream of depressurizing of the decks affected.

The huge alien mother ship disappeared. There was no notice of where they were going and where they would appear. But they had left Earldom space that much was certain.

Tanner was sick to his stomach and retched in his mouth, swallowing bile and regret. In trying to evade collision, he had caused just that to occur. He knew they would eventually be picked up after the battle, as they spun away from the now distant mother ship. As he retched onto the floor beside him, the balance of the crew was quiet. They had lived through the battle, and for them that was enough.

He would always remember this as the event that changed him; in trying to accomplish one thing, he had caused just that to occur. He suddenly wanted a drink, any drink, just a big one. And then another, and another.

This could all go away, he thought, as he knew he had to face the admiral later. And then there were all those letters to write, his first ones ever to the families and loved ones of God knows how many crew members had died today. He'd killed them; he knew that in his heart, and for that, he would forever be sorry. Even knowing that his decision was what any other captain would have done, given the same circumstances, didn't help at all. And in trying to protect the flagship, he'd caused her losses as well, good intentions notwithstanding; the deaths of many were on his hands today.

Later, when facing the admiral, he had tried to explain his actions but the Admiral knew that he had done what any of them would have done at that time and facing the same decisions. The fact that he'd made the right choice had not soothed him in the least, not even when the Admiral himself had tried to comfort him.

And much later, over a Scotch, a good, fine, aged Scotch, he noticed no ease of his guilt, but after quite a few he simply forgot. The cure for guilt he had learned lay in the application of Scotch, many, many of them, but he had the formula for relief, and he practiced it at first seldom, then occasionally, and then almost daily.

And of course, his crew noticed and eventually so did the admiral. He endured many lectures on duty and putting the past behind him and on assuaging guilt in other ways, but nothing interrupted that slide into the bottle for him.

Even when the admiral let him know he was leaving to take over the Rim Navy some 1200 light-years distant out on the Rim and wanted him to come along, he barely cared.

Somehow the admiral felt responsible for creating what he had become—the admiral's guilt perhaps over the results of the battle with the mother ship. Or not, he didn't know nor did he care. Nor did he even somehow notice the various transports out to the Rim; the almost three years on the Galaxy class passenger liner *Exerkes*, where he did try all kinds of Scotch and realized it didn't matter as they all worked to salve his guilt.

And the subsequent smaller liners that slowly worked their way outbound, each of them with another bar to sit at for a while or a room to sleep it off in, no matter. He became thinner and gaunter and never went to any of the various gyms on board all of them. He was haunted in his sleep, spinning and twisting, and as he turned, he saw the *Keenan* being hit over and over again, venting out crewmen and aliens alike. Dreams haunted him still.

When they arrived on the Rim, the *Sagittarius class O'Hara*, the smallest liner they'd been on, deposited them on Juno, and he'd slept it off in the Navy officer's barracks, snoring his welcome away. Days later, the admiral had settled in and he'd found himself ordered onto the frigate *Kerry* as a brand new lieutenant commander. The loss of two levels of rank, from captain down to lieutenant commander meant nothing to him. He knew that with someone else in charge, he'd have no worries about ever making a decision again. Happiness evaded him as did sobriety, but he could perform here on the Rim without either it seemed.

And he'd been able to cope. He had now been out here on the Rim for four years almost, and until the Pirate attack, he'd drunk enough Scotch to fill a cruiser's cargo bay. Now, four years later, he'd become the captain of a Navy ship, the *Marwick*, and with it all the responsibilities of command had come back too, and he shook off the memories of years ago.

He continued to dress each collar with its new silver eagle and put on his shirt last, noting the starch had been heavy and the pressing well done. Neat, at least, he thought and promised to look up the officer's times for the gym first thing, as he left his cabin and went up the stairs to the Bridge of his new command, his past Navy life now forgotten ... for now.

#####

"I'm telling you," Lieutenant Billy Doering said, his voice like chipped flint, "we can't lose. If we use my brother, then it's all about winning, and that's all you gotta know."

He swirled together the wet rings on the little black laminate table with his beer glass and didn't look up. Around them at all the other tables, in the ship's officer's mess, sat only two other off duty officers who quietly chatted after the end of their watches.

Lieutenant Fleen sipped his drink and then wiped his mouth with the back of his hand, the gold braid on his cuffs shining even in this dim end of watch light level.

"Win? We have to win, Billy. We were told to win, and that's how it is, plain and simple." His collar loosened and his eyes now holding a hint of a glaze after three drinks, Mel Fleen said what Billy already knew. The Baroness brooked no deviations from orders, and those orders had been very very simple ... win the Open Pro Class level at the upcoming VacJump Games. End of story.

Billy shrugged and pushed his beer glass away as he leaned forward to softly reply, the rocket whine now fading away.

"Mel, hell, I know that. Why'nt you think I don't know that? If we lose, then we're done, careers over for sure. Billy shook his head. Everyone in the Barony knew that, he thought, you either followed orders, no matter what needed to be done to do that, and excuses weren't even listened to. Everyone knew that. Billy sighed.

"And I've told you twice tonight why we gotta use my brother. I've told you that he has this ... this condition ... the reason why he's such an odd duck, and how we can use that this one time, to win that Open Class jump and to make a betting killing, which'd buy us out of the Barony Navy. The Caliphate casino won't want to pay off, but they will 'cause they must ... bets laid equals bets paid. Then we buy our way out of the Navy with this simple win and my brother. Or else we get used to never-never land out here ... with the rest of these wanna-be Navy types." He gestured around them at the other men sitting and quietly drinking.

"They're nobodies, Sam. Not like us. They will never go anywhere, pulling their duty for the Navy. Not us, Sam. If we can win, then we'll clean up. Odds against the Caliphate champ are almost 1100 to 1, and we can buy our way in if we bet big enough. And we know where to get 90,000 credits to bet with, now don't we?"

Billy straightened then and softly sipped the finish of his beer, putting the glass down exactly over the top of the wet ring on the tabletop in front of him. He looked at Mel and waited, as Mel pondered their options. They both stared out the window as droids swarmed over the merchant freighter beside them here at the Leudi Station, grappling hooks and conveyor belts swiftly moving cargo out of its holds. He wondered what kind of cargo it was and how one might boost it for a minute or two. Then he finally looked back at Mel who also turned back, his pale blue eyes looking for assurance as he licked his lips before he spoke.

"But only if we win, Billy. What makes you think you can even ask your brother to risk his life for us?" Mel tossed the dregs of his Scotch down and punched another round's order into the tabletop console. They waited quietly, while the droid brought the fresh beer and another Scotch to the table and then floated away.

"And more importantly, what makes you think that your retarded little brother can beat this Jocko, the Caliphate champ now for, what's it been, four months? Lotta vacuum there ... Your brother ever even been in a vacuum before? What's he know about it anyways?"

Billy knew Mel; they'd been friends since they'd shared a cell out on Halberd, the RIM's Max Security Prison planet. There, after three years of sitting and walking the island end to end to end to end just waiting to complete their sentences, they'd both been offered commutation of their sentences if they signed up for the Barony Navy with a mandatory five years of service. Hadn't taken a brain, Billy thought, to figure out that five years as a Navy man, even a lowly lieutenant, would be better than the rest of his twenty-year sentence for extortion on Neres itself. And Mel had agreed, and they'd signed onto the Barony cruiser *Newton* and now lay off Leudi, on a three-day turnaround from a long leg out to Far Away, more than twenty light-years out at the edge of the RIM.

Billy grinned at Mel.

"Oh yes, Mel, Junior knows what the game is, and I know how to make him the winner. You ever wonder why Junior is ... well ... like he is? What he's got that makes him so weird?"

Mel shrugged and sipped his Scotch.

"Why'n hell do I care? He's an idiot that I met once on ... Randi, wasn't it ... he's got a big head, right?"

Billy nodded.

"Yeah, Mel, he's an idiot for a reason. I went with him to most of those specialists to help and all those brain doctors and even to that big clinic on Eons with their Adept doctors, Mel. You know what he's got? It's called Proencephaly and it's 'cause when he was twelve and we had that cruiser punch the hole in our ship out in the asteroids off Ramparts, remember? I told you, anyways, the trauma caused cysts to appear in his brain ... and they had to take them out, which left him with these big sorta bulbs of just air in his head. His head is full of air, Mel ... and that makes him a winner!"

Billy sipped at his drink.

"Remember back months ago, Mel, when I went to the monthly games at the Caliphate Station, and he won his heat in the Amateur class? And remember he told me that he could have lasted minutes more or so cause of that 'pocketed' air in his head?" Billy sat back and took a swig of his beer, smiling at Sam.

"And we're gonna bet our lives on a head full of air," Mel queried as he nodded his head," is that what you want me to do?" He shook his head, but Billy knew then it was a done deal. Mel always nodded his head when he'd made a decision

"Mel, you're gonna love being rich, just you wait and see. Now let's go over the game plan one more time, okay? We pulled him then outta the Amateur class and got a bye into the Pro Class as that's the rules ... never mind no one ever had claimed for same before. We get grandfathered in! And Junior will win," Billy said, his voice now as low as could be. No sense letting any of these other Navy losers in on this, he thought. He almost smiled, as Mel ran through the details of Junior's pickup on Neria itself and how the plan was to work

Chapter Four

Four days later, after negotiating with the Port Authority on their departure and using InertialDrive to move out to past high-orbit and into the position to turn on their TachyonDrive and move toward the planet Conclusion, the *Marwick* was now space-worthy. At least, she'd been okayed by the contractors and signed off by both Tanner and the admiral eventually, he knew. The fact that their force-field generators were still not up to 100 percent nor it seemed was the turbo-lift operating at full efficiency, he still took her out only a day late, which in the larger scope of things wasn't bad, he knew from experience.

He had used the time, from early morning to late at night, to look over the installation and implementation of each and every piece of equipment supplied. He asked pointed questions and made demands that would have made any mother-in-law proud and had generally been a royal pain to the contractor and their project management people. But they had responded by upgrading some of the electronics and moving not-the-latest-model equipment out and installing the best in port. He'd blithely signed for the equipment knowing that the admiral would be presented with the bill for same but also knowing they'd be underway before the paperwork ever caught up with him.

After work had stopped for the day, he poured over the personnel files of each and every crew member on board, enlisted all the way up to officers. Each file was read, and in some cases, he checked with previous command as to items that worried him or in his opinion might cause him future concerns.

Can't work dry, he thought, as he sipped at his Scotch. His stewards had been instructed to keep his cupboard stock always at a two bottle minimum, and while he detected no sign of a raised eyebrow at all, the cupboard would never be bare. He sipped again and thought about the four crew members and only one officer replaced out of a total complement of 355 men he'd just okayed. He might have made some other choices had he had the time, and still might in the future, but for now he was ready. He sipped again, and again, savoring the smoky taste, the fired oak and the smoothness of the age.

Cruisers in the Rim Navy also carried one extra officer on the Bridge crew, an Issian Adept from Eons, who answered only to the captain and sat to his left side, between him and the Ansible officer. On the frigate *Kerry*, he'd not wanted the opportunity of getting to know one of these "mind readers" and the scuttlebutt around the yards had always been that these officers were along for the ride and occasionally had a comment to make but generally aided the ship little.

He'd been assigned a new one to the Navy, who'd never served, named Lieutenant Bram Sander, a too young twenty-two-year-old. Not right, he thought, but he quickly learned that like himself, this man had been dropped into this position as there didn't seem to be anyone else available. He had interviewed the young man and had chatted with him and yes, had tested him too. He, like most Adepts, could certainly read emotions and even could somewhat more than luckily guess on thoughts sent to him, but like all of them, their work required close distance to be of much value.

As he had thought, Tanner realized that having such an officer on the Bridge would mean little in any space confrontation, but would perhaps be of value when meeting with others on away teams. He would reserve judgment on the Adept's true value and see how the youngster made out in the field. He moved on to other pressing matters like upgrading the turbo-lift's controls or insisting the redundancy motors for the landing gear be fully diagnosed again. Being a captain in space was quite different than being one in dry-dock he soon learned and went after the tasks presented to him with a fanatic desire to outfit the Marwick as best as he was able.

Tanner left his cabin and bounded up the stairs directly onto the bridge.

"Captain on the bridge," his XO barked, and the on-duty crew threw him a quick salute.

"At ease, men ... back to your duties," Tanner said and eyed the coffee station.

As they reached high-orbit, he looked over at the Helm officer, Lieutenant Commander Bates, and inquired, "Ready in engineering, Helm?"

The Helm officer checked and then double-checked his display at his console. As he used his throat mic to speak to someone else on board, his fingers flew over the large rows of buttons and his hand then grasped the helm controls again.

"Aye, Sir. Engineering reports the candle is up and lit and ready to go," he said as he turned slightly to look at his new captain.

Tanner nodded and said quite simply, "Fine, Helm. Set course for Conclusion and engage ..." He leaned back into his chair. As he watched the forward display, he looked around at his officers on the Bridge and nodded to each of them in turn. The *Marwick* was underway for the first time.

As he again watched the main front display, he saw the few stars that shone begin to flutter as the TachyonDrive suddenly surged them ahead, and they went up to and past the speed of light in an instant. Still accelerating, well below them in engineering, the Tachyon candle stretched as the magnetos were dissipating the energy within the candle which pushed the Drive as it surrounded the ship and carried all up to the normal cruising speed of the Perseus engine that drove her. As the forward display now showed, the *Marwick* was Conclusion-bound at roughly the speed of one light-year per day and would reach their destination in another twenty-eight days.

"Helm, I want to know if anything, and I mean, anything, unexpected comes along with regards to the TachyonDrive, and you and your shift-mates are to contact me no matter what time it is or where I am on board. Make that our first standing order and post same. Tactical, for you, please have any and all CPOs or Master CPOs again contact you directly should anything else suddenly rear its ugly head. We're new, gentlemen, and this is our shakedown cruise, and I want to know about every loose screw and odd fellow that comes along. Everyone understand that too?"

They all nodded and added their "ayes," and Tanner left the bridge giving his XO, the

Tactical officer, his Conn. He popped down the stairs to his cabin and sat at his console. He had been instructed to not open his orders until they were underway, and this was the first chance at that opportunity. He quickly tore open the envelope that only listed his destination on the outside and opened up the single sheet of paper to read what the admiral had ordered him and his ship to do.

He read it quickly and realized that he'd just been charged with the duty of finding the Pirates' home world and reporting that back to the admiral. Not to attack them or to confront them in any way, but only to find them and report their whereabouts unless attacked, in which case they could defend themselves. That was somewhat unexpected, he thought, whoever was given those orders should also be charged with the duty to destroy them. This puzzled him, but the admiral seemed to have another strategy in mind, and he was just a captain.

Bigger fish to fry, he thought for a moment and then changed to go down to the gym as the officers-only time had just started. Work a sweat up and then a long shower and some food, he thought. For an instant, the desire for Scotch welled up in him, and he realized he would perhaps have to see if he could smuggle in a cup of his favorite into the gym. But he shrugged to himself and went to get his gym clothes out of the locker on the outer bulkhead, noting the slow movement and flutter of stars on their outward-bound trip to Conclusion.

Weeks later, as they came out of TachyonDrive and slid into high-orbit, Tanner suddenly remembered being here the last time, when he'd been so sotted that he hadn't even known they'd landed when he awoke.

As he dressed in fresh khakis, he remembered he had awoken and staggered around the end of his quarters noting that he had full gravity and wondered why the shipboard level was so high all of a sudden. It did take him almost an hour while he showered and slowly got dressed to realize they had already put down in the port, and the gravity that was making him feel so bad was due to that fact and not his hangover. He had taken three of those anti-hangover pills and swallowed them dry hoping they'd kick in before long and checked the console to see any standing orders and what Captain Richards might have asked from him, but there was nothing.

He had three days here for shore leave and that meant three days of Scotch anywhere on planet. He remembered he hadn't gone far and had taken a room as well at one of the port's gaudiest gambling clubs; he drank and he slept and then he drank again. Simple existence, he knew, but it worked for him. If you sat at one of those slot machines too, he knew, the girls would come around and offer free drinks. That way, he could wait until he needed a fresh one and then pump in a credit while the next girl took his order then not bother gambling again till the plas-glass was empty again. And because of whom he was, or rather what rank he was, they let him just sit there and drink the days away. Free Scotch ... could there be anything better, he wondered, knowing that was truly a redundant question.

He grinned to himself and shook his head. He wouldn't be visiting the planet like that in any way in the future. He slid back the doorway and went up to the Bridge.

"Helm, we heard from port authority as of yet?" he asked as he slid into the captain's chair.

"Aye, Sir, they're awaiting us at the bottom of the boarding ramp. Health, Customs, and our local Navy commander is also there ... and Sir, he's added a bit of a postscript. Seems that someone's doing a 'survey' of landing facilities and such and that surveyor and her 'entourage' is also there, but as an Observer, he says. No real data on that person though," Lieutenant Elliot responded and turned to face the captain.

"Fine, Helm. Send down word we'll be

right down, and Tactical, button us up from the trip. Elliot, Sander, and Greeley, you're with me.

As his away team made its way off the bridge and into the turbo-lift, Tanner wondered about things like Conclusion's weather and whether or not he'd be able to scan from a low orbit should it be necessary. He carried the authorizations for same for the local Navy commander, but did worry a bit about the possibility that the scans he might be able to take would be of any merit and if they'd help him find a lead to the Pirates.

Moving off the lift, they moved down the corridor to the boarding escalator ramp and rode down to the waiting figures below.

As captain, Tanner led the way and saw that right at the bottom of the ramp was Commander Lewis, the naval base commander, who stepped forward with the Conclusion natives standing to the side. He knew they were natives, of course, due to the large tufts of snow-white hair on each head and the furry backs of their hands too.

"Ah, Captain Scott, nice to meet you, Sir," the commander said as he saluted.

"Same, Commander," Tanner replied as he saluted back.

"Sir, if I might, this is Inspector Masson of Health and Superintendent Matthews of

Customs. They await your pleasure, Sir and—oh yes, not to forgot," he said, "This is the Right Honorable Lady St. August, who is charged with the duty of surveying all of the Rim's landing functions for the Council ... and um, her Adept officer—er—counselor, perhaps ..." he said with a degree of uncertainty as he half-turned and gestured for the young woman to join them. The Adept in black did not come forward but remained in the rear of the group facing Tanner and his away team.

The Royal walked up with a couple of short strides in her yellow jumpsuit, and with a very polite smile, she held out her hand to Tanner.

"Nice to meet you, Captain," she said, "but please disregard the Lady honors. I am simply Ms. August to all." She was obviously Royalty, Tanner knew from the title, but he wondered where she fit out here on the Rim. She was also pretty, though a bit thin with high cheekbones and an aquiline nose. Almost a full six feet or so in height, she filled out her suit nicely and looked for all intents and purposes efficient and interested in the goings on.

As he took her hand, he shook it with a bit of authority and was surprised at her firm grip back.

"Nice to meet you, my Lady," he replied using the title as was needed. "And if we can assist you in any way ..." he said almost dismissively as he half-turned back to the commander. Her survey was obviously a "make-work" project for a council sycophant, and he had no time for that on this mission. As he turned away to again face the commander, she added the following with an ironic tone in her voice.

"Yes, thank you so much, Captain, I may take you up on that kind offer." As she backed up and out of the circle, he noted that her cheeks were flushed and that her jaw was set. Too bad, so sad, he thought as he began to again chat with the commander and let his lieutenants take care of checking in with the port authorities and the necessary items to log them into Conclusion.

Her Adept companion, dressed as usual for all Adepts, who were not in a uniform, in their black robe, was a middle-aged woman of about forty or so, Tanner judged, whose eyes were locked on Tanner's. She gave no outward indication that anyone else was even present as she continued to stare at him while the Lady St. August marched back to stand at her side.

Later that afternoon, with all the paperwork taken care of and a courtesy visit over to the naval base with the commander,

Tanner found himself alone and eager to begin looking for the Pirates. Holding back planetary scans as a collateral thrust, he remembered a favorite club that was not too far from the port and took a robo-cab over there. Sliding his card in and then out of the cab at his destination, he strode up the walkway and into the gaudy looking building. In the lobby, he was scanned for weapons, but he had come down unarmed though as a Navy officer he was allowed to wear a sidearm if he preferred. He moved through the lobby quickly and into the main floor of the club and looked around as he ambled to the bar. Sitting on a very comfortable stool as he remembered, he twisted and looked out on the floor at gambling table after table. Closest were the craps tables with the whoopers and hollerers, and they ringed the roulette, blackjack, and keno players that generally were a little more reserved. Of course, a big win on any table meant that someone surely shouted out their glee, and he realized that only the losers were truly quiet. But they're all losers, he remembered, which brought him a smile.

As the robo-bartender asked what he preferred to drink, he did have a momentary bit of confusion. The planet was known to have the best of the best when it came to recreational drugs and liquors, yet for him there was one drink that he ordered time and time again,

Scotch.

Scotch made on any planet with any water and peat and smoke and oak ... they all tasted the same—wonderful! Soft with hints of smoke from the peat and sea-spray from the ocean and the grains that were picked it seemed by hand to make a blend that was the same. No matter neither the year nor the age, if you fell in love with a brand of Scotch, it was the same on any planet on any of the arms of the galaxy. His own favorite was Black made inward and imported by the Leudies; it was a blend that was always at least twelve years old from heavily charred oak barrels, and whenever possible, that was what he ordered.

So he ordered a double Black, water on the side, and was served quickly and without flourish. Just Scotch ... yes, the bartender had done fine, and he sipped as he watched the action out on the floor.

Over on one of the closest crap tables, a Ttseen was throwing the dice and winning it appeared. He howled up at the high ceiling each time the box man cried, "We have a winner!" As always, Tanner was reminded of a breed of dog long extinct, the boxer. Ttseens looked just like a boxer standing on its hind feet, about five feet tall with the same whiskers jutting out from its muzzle. Around the Ttseen were a dozen or so other bettors, all raking in chips as they won

too. One of the loudest was a Leudi that was
blue in color as they all were but flushed and
panting as he threw his arm up high and called
for more "sevens!" Around his neck, his coiled
neck snake raised its head and arched up over
top of its connected host. Wonder what'd
happen when the boxer no longer is winning,
Tanner thought, sucking the dregs of the Scotch
out of his glass. Good gosh, there's a group of
weirdos out here on the RIM for sure, and he
turned back to the bar.

As he called and swiped for a refill, he
was a bit surprised at how part of the solution
to his problem was presented to him, as well as
furthering the problem itself.

From his left side, and further into the
club itself, an obvious loser, another Leudi, was
struggling within the arms of the robo-bouncer
who had him firmly clasped and was dragging
him out of the club. No snake to see, Tanner
saw. Figures.

"Stupid," the male Leudi cried, "the
dealer was stupid and should have never
listened to me. I didn't want a card, I really
didn't. Look at me," he said as his shoes left
furrows in the carpet as he was dragged
inexorably toward the door. "I don't look like
someone any dealer should listen to—" He
continued to struggle and shout as he left the
area on his way to the door and outside.

The thought that came to Tanner was the man's last comment that he didn't look like someone who should be listened to, and he applied that to his mission and drew a breath.

Anyone on Conclusion who knew about Pirates, where they were or how to contact them —anything at all, would take one look at him, a Navy captain, or any of his men and clam up. The Navy was the opponent and as such would be privy to no data on the Pirates—not one iota.

He pondered on that for a moment and realized that basically this was true. He'd get not even a notion of any hint about them as long as he was Navy. He pondered that for a full half-hour before the answer to that presented itself, in person.

"Captain, Sir," said the voice from his right.

Tanner turned and gazed at Lieutenant Sander, his Adept officer.

"Yes, Lieutenant, what can I do for you?" he said as he peered at the young man beside him. His face still looked like it'd never been shaved with a wisp of hair at the chin, and his height as an Issian was somewhat short as he was eye-to-eye with his Captain perched on the stool.

"Sir, may I join you for a moment, and speak freely?" the Lieutenant asked.

"Surely," Tanner said, "sit down right

here." He twisted around to face the stool
beside him.

The Adept sat and cleared his throat.

"Sir ... I think that ... well, freely, Sir?" he
queried once more.

"Speak up, Lieutenant, as freely as you
want," Tanner replied and leaned toward the
young man. He put down the glass and sipped
the water that came with his Scotch for a
moment and then leaned even closer, trying to
create a small, intimate area that the Adept
would perhaps feel comfortable enough to
speak in.

"Um ... well, Sir, it appears like you've
just spent some time here and you still sit. Did
we come twenty-eight light-years to drink
Scotch?" His tone was pointed but Tanner could
see he was going somewhere with this line of
talk.

"Or, did you just realize that the method
in which you accomplish our mission will be
very much a part of the solution itself." He
smiled, and Tanner could see that he had just
opened up to his captain. That took a degree of
trust, he thought and took a moment to
compose his answer.

"The thing is, Lieutenant Sander," he
said as he was nodded to, "is that I have, yes,
just thought out that to uncover the tracks of
our quarry, so to speak, that as a Navy man that

may be impossible. And as yet, I don't have an answer for that problem, but have thought that an opportunity might present itself either to a non-Navy man, or to one that is obviously not acting like a Navy man. This is where I am right now. Your opinion, please?" he asked, thinking that as an Adept he'd maybe known this all along.

Sander nodded at his captain, as if to agree with him.

"I understand that, and yes, I too do see that there is a bit of a problem that lies ahead in your thinking. After all, soon as someone sees me coming with those little ringed planets in my collar, they begin to recite nursery rhymes to try to wall off their thoughts. And while that does work for a time, eventually whatever is lurking there will surface and we can generally see what's being hidden. So they run away quickly. As you know for an Issian adept, closeness is necessary for better success. And as a captain, with your rank in the way, even though you know every itinerary and port-of-call for every ship of the line and all the merchant lines here on the Rim, you too are someone that no one with any knowledge will ever talk to—unless ..." he stated and stopped talking.

Tanner sat still and then nodded.

"I see things much as you do, Sander,

and wonder what answer you've come up with—
you already know mine. For someone to talk to
me, they'll have to feel that they can get
information out of me. They'd need to feel that
they can 'play' me and take advantage of me and
gain in any exchange. Therefore ..."

"You have to be 'playable,' Captain. And
that means what?"

Tanner picked up his Scotch again and
took a long draw on the glass, slurping up the
sweetness down at the bottom. He felt as
though there was no way around this and
sighed as he tapped the bar for the robo-
bartender.

"Um ... 'nother double Black Scotch for
me, and for you, Sander?" he inquired and
turned to look at his Adept. Sander smiled, gave
the bartender his order for a vodka tonic and
don't forget the chunk of avocado either, and
leaned back.

"Captain, if it matters, we'll be fine. As
you know, alcohol doesn't affect my abilities at
all, and I'll look out for us. All I need you to do
is to change these for me." He held out new
collar insignias, the bar of a plain lieutenant,
and put the ringed planets in his shirt pocket
and buttoned them up until tomorrow.

"Right, Captain, now I'm plain
Lieutenant Sander." He smiled as he picked up
his drink and downed half in one gulp. And he

smiled again.

The next seven hours were a blur to Tanner, but his body had not forgotten how to handle the Scotch. He and Sander moved away from the club and over to a local brothel for a while and drank heavily there, enjoying the company of women from many of the worlds of the RIM. One female from DenKoss—if you could believe that—took a real shine to the lieutenant and wanted him to swim with her. The lieutenant was having none of that, but it did make Tanner have a fit of laughing so hard, he spasmed into a coughing spree that almost made him pass out, but not quite.

They asked for further locations to visit and received many recommendations and tried to infer that they wanted something a little "out of the ordinary." They ended up at a Jael fight out under the docks near an inlet of the local red-colored sea and watched with delight as two large, bear-shaped alien creatures charged and bit and clawed each other until the contest was done. Sander even made 500 C$ on wagering, as he was able to tell which animal didn't get the drugs to slow them down from the house bookmaker but couldn't mention that to Tanner as they were in crowds, and he'd liked the dull red one instead of the pink winner. Once that event was over, they didn't stick around for the man versus gorilla duel but instead robo-taxied it back to the port city and its string of night life. Two hours later, they were throwing dice at the strip's biggest casino and it was almost time to head back to the ship, as Tanner now had a bit of trouble standing up straight yet gripped the Scotch in his hand firmly. As he leaned on Sander and they wobbled out to the front of the casino and couldn't find a cab, they began to walk back toward the central square and in the direction for the port and the *Marwick*.

As they walked toward the square, they passed many fine-looking apartment buildings and condominiums and made some other sidewalk travelers take to the gutter to go around them. Tanner sang and Sander kept off-key harmony, playacting at being drunk but quite aware of those around him. He'd acted all night and now on the way home, he'd about fulfilled his duty.

As they came even with the corner and turned to the left to enter the square itself, a group of people just ahead were milling around a lineup of robo-taxis.

"Woohoo, Sander ... grab one o' thems..."

Tanner was able to whoop and slur at the same time by this point in the evening and then belched loudly as well. He pushed them past the waiting people in evening dress and bumped into several as Sander tried to keep them from knocking anyone over.

The crowd had come from the Embassy of the Barony of Neres; some kind of late evening event had ended and brought them all out onto the street at once to find their way home. The Barony was, of course, a charter member of the Council, and the Baroness herself sat on the council after taking over for her husband who had died a few months back. Certainly not the type of people to offend, and as Sander manipulated the now drunken captain to the head of the line, he blanched slightly and wished he could be anywhere else.

"Well, Captain, I see that you've been partaking of some of our city's finest night spots," Lady Helena St. August said meticulously, "and with a junior officer too. How nice your reputation precedes you ..." Her voice dripped with sarcasm.

She looked down on the two of them as Sander attempted to stuff the captain into the taxi seat at the back, but was being fought by him all the way. Her Adept stood at her side; the helping of their guests into the cabs had stopped, and she too stared at the two Navy officers.

"You are mistaken, my Lally," Tanner slurred again and tried to correct himself "Lardy ... my Lardy. We were out on a mission ... a berry serious ..." He fell into the back seat as Sander had arranged his rear and then kicked out his supporting foot. As he fell, he continued to try to say the word Lady and Sander slammed the rear door.

"I apologize for him, my Lady," he proffered and added, "and I am sure he will offer his own apologies in the morning. Good night all," he said and slid into the front seat and quickly gave directions to the taxi that zoomed off moments later. Behind the now leaving cab, the group slowly began once again to say their good nights to the Lady St. August, and slowly the row of cabs shrunk as the evening's festivities were over. Lady St. August and her Adept saw the last robo-cab off, and turned to re-enter the Barony Embassy, as the street emptied.

Closing in on the city's landing pad, Sander thought there'd be one heck of a hangover coming tomorrow, and he was glad he'd been able to help on this, and he'd actually picked up a bit of a hint that could help, but he awaited speaking to the captain in the morning before he'd really know if they'd learned anything that night. He sighed and watched the form of the *Marwick* as it grew as they got closer and somehow felt a part of the crew, a good part, and he leaned back to enjoy the final minutes of the taxi ride.

#####

The next morning came too soon for
Tanner as he struggled to find first his arm to
lean on and then his feet to stand. "Been here,
done this before," he said to himself as he found
his way to the shower and put it on cold only. As
the shock hit him, his head felt like it opened up
on its own and bit itself off just below the ears.
He left the shower and went across the now
slippery floor to the cabinet, found his bottle of
anti-hangover pills, swallowed a handful, and
went back into the shower. Swallowing
mouthful after mouthful of pills, the pounding
coldness of the water helped him get through
until the pills kicked in ten minutes later and
the hangover disappeared. He knew it was gone
like he'd always known, and he turned the water
quickly to almost hot and relaxed in the
refreshing spray. He killed the shower, hit the
dry button, and enjoyed very much the warming
direct zephyrs that dried him in minutes. His
mind returned to his escapade last night, but he
again tossed those thoughts out of his
consciousness and continued to enjoy the
breeze. Later when dry, he dressed himself and
then went to his console. Fingering the call
button, he requested that Lieutenant Sander
join him in his quarters and sat quietly awaiting
the lieutenant while refusing to think about
what he had done. When the door chimed, he
called out enter and the door slid open to admit

the Adept, who came to the desk and stood at attention.

"Sir, Lieutenant Sander reporting as ordered, Sir." His back was straight and Tanner saw that the ringed planets had been replaced in his collars. Looks like last night didn't even affect him, and judging by what he did remember, he doubted that it had.

"At ease, Lieutenant. Speak freely, please and fill me in on our romp last night. Did we accomplish anything other than my learning that I should always take the counsel of an Adept when it comes to betting on a livestock fight?" He spoke plainly and was interested in learning if they'd actually aided the mission.

Sander cleared his throat and nodded.

"Sure, Captain, we had a good time, and yes, next time—if there is ever a next time, bet with me and not against me. But as to what we accomplished, I know of only one thing for sure." He had a bit of an ironic look on his face, and Tanner wondered what that might be. He looked expectantly at his lieutenant and awaited the word on just that item.

"Sir, do you remember at the end of the night, when we tried to find a taxi back to the ship? Do you remember bumping into the Lady St. August again?" He offered up a small smile, knowing that the captain was not going to be happy with his tale as he could already see the captain had no memory of meeting her again last night.

"No, Sander, no memory at all of seeing her. I take it that was not a good thing, right?" Tanner looked a bit worried, but on the whole, the Council was political, and he was a Navy man who couldn't care less about their politics and intrigue.

"Sir, yes, we did meet outside the Barony Embassy. It appears that she is the daughter of the late Baron and step-daughter to the Baroness herself. And we did not impress her at all, Sir. In fact, she even stated that your 'reputation had preceded itself' as we even took a taxi right out from in front of her too."

Tanner cleared his throat and then raised his eyebrows a couple of times as he made himself try to feel better about this considering that as a captain he had a much larger profile to the Council and was worried if this might affect the admiral a touch. But then he shrugged and spoke quietly.

"Spilled milk, Sander. Anything else happen last night that is good news?" he inquired as his eyes again found the ringed planets in the lieutenant's collar.

"Um ... don't know, Sir, actually ... but perhaps. But it's not as plain as you might think, and it actually poses a new problem for the mission too."

"Well, out with it, Sander, let's both noodle this around," he said, staring now at the younger man who stood before him.

"Sir, at the Jael fights under the docks, you were pretty pie-eyed by then. We leaned up against the railings on the first level and I went —remember—to make our bets and I left you alone. When I came back, and only for an instant, I heard someone, like an Adept hears a stray thought, think something like the phrase 'can't see this guy ever beating Rhys' and then the image of ITO came into that mind. By then I'd moved around two guys arguing over the color of a Jael and how they use that in the wild, and I was trying to find out whom around you thought that, but there was so much traffic then trying to go around you and down into the stairwell I just couldn't figure out who it was."

Tanner, for a moment, stared at Sander and thought to himself about what that could mean and what kind of a lead ITO might be. And as far as he knew, he knew no one named Rhys. But he'd plug that into the Navy dBase later and do a search on that name then. For now, he suddenly realized what Sander had meant when he'd mentioned the new problem.

"ITO," he said. "That's a mining colony that just registered in favor of the Barony, so it's under the Baroness's control—and I just stole her daughter's taxi. Umm ..." he ended, knowing he now had a problem.

Something like that wasn't a good thing to do before you want to ask permission from them to visit the colony. The rules on colony visits were Navy rules, but still he had to abide by them. Until the registration for a new colony was at least one year old, the Confederacy provided that only the sponsor to the colony could visit same and they were charged with all duties for police action and more. That kept out the opportunists and the ones who were out for a quick buck in moving into a new colony and taking the colonists for everything they had. And if Tanner remembered, the colony still had almost five months left until it would accept touch-downs from anyone, Navy included. Until then it was sponsor or the Barony only.

"Right, Captain. We need to follow up this lead with a trip to a place we can't visit, well at least not without permission from the Baroness herself. He smiled at the captain and looked like the cat that swallowed the canary for a moment.

"But Sir, when we get to Neres, I can certainly delve as only I can and see what the Baroness herself might know—and that'd be a good thing, yes, Sir?"

"Most likely, Sander. Thank you. Dismissed," he said and watched Sander salute and then leave his cabin.

Moving to the large view-port that now overlooked the tarmac and the various ship, that were down there, he glanced at the Skoggian frigate Remembrance as she slowly rose on her InertialDrive moving slowly up and up until he couldn't see her anymore. Bound for somewhere, he thought as he now contemplated somehow being able to set down on ITO and what he might find there. As a home for the Pirates, he somehow doubted that, but he knew they would be somewhere here on the Rim, and that was as good a place as any to make his next port-of-call if he could arrange to set down. And that would be up to the Baroness herself. Royalty, he thought and winced, and politics all rolled up into one. Damn, give him a Navy ship to run without the bother of those two and a case of Scotch, and he could be happy until the end of his days.

He smiled and watched more loading going on over on the merchant passenger ship Cunningham as cargo was run up the conveyor and passengers walked toward the ramp to board. Over on the far side of the landing field lay the Barony Navy ships, the cruiser *Newton*, the frigate *Sterling*, and the cruiser *Whitney*, all being chandlered as he watched. Lines of automated conveyors moved stores of food and materials into the ship as he watched.

Yes, Neres was next, and that should be

better than the last time he'd been there.

#####

On ITO there was still only one town of
any size, and in it, most of the citizens of
Emmanuel were employed by the mines upon
which the success of the colony existed. The
small town held only 14,000 colonists, and of
them only a few hundred or so were kept away
from all others in the walled-in mine area just a
dozen or so miles outside of town in the
mountainous region to the north. The one thing
that these separate hostages had in common
was that they were the kidnapped ex-passengers
of various commercial, freighter, or merchant
liners who owed their current existence to the
Pirates and to the anonymous guards that
oversaw everything they did, morning to night.

Led down to various levels of the mine
daily by those guards, they were the ones that
actually mined. With drills and pick-axes, they
mined the ore, its purple-colored vein plainly
visible even in the low light surroundings of
their guarded separate shaft. Each of them
mined; the men doing the harder physical
digging and drilling while women and children
filled the ore carts called goats and pushed the
carts back down tunnel number two to the level
terminal where still others moved the ore and
rocks into the lift carts bound for the surface.

It was hot, humid, and dirty work, like swimming in hot mud, as each of the kidnapped miners fought with their environment to barely survive. And not all did. Some fell at their posts and were resuscitated by friends and family as quickly as possible so that a roaming guard would not find any fallen. To be found by the guards in that state meant a quick trip up and to never be seen again; they all knew that perhaps the only way out of this was to mine the ore and to survive, perhaps.

Choking billows of dust often drifted throughout the tunnel around them as they worked in their drudgery, slogging the full carts one way and the empty ones back in their place. Food was not provided until work was done and they left the mines and returned to their own separate walled compound, and while it was plentiful, it was plain and barely nourishment for one and all. After cleaning up, each was to be locked up overnight in their barracks, and no one even thought about escape as it was plainly visible to all that the guards would simply kill anyone who even thought about getting out.

Roison and her aunt were hostages who were also Adepts, and while they'd only been there a few weeks, already she'd learned to turn off her mind when confronted by a guard. Once one of her crew mates had tried to ask her what she could "see" and what was planned for them all, but that young boy had been grabbed by two guards and beaten before Roison could even try to find the answer from those around her. Adepts can see but she knew the time and the place to try, and so far, both had not presented themselves to her with enough security to escape any backlash. She waited for her chance ... it would come she knew ... but not soon ...

Leaving high orbit, the Baronial frigate, the *Sterling* with it's Royal Crest glowing prominently on the bridge nacelle, moved off DenKoss and pushed out of the planet's gravity well to begin the TachyonDrive to jump to Elbo. While on board, Lady St. August seldom ever went to the Bridge and today was no exception, as she was in the gym on Deck Eighteen when the klaxon sounded warning the shipboard inhabitants of the imminent jump to FTL.

"Damn," she said, stepping off the treadmill onto the side supports and mopping her brow with a quick toweling off. She stood still while beneath her the track continued to move at her nine miles per hour rate, and she looked around to see who else might have been present. No one, she thought, not another soul here in the gym except for her two constant companions her Barony EliteGuards in their black and china blue booted uniforms. I wonder if everyone else knows that I usually come here to the gym soon as we embark, and they stay away from me because of who I am? Or are they all busy with shipboard duties? She shook her head ... not important enough to waste time on. There were other more important—

As the TachyonDrive candle kicked in, she felt the momentary feeling of falling and then that feeling disappeared. They were at FTL and she smiled as she stepped back onto the treadmill and quickly accelerated as she got back up to her normal workout speed, the sweat already dripping down her china blue leotard, making it two-toned. She ran for the full half-hour and worked hard after that routine on the free weights and the isometric leg lifts, and then she was done.

As she once again toweled off and wrapped herself in her robe, she left the gym and moved off to the turbo-lift to rise four decks to the Royal's stateroom which she claimed as usual on this ship. I could, she thought, use any of the Barony cruisers as my right, but the Sterling seemed to "fit" her sense of what she wanted, at least at this point. Not that a frigate was beneath her, but she had been told —"TOLD," she said to herself, "that she would only ever be able to use a Barony frigate and not one of the two Barony destroyers." The destroyers like the *Compass* that the Baroness reserved for only her use, with their bigger quarters, better gym, and where she could have brought her own kitchen staff instead of just her personal chef and a couple of cooks. A breath escaped her and she pursed her lips, but her bodyguards also in the lift paid carefully no attention to anything as a matter of course. That was their role, to totally ignore her and anything she did, but to protect her at all times in all situations at all costs. Which she noted was a good thing as her face darkened then for a moment as she thought about her step-mother, the Baroness, who had taken over the Barony after her father's death.

"Damn her," she said to herself and almost stamped her foot, her bodyguards still looking straight ahead, noting nothing. That woman, she thought, was not even Royalty ... not now and not ever. She swept out of the opening lift door and walked counterclockwise to her stateroom door, pausing only long enough to let the auto-door acknowledge her ID via the ship's AI and into her rooms, as the bodyguards took up their duty positions on either side of the doorway that was now closed.

It was almost an hour later after a shower and drying session that the door chimed, and Lady Helena admitted her Adept, Gillian, her veil and hood dropped in this environment, glided in to stand in front of her.

She searched the face of the Issian and wondered about her life, the life of an Adept and how it progressed from childhood with those strange thoughts that must come to adulthood and knowing what will happen to yourself and to others too. Must be quite a thing, she acknowledged to herself and must be even more interesting to the parents too as those powers developed. She shrugged; wouldn't happen to her, she knew, and children were still a long way off ... and she sighed.

"Gillian, yes, you asked to see me?" she said to the black-robed woman in front of her. Gillian's face pursed as her lips drew tighter, and she seemed to gather her thoughts ... and then spoke slowly and succinctly, her tone almost apologetic to her Lady.

"Mistress, I come to you tonight, to speak of a change that is coming, to you and to the Barony and RIM. And this change, Mistress, will not be a controllable one, but one that we can help you to play a major role in enabling its success," she finished up quietly. Her head nodded a few times, Helena noted, and she waited for word back, but Helena said nothing. More to learn here, she knew, and as her father's daughter, she knew that listening was always a great strategy when faced with news. So she waited.

The Adept swayed from one leg to

another, as she too awaited something back from her Lady, and while her eyes never left the blue eyes of Helena, she was uncomfortable it appeared to Helena as she stood there, still swaying.

Helena gestured her to sit off to the side in a tub chair, and her Adept did so quickly and then stared once again at her. And she stared while Helena did the same, until she couldn't wait anymore.

"And just what do you want me to say, Gillian," she said quietly as she continued to look directly at her. She knew there was more coming from Gillian, and she knew that just from the severity of this initial discussion that something was going to take some real hard thought.

"And what role might that be, Gillian," she said putting just the tiniest bit of steel into her voice. She was the next in line to the Barony; she was the progeny of the second Baron of Neres, and as such, the rightful ruler of that nine-planet Barony and no interloper would ever—

"Mistress, please ... understand me that I come on Issian command, from the Grand Master Adept, with news and a request to you ... not to order you, Mistress, to do or to help, but to ask that you aid us to gain back our recent hostages taken by the Pirates just a few months ago. Please, Mistress, may I explain?" the Adept said plaintively.

Helena nodded and waited. Here it comes.

"Mistress, we know via our Adepts all over the RIM that there will be a way to defeat the Pirates that involves you, if you allow this, and one Captain Tanner Scott of the RIM Navy, whom if you remember, we met back on Conclusion—"

"Remember, I do! Do you not remember, Gillian?" Helena said stridently, almost barking at her. "We met him when those damn prissy Navy men landed and then later that night when they showed up drunk and took one of our robo-cabs as our guests were leaving after the banquet in honor of the Ambassador of Leudi! He was rude and he was drunk, and he cannot even help himself let alone help get back the Pirates' hostages. I can not believe that you —even an Adept—could council such an idea! This is impossible, Gillian ... this cannot be any kind of a workable idea ..." she said as her anger waned a bit and she quieted but continued to shake her head at her Adept.

"Mistress, please let me explain," Gillian said quickly, and she pressed on with the tale, stopping often to provide a degree of explanation when needed, but pressing on nonetheless. The whole discussion took more than an hour and was oft interrupted with a rant of anger from Helena, but eventually, she was left with nothing to disagree to ... and that perhaps was the worst part.

"Gillian, I am sure that this is supposed to work, and yes, you've explained it as well as can be hoped for, but your whole plan hinges on this drunk Navy captain. And that, I'm afraid, will be the downfall of this plan ... you mark my words," Helena said, and she stood to end the talk.

Gillian also stood, smiled at her Lady, and offered up one last thing.

"Mistress, one thing we do know is that this officer will play a major role, not only in the hunt for the RIM Pirates, but also, Mistress, in your future too!"

She turned and left the stateroom as Helena just stared at her back, and in the turbo-lift down a deck to her own quarters, she smiled to herself. A drunk indeed, she thought and waited as the lift dropped below her ...

Gillian sat and waited for the linking, and around her the cabin was quiet. On a shelf near the computer terminal that had never been used sat her black sculptured icon, a single obelisk that stood almost two feet tall, plain and unadorned except for a single symbol on the front side. There, the ringed planet of Eons was carved within that face, in faint but distinct relief, the symbol, of course, of the Issian Adepts. No matter where on the RIM they were, that obelisk went with them to be displayed.

The rest of Gillian's quarters were what can only be described as bleak with a lack of any personalization or owner's contents or furnishings. Clothes were kept, all black and as few as there were, in the wall panel and built-in drawers, and the nightstands on the side of the bunk were empty of any items save the ship's communication console. Without that single black icon, the room looked like it was uninhabited, truly the Issian way.

She drew in the three deep breaths to quiet her psyche. She sat still on the edge of the bed, her ankles crossed below the hem of her black robe. She waited ... and fell and waited and fell and waited ... and suddenly, she was not alone.

Linked to her consciousness were others ... other Adepts, their personas seeming to fill her mind like a circle of friends at a séance. She nodded to their faces all un-hooded that seemed to shimmer around her. As she glanced at them, she knew them all ... except that one, she noted.

That one's mind said her name was Michelle. Michelle with the dirty face and not even clad in black but in a simple dull beige jumpsuit. Michelle the miner on ITO she was; a strong mind there and knowing more about the Pirates and the mine there than anyone else.

Now that the circle was complete, the Grand Master Adept at the center of the circle dropped the hood away from her head, smiled at one and all, and spoke in her mind.

"Adept Gillian, a well done I see is in order for your talk with the Lady St. August just a bit ago. She now realizes her place in this quest to rid the RIM of these Pirates," she said slowly, her voice strong in Gillian's mind, as if she were sitting here in her cabin. She nodded back to the Grand Master Adept as did some of the other Adepts in this link from this ship through other worlds and back to Eons itself.

"And, as needed, she knows not yet of the Baroness's involvement, and that must not become apparent to her until the very end game," the Grand Master Adept intoned once more to more nodding heads, Gillian's among them.

"We then await the next step..." she said quietly, "and that comes soon ..." She finished, and slowly as the Adept link faded, she and the rest of the circle members faded ... and Gillian felt the disconnect as she always did, as a momentary blackness before her eyes. And the link was gone.

She stood then and moved to the door to

leave her quarters, the thought in her memory that all was right so far ... and would be as long as the Lady St. August could be led. She moved to the lift to go to the ship's dining room to join her charge for a meal. And she smiled ...

Chapter Five

Entering high-orbit around Neres, the *Marwick* quickly began to circuit the planet with its pale indigo blue oceans, cluttered it seemed with small continents and archipelagos that stretched out almost one into the other. As Tanner looked down, he suddenly realized that he'd not noticed how beautiful the planet looked, and he wondered how he'd missed it the few times he'd been there before.

"Must have been the beauty of the Scotch," he said to himself as he sipped his freshly-spiked double-double in the captain's chair on the Bridge. Gained a couple of pounds, he thought. He added going to the gym to his list of items to do. Or maybe just another Scotch.

As he turned to the Ansible officer on duty, he simply asked him to ask for their permission to land, and they awaited word back from the port authority on when and which landing pad they had been assigned to.

After almost an hour awaiting word, he began to fume and asked for an update on their landing request, and again the Ansible officer made the call down to the planet. Again they awaited word, and he was thinking about saying the hell with it and landing anyways when the Ansible officer announced they'd been granted clearance and assigned to landing pad sixteen.

After giving the command to land to the Helm, Tanner sat back and tried to recall all the information he knew about the Baroness and her recent rise to lead the third largest member nation of the Confederacy. From what he knew, or rather from what he'd heard, she was a beauty that had married far, far above her station and had used the marital bed to end her much older husband's life. He did know there had been about forty years between the two of them, and he did know that she had come from inward about five years ago and had once it was said worked at the best brothel somewhere in Pentyaan space that catered particularly to humans only—no Pentyaans allowed. Whether or not this was true, he couldn't say. Navy men talked about women out on the Rim like anywhere else, and that meant that one that had been a gold-digger and turned herself into the richest woman in the Rim would always be talked about ... and despised too, it seemed.

At the bottom of the slow movement down toward the surface lay the huge painted number sixteen, and as they settled on the landing pad, Tanner received all the closing-down reports from the XO who happened to be at Tactical this shift and motioned to him.

"Commander, please join me on the away team. Give the rest of close-down to the Helm, and Sander, join us as well."

He rose and went to the lift to disembark, and as they moved downward in the lift, he took a moment to caution the two officers with him.

"Gentlemen, the most important thing that can come out of our meeting today with the Baroness is the permission to visit ITO. It is imperative that somehow we get that permission, and I will do just about anything to gain that permission. Please, if anything should arise that you see that might imperil that opportunity, please nudge me or give me a high-sign." With that caution, they both nodded to Tanner and left the lift to take the boarding ramp down to the tarmac where port authorities awaited.

Not only port authorities, Tanner saw, but also four members of the Baroness's EliteGuard, dressed in their midnight black and royal blue uniforms with the highly polished china blue boots and those Sam Browne leather belts that were ivory white. They were led by a major if oak leaves meant the same here as other places. Tanner was at first surprised and then realized they were probably their escort over to the Baronial Palace.

At the bottom of the ladder, RIM Navy base Commander Heath saluted and then went to introduce the officers from Health and Customs but was interrupted immediately by the EliteGuard Major.

"Captain, is this man," he said as he pointed directly at Sander, "an Adept officer?"

With the ringed planets so plainly visible, Tanner didn't think he could lie, nor he realized did he have to do so either.

"Yes, Major, he's an important part of my away team. Why do you ask?" he replied cordially to the major.

"No Adept officers are allowed to enter the Palace, Sir. This is a directive direct from the Baroness herself, and part of my job here is to enforce all standing orders, Sir," he snapped back.

"Well then, perhaps we're at an impasse then, Major. Looks like the Baroness will not get our visit this time around," Tanner said as he looked at the port authorities, his Navy base commander, and his team. No one spoke for a full minute. Feet were looked at and hands put in pockets as the silence grew. Moments later, the major then cleared his throat.

"Sir, it's my understanding that you requested this audience with the Baroness yourself," the major said, and that fact now lay out for all to see.

Tanner was at a loss. Yes, he needed to see the Baroness to get permission to go to ITO, and yes, it was as he knew very important, but now he couldn't, it seemed, take along the one person that would help him get the permission he needed. He sighed. This would have to work without the advantage of using Sander, and he turned to his lieutenant.

"Lieutenant, please return to the ship and monitor everything from there and make full notes as usual." He had no doubts they were under the watchful eye of the Baroness here on the tarmac, and while what he'd just said couldn't work, he knew, he also knew she didn't know that for a fact. Some Adepts, admittedly less than a tenth of one percent, could still read people over a distance. He was sure the Baroness had no data on Sander as he'd just come into the Navy a few weeks back and was fresh from the naval training base on Eons before that. What the Baroness didn't know wouldn't hurt her, he figured, and this way she'd be too busy thinking about Jack and Jill to be able to think about refusing his request to visit ITO. This might work, he thought as he took the lieutenant's salute and then turned to the naval base commander.

"Commander Heath, our check-in team will be right down. Please await them while the commander and I accompany the major to see his mistress." He again saluted and then followed the major and his squad over to the open-topped troop carrier. Tanner climbed into the rear seat behind his commander, and they moved off the tarmac and toward the long, wide boulevard that would take them to the east and the palace in the distance. As they moved along, the commander gave him a wink, and Tanner grinned out the window. They were down for a moment there, but far from out as yet.

#####

As they were marched up and through the entrance way, Tanner realized that even wearing a ceremonial sidearm might have been a bad idea. At the doorway, flanked by the first of many pairs of EliteGuards, AI chimes rang twice, as they did again inside the elevator during the complete ride to the top with the major taking no notice. Once off the lift, they were escorted through a long corridor guarded by more pairs of EliteGuards and full of life size paintings of previous Barons, Tanner surmised, and then through a large hallway into a rotunda that held one of the biggest vases that he'd ever seen on a table that appeared to have been made from one slice of a tree trunk that must have had a girth of at least twenty feet. They passed by more EliteGuards and beyond the vase room lay another long corridor that when walked made the ceremonial slug thrower at his hip seem like it tingled. He worried for a moment that it might even go off as the AI scans continued for the full corridor's length.

But once through that corridor, he realized they were now entering the audience hall and noted that here the numbers of EliteGuards almost doubled. The carpet now was a soft, light brown and the walls were covered with tapestries and paintings he assumed were landscapes of various scenes here on Neres of mile-high waterfalls and rounded hills. As the EliteGuards snapped to attention, the escorting major stopped at a side door off the room, opened it, and waved them to enter.

"The Baroness will be right with you, Sir. Please go through this anteroom, take the door at the far end into the Baroness's sitting room, and there make yourself at home in the meantime," he finished and closed the door behind them.

Taking the lead, Tanner strode through the anteroom noting its soft settees and matching blue footstools, its complementary seating placements of facing love seats and low coffee tables, and its feelings of comfortable surroundings. There were many doors off to each side, but he continued to walk toward the only door on the far wall, and he opened that

door and walked into the sitting room, again
with some couches facing each other and no
guards he could spy. In the far wall, a fire
roared over logs big enough to have come from
the same tree that made the large vase table
he'd just seen. Looking, he also noted there was
no other door to the room, so he and the
commander picked a setting of couches and
took the side that faced the door. They'd see her
as soon as she came through, and he'd jump
immediately to his feet and earn at least her
respect for his manners.

"Good afternoon, Captain," a voice said
behind him.

As he rose and turned quickly to face the
voice, he was a bit perturbed that she'd come
thorough an unseen door and caught him
sitting unaware and quickly closed the distance
between them. She held out her hand quickly to
stop him.

"Please, Captain, you will only be allowed
to come so close by the AI auto-defenses in the
room. Please do try to remember that, and oh
yes, I also might caution you not to at any point
take your weapon out of its holster. One can do
only so much with the AI programming of these
defenses, and I am sorry that the AI we use is
still somewhat outdated."

As he saluted her, she nodded and then
motioned them to take the opposite couch as

she sat where they just stood. She smoothed the long black dress over her thighs and then toyed for a moment with the ends of her hair beneath what Tanner could only say was one of the prettiest ears he'd ever seen. He watched for a moment more as she turned her attention now to him, and her face looked as if there was a question that lay between them. He cleared his throat.

"Um ... Baroness St. August, we are so delighted that you were able to receive us today, and we'd first like to thank you for that honor." Politics and royalty, he thought, too bad Sander wasn't here to hear him. He paused briefly and then continued. "Part of the reason that we did ask to see you, Baroness, was to deliver the good wishes of the Rim Navy and our admiral and each and every ship of the line." Bullshit, but then maybe a bit of flattery would work on her, but maybe not.

"Thank you, Captain, but surely you've not come all this way just to thank me?" she said, her left eyebrow arching slightly as she looked over at him.

The Baroness was only an inch or two short of six feet and had eyes the same color of the blue in the EliteGuards' pants. This is one pretty lady, not at all unlike her step-daughter, the Lady St. August, although from different genes. Both of them, or rather either of them, would be more than a match for any man, and he again grinned to himself as he wondered under what circumstances he might have been that man. He nodded and bowed his head for a moment and looked directly into those royal blue eyes.

"Your Highness, we would very much like your permission to visit ITO on a Navy matter, and we know that our even contemplating this all depends upon your good will due to Council Statutes."

"And why would you want to visit this new colony of ours, Captain? Surely you realize that the port is still under construction, and as yet there aren't even any port authorities there nor provisioners or any matter of creature comforts for your crew. Why the attraction, Captain?" she asked, as she crossed her left leg now over her right, the dangling foot bouncing ever so slightly.

Tanner considered and answered as he thought he should.

"Baroness, it's a matter only of trying to solve a small Navy matter too tiny to even mention here. I can assure you that we will touch down only at the mining city of Emmanuel, and we will cause no harm nor will we take any sides if there are any complainers, Baroness. We don't intend to interfere at all, just to speak to a certain few." He lied fairly well, but it would remain to be seen if the Baroness agreed.

She looked over at him and smiled.

"Perhaps I should have told you first, Captain, but all traffic up and down to the colony is now suspended. There's been an outbreak of Natrium Flu, and until that is cleared up by the local health authorities, I'm afraid all access is closed— well to anyone but myself or the Royal family," she said, her eyes tightening as she seemed to freeze for a moment. She looked away then and blinked three times or more and then looked back to Tanner as she played with the material that now gathered on her raised left thigh and then smiled again at Tanner.

"But of course, that's just myself—well, myself and I would suppose our Lady St August, as my husband, the Baron, has passed on," she said with the slightest hitch in her voice and tone. He looked down at his hand for a moment and wondered about the veracity of her claim and then nodded to her politely.

"Well, we understand completely, Baroness. Would it be okay then just to stop by the Landers Station and do our inquiries there?" he asked, grabbing any chance he could to get as close as possible to ITO. Even though the station was in low-orbit, it would still house or hold colonists due to go down once the flu's quarantine was lifted. It might also be the source of more information and on that Tanner hoped he could at least save this small victory.

The Baroness rose as they rushed to do the same, and she spoke to them quietly, her voice firm in Tanner's ears.

"But of course, Captain. Please do visit the Landers Station, and if you have questions there of any of our citizens or my staff, just ask them. I will ensure that you get full cooperation from everyone. And even though the Station is now very crowded, I understand, room will be made for you should you need to stay over. Please just see the station commander, and I will ensure that he is expecting you." She bowed again to them both slightly and then stood there waiting.

Tanner realized that she was awaiting their departure and bowed once to her much deeper than he wished and then saluted and spun along with the commander on their heels and left the room the same way they'd entered. They marched back through hallways and the rotunda and more hallways again, now flanked by a squad of EliteGuards and eventually ended up back in the troop carrier on their way over to the port.

"Some palace," Commander Templeton commented.

"Right. Some palace," Tanner

commented to himself and the rest of the return trip was silent.

Back on board and in his ready room, the commander could not offer up any more depth to the audience than Tanner himself had to give, and both could not say with conviction that the quarantine was a total fabrication invented just to stymie their attempts to visit the planet. Neither knew and neither really had any proof of anything that had been stated was not true. At least not now. At least not yet.

After taking on provisions and spending the night in the Officers' Mess on base, Tanner and the rest of his crew were ready to leave to go to ITO and its Landers Station the next day.

He spent a bit of time on the ship's computer, looking up the incubation time for Natrium Flu and learned that it took at least two weeks to infect a new patient and that the quarantine seemed to have been in effect now for at least three days, so the Baroness's story seemed to hold water, but with Royalty, one could never tell.

He spent a bit more time at his view-port window, staring the few miles to the distant Palace and wondered about its occupant as he sipped another Scotch. He thought about where she had really come from and what she thought her role here on the RIM was and what it wasn't. He wondered whether or not she would be a good woman to kiss and what that would be like, and more challenging thoughts entered his head. He often had to shake his head to make them go away. So he sipped again.

The fact that the same thoughts had already occurred to him about the Lady St. August was not ignored by him, but he shook his head of that remembrance and went back to looking at the far Palace turrets. Truly a medieval castle for a medieval lady.

As he awaited the final provisioners to finish off later that afternoon, he was called to the commander's desk over at the Command HQ on the naval base. Arriving shortly after being called, he made his acquaintances with the commander's adjunct and the rest of the base office staff, some of whom he'd remembered from the night before as really enjoying their night together and still others were new to him. As well, there were two Provost guard MPs stationed outside Commander Heath's door who ignored both him and the rest of the chatter. As they chatted, Tanner wondered as to their presence and was glad that it wasn't for him since these were two awful big lads, both carrying neural whips as their standard sidearms and both holding batons the size of small trees.

Right after the commander's adjunct's intercom went off, he was told to enter the office and did so between the two MPs, closed the door behind him, and turned to face the commander who'd risen from behind his desk. As he did, Tanner crossed the distance between them and realized that one of the chairs before the desk held an officer, a lieutenant he didn't know or recognize. He saluted back to the commander and was asked to sit which he did, and the station commander spoke up quickly as he sat. Beside him the lieutenant still stared straight ahead. He gave no indication that Tanner had even entered the room.

"Captain, I have a very large favor to ask, and I do realize that you are more than free to refuse me. May I explain, Sir?" he queried and then awaited word.

Tanner thought for a moment. As long as this doesn't take me off mission or delay it, I would love to have the Commander obligated to me personally, as his men would visit Neres often, and in doing so in the future, he might need to ask for the favor in return.

He grinned at the commander. "Certainly, please just ask." He listened to the commander as he began to talk.

"Sir, with respect, this is pretty simple. This is Lieutenant Dieter Huber. Lieutenant Huber was our base CTO and as such, was a perfect officer, excellent performance ratings every quarter, Sir."

The commander squirmed a bit in his chair.

"However, the lieutenant ... um ... well, the lieutenant plainly speaking is also a bit of a 'ladies' man,' Sir. And he was wooing one of the Baroness's favorite nobles, a countess or some such lady. Or rather, a daughter of same, and in doing so, we're afraid he's made some enemies."

The lieutenant stirred and sat up a little straighter in his chair. He glanced over at Tanner and then went back to eyes straight ahead. Tanner thought he shook his head imperceptibly but wasn't sure.

"In any event, no matter what happened, we've been told that the lieutenant needs to be off-planet by the end of business today—and as you're the only ship in port right now, the favor must be asked, if you could transport him over to the naval base on the Duchy of d'Avigdor. Big favor, Sir ... but one that would be a comfort to both the lieutenant and to myself," the commander said as he picked up an envelope from his desk.

"I see, Commander. Well, Lieutenant, what do you have to say for yourself," Tanner asked, half-turning toward the younger man. Seems calm and composed with even a hint of a smile on his face when getting thrown off-planet.

"Sir, may I speak plainly, Sir?" he queried.

Tanner held up a hand to silence the commander who was trying to break in. "Yes, of course, Lieutenant."

"Sir, I was very much in love with Lady Jane Allenby, and no, Sir, I'm no ladies' man. In fact, anything else but—Jane and I really hit it off great, and we were seeing each other almost every day. I often visited her at the Palace, and we'd sit in some of the gardens and in the waiting rooms quietly just talking like we weren't even there. And I've no idea why the Baroness would suddenly want me off-planet— never even met the woman though I have heard her voice. It's a mystery to me, Sir. Totally."

Tanner considered what he'd heard and realized that the Baroness could order anyone off-planet, so the lieutenant would have to leave. And he'd have to see to it. He held out his hand to the commander.

"Commander, his orders are cut?"

"Cut, Sir, and right here," he said as he handed over the envelope to Tanner who nodded and then handed it to the lieutenant.

"I suppose this includes the paperwork you'll have to turn over on d'Avigdor to our base station commander there?" he asked, and the commander nodded in agreement.

"Then this is really just a delivery job, Commander, and I'm happy to do it for you. That all, Commander?" Tanner added, knowing the slight out-of-the-way side trip would cost little in time and effort.

"Not at all, Sir. Very glad you could aid us in this, and if ever ..." He closed off with the traditional Navy reminder that all Tanner would have to do was to ask and whatever it was would be granted.

As Tanner stood, the lieutenant also rose and came to attention, saluting the commander.

"Sir, permission to speak to the station commander one last time?" His back was as straight as a steel post and his black hair shiny under the lights in the commander's office.

"Um ... go ahead, Lieutenant," the commander said.

"Sir, regardless of what the Baroness thinks happened, I can honestly say, Sir, that I was a gentleman at all times. I am innocent of all charges, commander, and only time will prove me out. You will know then, Sir, that I am not guilty of any misconduct, to the Baroness, Lady Jane, or to you as my commander." He spoke softly for a man kicked off-planet for misconduct he didn't commit. Tanner watched as the commander shook his head and said nothing. In came the MPs who escorted the lieutenant as they marched him out of the office and over toward the port where the *Marwick* stood.

"Can't believe him, Captain. The Baroness has never been wrong before," he stated and then saluted himself.

"Yes ... um ... of course." Tanner nodded and saluted back as he then left the office to return to the *Marwick* to plot the change in course to the Duchy of d'Avigdor. Side trip, he thought, but one that might prove interesting at the same time. He pondered the newest addition to the ship and walked out of the offices and toward the port.

Chapter Six

D'Avigdor was one of those planets you'd like to think you'd visit, but most likely would never settle on. It was slightly bigger than most of the settled worlds out here on the Rim and therefore almost all but its inhabitants worked hard at the extra gravity. Almost half the world was oceans; big, very deep oceans that housed surprisingly little sea life. But the land masses that were spread across those oceans like leaves on a pond were really mostly all small sub-continents in size; each had had a set of feuding nations and war after war had raged on most for the past thousand years. The wars had continued until the current Duke's father, Duke Jonathan d'Avigdor, had combined via marriage with the other great house on his own continent and had eventually brought peace and prosperity to the planet as a whole via a consortium of support from all the royal houses on the planet. Advancing on other worlds within their reach had meant that the Duchy had grown now to a realm of six planets all controlled by the current Duke, David D'Avigdor, now in the twelfth year of his reign. His own space navy was about equal with that of the Barony, their competitor in this sector of

the Rim for supremacy and new colonization.
While the Barony had two destroyers to the
Duchy's one, the Duchy did have two more
cruisers than the Barony, and each had a host of
frigates and all the allied support ships needed
by the line. Both were about evenly matched,
and that had the Duke at some degree of
frustration, especially today.

"So, Captain, you visit us after a visit to
the Barony?" he asked as he leaned back in his
simple office chair.

Tanner squirmed slightly on his straight-
backed chair and carefully composed his
answer. They were meeting in the ducal palace,
in a small waiting room off what could only be
called the audience room. After being ushered
into the room by the Rim naval base station
commander and introduced to the Duke, he'd
been waved over and into this side room almost
immediately. Now just he and the Duke sat at
either side of a plain desk, apparently to chat.

"Sir, yes, that is true, Duke D'Avigdor—"

"Please, here and always in private,
Captain, just use my given name. No sense on
standing on ceremony in private," the Duke said
as he smiled at Tanner, who could see a slightly
crooked canine tooth at the bottom of that
smile.

He smiled back. "Uh ... yes, Sir ... er,
David, Sir," he said as he made a mess of the

whole thing.

The Duke paid no attention. "Captain, what can you tell me of the Baroness and your audience with her? Any items of interest there at all?" he asked quietly, but Tanner could tell that he was very interested in anything about the Baroness.

"Umm ... David, Sir, yes, we did meet and we did chat for about ten minutes or so, which is not a lot. She told us that our request to visit ITO would have to be postponed due to planet-wide quarantine as they've had an outbreak of Natrium Flu. But we are allowed to visit Landers Station in high-orbit and look into Navy matters there, no problem ... uh ... Sir." Tanner disliked very much having to call the Duke by any other name or title than plain Duke, but was reminded again.

"David, Captain, will do fine. So, the colony is under quarantine ... interesting, let me ponder that for a moment," he said and he stroked his chin. He looked away for a moment, and to Tanner it was as if he was looking out at ITO himself, studying what lay below and guessing as to the truth of the Baroness's tale.

While he looked so far away, Tanner took a moment to note the beautiful wall hangings of what looked like a hunting party with huge trophies on one wall and at the those same trophy heads mounted for all to see on the other wall. There were three oveds in a row, all with larger horns than they looked capable of carrying, yet Tanner knew that these large four-legged, hoofed, elk-like mammals from Anulet, one of the Duchy worlds, was a prized trophy and carried those horns right into battle. And beside those three was a giant head of a Jael, the carnivore much like a bear that preyed on oveds. Both were natural enemies. The Jael on the wall would have stood at least eleven feet tall and charge at over forty miles an hour, Tanner knew. Jaels were the talk of the Rim when it came to hunting, and while he had hunted smaller game before, these creatures were just too big to hunt with anything less than a cannon. He remembered the savagery of the Jael fight back on Conclusion, at least he thought he did and was brought back to the present as he realized that the Duke had just shrugged and turned back to focus again on Tanner, his eyes bright in his middle-aged face.

"Yes, I see you looking at the trophies on the wall, Captain. Tell me, do you hunt? I mean other than Pirates?" he said as he smiled. Looks like my reputation has preceded me again. Tanner grinned back.

"Sir, yes, I have hunted before, but for much smaller game. Winged birds on the fly and small boars much inward from here. I'm afraid that anything as big as an oved would take a much better shot than I to bring it down," he said honestly. Hunting game is only so much fun, he thought, and invariably it had its challenges and sometimes its consequences too.

The Duke grinned then at Tanner and pushed a hidden button as a door flew open at the far end and a Duchy naval officer marched up quickly to stand at attention and salute the Duke quickly.

"Nelson, never mind the formalities. This is Captain Scott of the Rim Navy. He's going to come with us on our latest hunting expedition to Anulet. Book his passage and quarters—next to my own, mind, and get him a complete set of gear from my quartermaster," he said, rising from behind the desk.

"Captain, we leave tomorrow at dawn. Please report to the Duchy port pad number one, at 0600. Bring what you will, but you will need for nothing on this trip as it will all be supplied. Oh yes, I know that you will contact McQueen about this—tell him I insist—and I do! We haven't had a real Navy man along in years!"

Tanner was ushered out and escorted back to the port in a matter of minutes, knowing that he'd be expected to go after talking with Admiral McQueen via the Ansible. Keeping on the good side of royalty was de rigueur for all naval personnel; Tanner had heard that time and time again. So hunting he would go and the admiral's last words sounded in his head. "Careful ... be calm and very careful ..."

#####

"Sir," Craig the XO said crisply back on the *Marwick*, "permission to take Lieutenant Huber over to his new command."

"Is it normal for a mere lieutenant to be escorted by a commander when dropped off on his new station, Commander?" Tanner inquired as he put down the PDA with the landing reports and turned toward his XO. Sounds a bit odd, he thought and wondered why he'd gotten such a request.

The commander smiled.

"Sir, our commander here is my brother, Nathan, and I'd just like an excuse to say hi— and might as well have the lieutenant tag along," he said reasonably.

"Permission granted, Commander. Please offer my own pleasantries and let him know that next time through, I'd like to spend an evening out with him at his Officers' Mess." Tanner knew he'd be drinking whatever passed for no-alco local juice on this planet.

The commander smiled, turned, and left the bridge to gather up their passenger and leave to go to the naval base station commander's offices.

Tanner busied himself with other duties and signed off on all the items that kept a captain busy when landing reports and provisioners reports were due to be handled. He worried slightly about his hunting skills and was determined not to let the Duke down with poor marksmanship or hunting etiquette either. He would look into both later via the base commander perhaps, grinned at having such a resource as a brother to his own XO, and turned back to the PDA and signing the reports. He was busy for more than an hour and was surprised when his XO returned.

"Um ... Sir?" Commander Templeton said with a questioning tone.

"Quick trip, Commander. What is it?" Tanner said as he laid down the PDA with the final reports that still needed checking and signing.

"Thought you should know earliest, Sir, about what the lieutenant said over at the base commander's office."

"And what is that, XO?"

"Sir, he was questioned by my brother pretty completely and offered up no real new information than what you already told me. Except for one thing, Sir. It caught me by surprise a bit, and I thought you should know soonest," he said.

"Sir, you mentioned that he'd been run off Neres, and as you stated, he had no idea why. My brother asked him if he'd ever met the Baroness herself—"

"And he replied no, he'd never met her. I think he said he'd heard her is all. Has that changed at all?" Tanner said.

"Umm ... Sir, all he added was that he'd not heard her on a public address or anything like that. It seems that he and his past girlfriend were sitting out in that anteroom we passed through. Remember the one before the sitting room where the Baroness surprised us?"

Tanner nodded; he'd not forgotten that and its waterfall tapestries.

"Well, he and his lady were sitting there at the last set of love seats right near the door to the sitting room, and while they were just talking, an EliteGuard came out of the Baroness's sitting room. As he opened the door, the lieutenant could hear shouting from inside the sitting room; the Baroness was yelling at someone. And he remembered what he'd heard ... she yelled something like '... you're NOT supposed to take on the damn Navy as yet ...'"

Tanner pursed his lips, sucking on the fleshy lower edge of his bottom lip. He thought about that for a moment and then nodded.

"Why didn't he say this before, Commander? And does he have any idea who else was in that room?" Tanner said.

"No real way to tell, Sir, he said. And he did admit that he may not have been close enough to hear those exact words. He also said he might have gotten that wrong, Sir, perhaps he had mixed the words or some such thing. I think pretty much he had his girlfriend on his mind and not something he might have just overheard. I don't know either, Sir, but I thought you should at least get that soonest," the commander said, saluted, and was dismissed.

Tanner sat thinking for a moment before he picked up the PDA again to finish off his landing chores. Wonder what he really did hear, he thought and sighed as he turned back to signing reports to close off his day. The Scotch in his glass called to him, and he chugged the balance in a quick down the hatch motion. Pouring another, he thought for a moment about the amount of Scotch he'd consumed in his short life. Hundreds of bottles he judged as let's see, a bottle a day for what, five years was umm ... about yeah around 150 plus cases. Lots. Perhaps too much for some. But not me. He nodded his head. Not too much ... Scotch can make one's temples pulse and that's not so much fun. He sipped and sipped again.

#####

The trip via the Duchy cruiser *Achilles*, which was really the Duke's personal yacht, was uneventful and fairly short: lift off of d'Avigdor, InertialDrive out to past high orbit, and then the switch to TachyonDrive to the planet Anulet less than three days away. Tanner was given enough time to familiarize himself with the yacht and he was impressed.

Seems like royalty has no bounds, he thought as he moved upward from deck to deck, looking at how this cruiser had been outfitted differently than his own Marwick. Instead of quarters for almost 350 men, she held only 90 or so for crew and a company of 75 of the Dukes Guards led by a guard captain who Tanner noted was handling calisthenics for a platoon in the very large and spacious gym on Deck Twenty-seven. Everything on board he noted, from fittings to brass, from steel bulkhead to floor plates and grids, from transit conduit to deck control panels, was not only clean but polished and shiny bright. On the *Marwick*, he knew, it was at least clean and somewhat shiny due to the last refurbishment but nowhere as shiny and as rich looking as on this cruiser-yacht. Difference between a ship of the line and a yacht, he surmised and continued to work his way upward. When he went by one of the officers' mess rooms, he noted that it was full of Guards again, all chowing down on breakfast, grousing and hurling around complaints and quips galore. At least something's the same as our ship. He grinned and continued to tour the ship upward until he reached the Bridge at almost 8:00 to meet with the Duke as per his request when they'd boarded earlier that morning.

"Captain, permission to enter the Bridge," he barked out as he snapped a salute to the Achilles captain.

"Permission granted, Captain; Willis is the name, Willis Fearman," he said, rising and proffering his hand. As Tanner shook his hand and made small talk with the Duke's captain, he looked around the bridge and noted it was the same layout he was used to and grinned.

"Ah, much the same as the *Marwick*," he noted.

"Right, Scott, surely is. Same basic layouts, though I suspect that you noticed we've made some interior changes. Added another landing bay and put in a ballroom, library, and an armory bigger than most. We also have reduced crew and officers, though we always carry a company of the Duke's Guards every trip. Questions, Captain?" He offered a seat near his own, and Tanner took it awaiting the appearance of the Duke himself.

"Not really, Captain. She's still a ship and I expect she handles the same, even though her innards may have been altered," he said, noting the Ansible, Helm, and Tactical officers were all at their station, while the Science officer was absent. Oh, he thought, and there's no Adept station. Guess they don't like them on board.

"Not exactly, Scott. Because the Duke as you know sits on the Rim Council representing his Duchy, he must travel to Juno for those monthly and special meetings. One day per light-year is a bit slow I guess he felt, so we've added in some modifications to the Perseus class engine; we can now make a light-year in just eighteen hours—if needs be. Costs run astronomical to do so, and we must set-down for anti-matter fills every ten days or so. Which means, of course, that it's really only meant for bursts of speed and it's not our cruising speed at all. Helps thought when the Duke wants to get somewhere a little quicker." He nodded to himself as he signed another report on his console's PDA and turned back to Tanner.

"But if the Duke wants to get somewhere fast, why doesn't he just use the *Ajax*? With her two Perseus engines, she gets around one light-year in twelve hours, right?"

The captain nodded and shrugged.

"But the costs of running that Destroyer at full cruising speed are enormous; more than a handful of trips in the Achilles still isn't close to one trip to Juno on her. And while I'm sure you appreciate that the Duke does have unlimited funds to work with, he doesn't like to spend too ostentatiously for his own needs. Spends it on the whole Navy and his worlds instead," he said quietly. "He's the best royal out here by far," the captain added proudly, "at least for a Navy man."

And Tanner knew that the captain was right; the word on the RIM was that the Duke was very involved in his six worlds and their governance, and his real favorite was his Navy. He was the kind of leader that any Navy man would follow, much like McQueen was to himself, and for a Navy man, it couldn't be better. Might bear remembering too, Tanner thought as he filed that away under the heading 'future job.'

The lift doors opened just then, and in strode the Duke in his hunting mufti, and on seeing Tanner, he came right over.

"Well, Scott, has our captain been entertaining you? Sorry to be a few minutes tardy; had to finish off with affairs of state via Ansible this morning—let's get going, shall we?" he said as he half-turned toward the lift doors with his arm outstretched.

Tanner nodded his thanks to the captain and followed the Duke into the lift.

Moments later, they got off on Deck Twenty-two and moved away from the ship's

axis counterclockwise until they reached a wide
set of double doors. Placing his hand on the
door reader, the Duke grinned at Tanner, and as
the door opened, he said, "so, let's get you
outfitted, shall we?" and led the way into the
Armory.

All Navy cruisers had an Armory, but this
was three times as big and stuffed with rack
after rack of various weapons and other deadly
items. As he walked inside the room, Tanner
thought that the *Marwick's* Armory held only
small caliber projectile rifles and crowd control
shotguns and various sidearms in holsters for
both everyday and dress use too. But this was
totally different and much more than he'd
expected.

"Right, Captain. Now I think you said
you had hunted before, correct?" the Duke said,
moving down the center aisle of rack after rack
of rifles, carbines, and shotguns. Most as
Tanner saw were brands and calibers he
recognized as weapons that the Duke's Guard
would be using, all unsuited for any type of
sportsmanlike hunting trip. But as they moved
past the racks, they got to the center of the
room, and the Duke faced the starboard
bulkhead. There, suspended against the wall,
were various weapons that were all slug
throwers Tanner noted. They moved past the
cleaning benches and ammunition lockers to

stand right in front of the display.

The Duke studied the selection before them and then took down a rifle and checked the breech and magazine and worked the action a single time to ensure that the rifle was unloaded and handed it to Tanner.

This first rifle was a basic weapon: a Fabarm single-shot rifle that used plain projectile .238 caliber bullets. As Tanner hefted it, the Duke offered that he may want to use this one if he thought his accuracy was pinpoint as oveds had only two small kill-spots and only the best hunters used this rifle.

Tanner nodded at that and said, "My hunting might be a bit rusty so my aim might not be so true," and handed the weapon back to the Duke.

Perusing further, the Duke took down a Merkel over-under .45 SUPER carbine that could bring down a large oved at full charge and put it down beside him against a cleaning table leg.

This one, Tanner knew, had one hell of a kick but would most likely be his choice. . He hefted and practiced bringing it up into firing position, fingering the double triggers as he asked about what might be better for him.

The Duke looked back to the wall and took down what Tanner could see was quite a weapon. It was a .405 Hornby semi-automatic.

It could punch through almost any animal on any planet, Tanner thought as he slowly took the proffered weapon. Haven't seen one of these in years, he thought as he glided it up and into his armpit and squeezed his cheek into the stock to take aim at the far bulkhead. The round from this moved at more than 3000 fps and at almost 600 grains would pack enough power to not only knock down an oved stone-cold dead but would take out most of the chest of the big animal at the same time, if he tried for a heart shot. He grinned at the Duke and handed it back.

"Not for me, Sir ... it's too much of a weapon, and I'm not skilled enough to handle it. I think this Merkel will do fine—do you agree?" he said, once again hefting and pointing the over-under carbine. Light, easy-to-carry, and a good bush gun when trekking through the foothills where oveds gathered; this one would do fine. Beside the rifle was a bandolier with more than twenty shells, and Tanner knew he wouldn't need more on this hunt.

"I concur, Captain. The Merkel is a strong weapon and you'll do fine with it. Personally, I use the Fabarm, as it is not outside my own skill to take down an oved with one shot. Together then we will be fine as a team." He busied himself with setting up the cleaning supplies and items to break down each weapon and clean and polish them. As Tanner helped, he thought to ask about the other teams that would be hunting with them.

"Sir, can you offer what the teams are, and who's with whom?"

The Duke nodded as he rammed the cleaning cloth into the barrel time and time again, seeking to ouster every bit of dirt and dust therein.

"Yes, Captain. There will be you and myself, as team A. My bodyguards, Guard Lieutenants Phillips and Norman—though much put out by not being paired with me—will be team B, and the last one is team C which will be one of my naval officers, Admiral Kent and our Guard Colonel Harrison, two fine officers in my own Duchy forces. Here, use this," he added as Tanner was having trouble getting into the breech of his weapon with the cloth, and he accepted the cotton swab gladly. Moistening it with alcohol, he was able to gather up the few grains of grit he found and left the area shiny and polished. They continued to clean their weapons, trading hunting stories from mostly the Duke's past, and Tanner realized after awhile that while the Duke was, well, a Duke, he wasn't a bad sort after all. They ended up joking about some novice hunters and how they'd choked up when being charged by even small game, and soon the weapons were clean, polished, and ready to be used. As the Duke packed them back and away into the weapons tote for tomorrow, he commented to Tanner in a friendly manner.

"If you have any trouble standing your ground if an oved charges, Captain, remember that Merkel will punch a hole right through him if you shoot him in the chest, though it will spoil the meat we hope to take back ..." He grinned and as they closed out the lights in the cargo hold where their gear was assembled, he led the way back up to the Officers' Mess and signed for a round for all found therein. Tomorrow we hunt, Tanner thought, and he had only one glass of Jovian ale and then turned in to await the morning.

#####

Anulet was a world like few others. A small planet of only about 5000 miles in diameter meant that all humans would be working against much less gravity than on Juno. This would allow them to feel much stronger, have more endurance, and of course, be able to take long bounding strides of almost twelve feet at a full run. But it wasn't that that was so different. It was the planet's double suns that made it such an oddball. Anulet was the fourth planet of one of the binary stars, a red giant named Oz by earlier colonists on Anulet.

Being a red giant, the light that fell on Anulet for the most part was reddish light, which deepened the shadows and made contrasting shades that could hurt your eyes to some degree after exposure for a few days. Of course, the colonists had become inured to that a few generations back, and all Anuletians paid the problem no attention.

But that was not the only sun that shone down on the planet, for eons ago Oz had also captured a smaller main sequence star called the Wizard, and with its yellowish light, the shadows it was said on Anulet were often muddy, deep in brown tones. Every four years the paths of the suns lined up to shine on Anulet, and right now, only Oz shone down on the planet as the Wizard was eclipsed. All shadows would be a deep red color and the contrasts would be bright for months to come.

It was also a planet that had grown little life in its infancy and one where evolution happened so slowly that its oceans were barely populated and its land masses mostly empty. However, at the top of the food chain were the Jaels, those bear-like creatures that hunted oveds and smaller animals called owphi that resembled six-legged mountain goats that lined the heavily eroded mid-latitudes on the largest land mass, where the colonists had settled centuries ago. Now used by the Duke as a major raw material planet, the colonists now were farmers, forestry workers, and small open pit miners for the most part. The planet went far in feeding much of the rest of the Duchy's realm, and its inhabitants, while not rich by any means, all enjoyed many comforts that other planets did not offer under the crimson skies above them.

As well as the colonists under the Duke's banner, there was also a small tourism group that ran hunting tours for hunters from all over the Rim. Beautiful lodges had been built with the huge beams of the planet's forest kings, the tossprho tree with its red grains and buff tones. The huge halls and resort rooms were well worth the hunt it was said by all who came to enjoy Anulet. Each resort was backed up by able staff, and guides meant that many a Rim citizen had come to Anulet to hunt for oved or Jael and had left with a trophy mount to follow them some months later, to be hung on walls all across the Rim. One of those hunting lodges was owned by the Duke's family, and it was down to that lodge that the whole hunting party and gear were taken by the Achilles tender upon their arrival. The gear was quickly stowed away and the guests were taken up to the lodge dining room for breakfast. After finishing far too many oved sausages and cups of coffee, they all moved over to the commons room to discuss the day's upcoming events.

"Right, if everyone's got their coffees, please may I have your attention to run through the drill for today," the senior guide, Koenig, announced as he stood up near the large display panel opposite the fireplace that even now roared with a log fire.

"Right, teams, you all know and I know that you all know to stay with your teammate at all times. This is Wizard eclipse month so you may well be using goggles and remember that shadows under Oz light don't look so deep—but they truly are. No leaving your teammate, no investigating any caves or slide areas, no leaving the assigned areas for your team. If everyone follows that, we'll all do just fine. Known you were coming now for about a week, Sir, and have closed off lodge boundaries to all via the subsonic fencing, to take some pressure off your bodyguards," Koenig said, grinning at the two of them on team B who shrugged as if to say that didn't impress them. The Duke nodded, and the hunting guide continued.

"Right, so here's the areas that we've seen oved trail in the past week," he said as he turned on the display and a 3D map of the hunting area appeared behind him. Tanner could see that the terrain was traversed with deep gullies, eroded water channels from ages ago that now were fully grown over with trees and short ground cover. Each of the almost parallel five gullies emptied into a larger canyon to the far right side of the display, a distance of almost a mile Tanner figured. Down the middle or so of that canyon was what appeared to be a river that twisted and scoured the canyon on its way somewhere else.

"As you can see, the tops of the mesas here are pretty flat and only hold grasslands mostly. Much thicker vegetation is located in the gullies themselves, and they all end up in the canyon. While we won't be down that far that way, know that the river is much swollen with the rains we've had in the past few days; don't even think about swimming in it, lads, as it's treacherous and full of rapids, short waterfalls, and eddies that will kill you before you go 100 yards." He went on as he zoomed in on one of the mesas between two gullies.

"Here's what we're working with today. The mesa is the oveds' preferred foraging area. They do love their grasses. But the Jaels know that and haunt the tops of the gullies, charging out to snare the weaker or disabled oveds whenever they can. Course, we've put out subsonics to bar the Jaels from even getting into this area, and we've monitored those mesas for the past week or so," he said, turning toward the Duke who now had a scowl on his face.

"Guide Master Koenig, I do hope that

you realize that the last thing that any good hunter wants is to be so coddled that there is no risk to anything one attempts at all. This is a hunt, man, not a kindergarten party," he said, with less force than Tanner expected.

"Granted, Sir. But we are looking at oved only on this hunt, and as you and I both know, Sir, they too can do quite a bit of damage if cornered. We kept the Jaels out only as a precaution; who knows, Sir, maybe some of them still snuck in around the subsonic fences," he offered, a small smile on his face.

The Duke waved him on, Tanner noted, as he realized that sub-sonics would keep the devil himself from your door; Jaels could not withstand them he was sure.

"Right, Sir. Then we leave in twenty-five minutes, lads. Please get your gear, unloaded arms only in the heli, and we'll meet out at the pad then. Off you go," he said and watched as the six hunters left to get their gear.

Tanner was upstairs in one of the prettiest bedrooms he'd ever been in. Rustic red tossprho wood beams were supported by half-round log walls with forest green curtains around a bay window that pointed out to the great red outdoors. His bed was big enough to hold a platoon, he figured, and his desk had a comm up-link he saw as he got on his camouflage clothing and grabbed his boots from the bottom of his duffel bag. Once his boots were on, he took his rifle from its tote as he grabbed the ammunition bandolier, his goggles, and a toque in case the day was cool and made his way out to the lodge pad.

There, tucked well away from the Achilles tender, was the lodge helicopter, big enough for a dozen or so at least and in good repair. The red light threw him for a moment as he thought there was trash or debris below the craft on the tarmac pad, but as he got closer, he realized that it was just the red light shadows that had fooled him, and he hoped the goggles would help some out in the field.

He climbed aboard and took a window seat beside one of the bodyguards and waited as the pilots warmed up the engines, and they lifted off for the days hunt. At about fifteen knots or so, Tanner felt the shuddering as they left the cushion of ground effect and made it into clean air, and the pilot surged forward and upward toward the hunting grounds.

As they sped along, above first the heavily treed lodge grounds, up and over a ridge a mile away, Tanner saw that the red-lighted shadows below him would aid the oved no matter if he was wearing goggles or not. The shadows between the tossprho trees below were dark, deeply red in color, and there was almost no contrast at all. Yet the trees themselves, some kind of strange conifers, were almost like shiny tinsel trees, all gracefully blowing in the mild winds below. He struggled to get on his goggles for a better look at what he'd actually see and was happy that at least the tinsel below was now much muted. Those shadows, he thought and watched as a mesa loomed ahead, and the pilot took them up almost at that instant to gracefully turn and arc down to land on a cleared landing spot that awaited them

"Right, lads, out we go," the Guide Master said and led the way beneath the still turning rotor blades and off to one side. As they all gathered, Tanner noticed that most weren't wearing their goggles yet, so he pulled his down to his neck and stood while the heli lifted off and curled back and toward the lodge.

"Right, so everyone okay from the ride, first?" Koenig said and looked at each for a nod.

"Okay, next, maps to each team, here … here you go," he said as he handed out a map to each team leader. The Duke took Tanner's team map, and Tanner glanced down at it at the same time, noting that their team A had been assigned the farthest over mesa and the gully just before it as their own grounds, which meant a traverse of three other gullies to get to where they were assigned. A long walk but farthest away meant less impact of the heli on the game at least.

"Right, lads. First mesa and gully are buffers for the heli; next gully and mesa, team C and guide Williams; next gully and mesa, team B and guide Brown; and last gully and mesa, team A and myself. Off we go, please a reminder to walk the gullies quietly as that's where the oved will be lingering before coming out to dine on the grasses for the day. Off we go." He led off at a brisk pace across the heli-pad mesa and toward the buffer gully beyond it. As the hike settled in, Tanner noted that the grasses were not too bad on the eyes if you slightly turned your head a few degrees to one side of the spot you were looking at and let that red light creep in from the side. As they walked, they fell quiet, and after a few hundred yards, they were at the edge of the buffer gully where Tanner noticed a subsonic beacon planted right at the edge of the gully stuck into the muddy edge of the mesa. As they slowly moved down on the muddy path, he spotted a couple more of the beacons when they skirted the bottom of the gully and began to climb the far side. Narrow one and I'm not out of breath either, he thought as he climbed the lower gravity far side and eased up on top of the next mesa, another buffer he remembered.

Crossing mesa after gully after mesa, the hunting party peeled off by teams until only Tanner, the Duke, and the Guide Master slowly moved through the top of the mesa beside their own gully and suddenly, they stopped cold.

The Guide Master at the head motioned them to come up to see what only he could so far see over the gully's edge. Rains from the previous few days had poured into their gully right where the path lay, and the heavy torrent had eroded the ground around the path. Lying on its side, its grid of speaker holes clogged now with mud, a subsonic beacon lay. Peering ahead, Tanner could see that the small landslide had taken out much of the path, and ahead he could see only the bottom of another beacon poking out of the mud below.

Shaking his head, the Guide Master turned to the Duke.

"Sir," he whispered," looks like we've lost some sub-sonics here at the edge and down a bit. I don't like that at all, Sir, and would recommend turning back; we can't count on the area being empty of Jaels." He wasn't wringing his hands, Tanner thought, but it was obvious that he was somewhat cautious. Most likely as he's really in charge of the Duke's safety, and now he didn't have a lock on that at all.

The Duke shook his head.

"Not at all, Guide Master. We push on, and if there are any Jaels, I wager I'll get him before he gets me," the Duke said as he smiled and slowly began working his way by the guide and down into the gully.

Tanner looked at Koenig, who just grimaced and motioned him to go ahead, he'd bring up the rear, and Tanner moved down the slippery mud-covered side of the gully. Ahead, a wall of trees loomed up in the reddish light, and the Duke moved slowly between the trunks as he tried to still move down parallel to the path but to its right. At a small clearing ahead, he motioned them to come closer as he began to load his rifle.

"Scott, you take my right flank. Guide Master, you get the left. I think we'll angle down slowly, through the trees towards the bottom of the gully, but also towards the canyon too. That way, we can stay away from the mud slide and try to drive whatever might be ahead lower towards the gully floor. Clean shots, fellows," he grinned.

Tanner reached for his goggles and held them up questioningly to the Duke.

"Not me, don't like 'em," the Duke said, "but if you want to wear them, go ahead. Now let's hunt," he said as he smiled once more and moved off slowly with his gun at the ready.

Tanner loaded both barrels of his carbine, thumbed on the safety, moved slightly up and to the right of the Duke's path, and worked his way away from the other two, angling right and down eventually. Ahead, those tinsel conifer trees were clumped together while low bushes tended to be alone in between. The ground for the most part was dead leaves and those conifer tinsel needles if he could believe his eyes with the goggles. But the shadows ahead between the trees were just too dark red for him to make out anything lurking there. He tried to move around the tree clumps at first, figuring that if there was a Jael there, it would be too much of a surprise as he wouldn't see it. But after a few minutes went by, he found himself almost able to make out tree trunks within the shadows, so the next clump, he entered slowly as he moved downhill. Trunk after trunk went by, mostly tinsel conifers though there were some broadleaf trees that grew from very twisted trunks of twice a man's breadth. As he made his way around big rocks and over roots that had pushed up from the earth, he took care not to slip on any and left that first clump feeling a little better and trusted his eyesight a whole lot more.

Swishing through the long grasses and crossing the next little bush-littered clearing, he paused just inside the edge of the next big clump of trees to listen for a moment. He judged that the Duke was no more than hundred yards to his left and the Guide Master a farther hundred. He could hear little, except the slight blowing of broad leaf leaves within the clump ahead. No wildlife sang that he could

tell nor moved with noise either. The shadows
of the clump of trees around him was thicker
than the last one, but still he could see the
broad leaf trunk almost dead ahead. Beside it
low bushes had grown to almost hide a big rock
that lay there. As he began to make his way
around the rock and the broad leaf trunk, an
arm like a railway tie, with claws extended,
swung at him from above the rock, and he was
knocked down onto his back. The realization
that he was in deadly trouble was on him in an
instant, and he rolled and rolled until he hit
outstretched roots and only then looked back up
at the blood red Jael who had clambered down
off the rock and was charging him head on.

Even on the ground, and on his back, he
knew that the animal would pounce on him,
teeth searching for his throat, trying to kill him
with one bite. And as he raised the Merkel, he
thumbed off the safety and let go with both
barrels directly at the charging animal.

The double explosion of the gun when it
fired, coupled with the tight confines of the
clump of trees made the sound of the weapon
seem thunderous, as Tanner watched the Jael
take both shells in the chest. But the
momentum of that charge meant that it only
slowed the Jael, and it fell half on top of
Tanner, its right paw striking him still hard
enough to almost break his leg. As Tanner

scrabbled backward to get away from the Jael, he realized that the animal was nowhere near done as it dragged itself after him using only it's front legs, claws digging at the ground and roots to find purchase. Its jaws gnashed as the big canines cut the air, searching for flesh as its eyes bored in on its prey. As it clawed feverishly after him, Tanner was now backed up right against a tinsel conifer, its scaly bark jammed up against his spine, the knots and twigs that low on the trunk piercing his shirt and even his skin. The Jael was still not dead, he realized as he leaned forward to grab the carbine out of the dirt, ejected the spent shells, and rolled to his knees, jamming the new shells into the breech, knowing he had only moments to re-load.

The sound of the Duke's Fabarm barked once, and the top of the Jael's skull exploded. Its head flopped down onto its forearms, as black blood under the red light flowed from its crown; it was finished. Tanner took his first breath of relief in what must have been a minute or so and looked to the Duke who grinned at him as he slowly stood up.

"Sorry, Scott, but that's my kill, agreed?"

Tanner nodded vigorously.

"Absolutely, Sir. Your kill without question. And soon I'll have my heart slowed down which will be ample reward enough," he said as he rose shaking from the adrenaline rush he'd just gone through.

As the Duke moved closer to inspect the carcass, Tanner moved away, and thumbing the safety, he put down the carbine that had saved his life. He shook for a few seconds then drew a few deep breaths, and suddenly spying over the top of the Duke, he saw the Jael's mate coming around the other side of that same rock just before she charged. As he dropped to his knees, he swooped up the carbine and again let both barrels go into the right side of the bear-like animal just before she knocked the Duke down.

Without hesitation, he used the now empty gun like a club and swung it with all his might at the head of the Jael, who had bitten into the Duke's shoulder, feeling the impact as he struck the animal's temple. It must have stunned the animal as she rolled off to the far side of the Duke who now lay quietly on the ground as Tanner struggled to find more shells in the bandolier.

As the animal shook its head and began to stand, Tanner realized that she was far from out of the fight and skinned his knuckle jamming a single shell into the lower chamber. He looked up to see the Jael, screaming its rage, towering over them both, as he knelt at the Duke's side. One more, he thought as the animal roared and began to pounce down at him. His carbine came up cleanly, and he fired into the Jael's neck as the animal's jaws snapped at his own, and he went over backward with the Jael on top. Then all he saw was black ...

Chapter Seven

On board the frigate *Avalon*, Rhys sat and champed on the hangnail on his thumb. His attention to the view screen was focused, but his gnawing didn't stop as the cuticle bled.

Ahead was a freighter that was carrying about fifty emigrants on their way from Carnarvon to Merilda. With all their worldly possessions, he thought.

Emigrants to Merilda were always suspect, Rhys thought, as anyone would be on their way to live on a planet that was a raw untamed world. More than 13,000 miles in diameter, its gravity was almost two times what was on Neres; its continents were huge, and its seas small. Much of the planet was undiscovered and unexplored, Rhys knew, and that was probably because the total population of this planet was less than 100,000. No cities, barely a few towns, and from what the rumors were, almost no chance of reaching out for Confederacy membership for at least five generations. "And if we take those fifty hostages, that'd take a bit longer," he said to himself and smiled, his thumb painfully red.

From the Helm chair came word about the matching of the TachyonDrive from the rear as they came up dead astern of the freighter. As the *Avalon* had been fully customized by the Barony engineering labs, she had been sped up to be able to do one light-year in eighteen hours instead of the normal twenty-four hours. Specialized modifications that coupled the Argosenium with the Tachyon pulse that drove the ship at light-speed had been added. There were few ships outfitted with the Tachyon over-drive, and only the *Avalon* had the Argosenium customization.

"Matching is optimum, Captain," the Lieutenant said as his hands cautiously matched the vector heading to come up astern.

On the bridge view screen, the Perseus engine on the freighter ahead showed the dull ocher color as usual and then flared brightly as klaxons came on all over the *Avalon*.

"Status report, XO," bellowed Rhys as he swung to starboard to look at his number two in command. "Shut off those Goddamn alarms," he added, and as they died, the XO spoke up.

"No idea yet, Captain," he said back as he scanned the screens on his own station's consoles.

"Damn it," Rhys said, "they're moving off ... what they hell has happened?" He spoke quietly now as the *Avalon* appeared to be slowing ... the freighter moving away quickly. At light-speed, the ocher rear-facing Perseus engine pushed ahead quickly, and they were moments later out of sight ... a growing smaller dot well ahead.

Dropping out of light-speed, the *Avalon* popped back into real space and the stars suddenly appeared. Aimed as they were toward the galactic core, there were dozens of tens of thousands of them, with the huge black channel of dust and detritus along the Orion Arm and the inner core.

Feverishly working on their screens with the sound of keyboards clicking and muttered curses, Rhys waited as the ocher dot ahead disappeared.

"Anyone? Someone? What the hell happened?" he said.

After a wait of more than ten minutes more, the XO turned to him and shook his head. And then he shook it again.

"Sir, it appears that the candle went out on its own, and we've no idea as to why ..." His disgust was real and his lack of a reason bothered him too.

"Fine, start her back up and let's head home," he said and leaned back to gnaw on his thumb again, worrying on that cuticle.

Moments later, the keys again were clacking and the view screen was still solidly the same.

"Helm?" Rhys said,"have you—"

"Sir, there's a problem with the engine ... we're not getting any candle at all ..." his Helm lieutenant said. His hands flashed again on the ship's controls on his desktop and yet nothing appeared to be happening.

"Sir ... I'm at a loss too. We appear to have no issues with any of the engine; anti-matter fine, helm control fine, heading and locks fine ... in fact we should right now be at light-speed, Sir. But we're not ..."

Rhys sat back and squared his shoulders.

"Get engineering on this immediately as I want to go after that freighter ASAP."

The XO he saw was on his throat mic, and judging by the jerking of his head, he was yelling down to the engineers. Rhys smiled to himself and licked his thumb to salve the irritation. This won't take long, he thought and turned back to the Bridge view screen to watch the stars ... at least there's a light show to watch. And another freighter to find too.

He woke with a start and realized that first, he had lived through the Jael's attack and then that somehow his right leg wouldn't move. Groaning, he continued to try to sit as he wiped the grit from the corner of his eyes, and he was pressed back down into the bed gently.

"Take it easy, Sir. You're fine ... all you

need is a bit more rest and another day with your leg in the auto-Doc," a soft voice said.

As he fluttered open his eyes, he was able to focus on the form beside his bed. It looked like a nurse.

"Uh ... where am I," he croaked out, "and how long have I been in Sick Bay?" he asked as he glanced around the room. Beside him was the stand for his IV, and down by the right side of the bed, a machine housed his complete right leg from mid-thigh down to past his foot. While he knew what an auto-Doc was, he'd actually never had an injury before that would have required using one.

"Captain, you're on the *Achilles* and we're making quick time back to d'Avigdor and the rest of the Duke's party directly to the tender, and we took off just a few hours ago. Our ETA is tomorrow night, which is a good thing as that will give your broken leg the full thirty hours it needs to be mended." She fussed with his sheets and smiled down at him, patting his arm and handing him a glass of water.

"And if you don't remember, the Duke has told us all that you saved his life on that hunt," she added. "And to those of us who know the man, we are all grateful that you did just that too!"

"Uh ... the Duke? Is he alright?" Tanner asked, sipping the water carefully from the straw.

She nodded at him.

"Yes, he's fine—oh, he's got lots of scrapes and a few bruises and lacerations from the beating he took. And his shoulder had big canine teeth bite marks that more than 100 stitches and an hour in the auto-Doc fixed up quickly. But on the whole, he's fine. He said for me to let him know soon as you were awake too," she said as she moved away to the wall comm unit and talked quietly for a moment into it.

She then busied herself with the auto-Doc settings, checking various dials and vials that he could see. He'd heard that an auto-Doc could fix just about any major wound or broken bone that any human might encounter. And while he'd never had the need for one, he was sure that his leg would come out of the machine whole and ready for use. At least he hoped that was true, he thought as the door to Sick Bay slid open and in came the Duke who smiled at Tanner and walked immediately to his side.

"Captain, never did I imagine that including you on my hunting party team would be the best decision I'd ever make. My thanks, Sir, your quick thinking saved my life—both of our lives, I imagine," he said as he smiled down at Tanner's face.

"Um ... Sir, I really don't know what to

say. I just ... well, I just did what I thought was best at the time. And I'm glad we got out of there with our skins," he said, a bit embarrassed at the Duke's honest thank you. He really didn't do much, just what anyone would have done in that situation.

"Nonsense, Captain. You saved us both. And I am more than thankful. I have Ansibled that news to your superiors in the RIM Navy; I have requested that you receive a full week's worth of recovery time on d'Avigdor at my palace and my expense, and I've arranged for a festival to be held in your honor in a week's time."

"Sir, I really don't think that I—"

"Save it, Captain. I also have a seat on the Council, so as you can imagine, when I want something done, it usually is done," the Duke said, still grinning down at Tanner. His smile was a nice one, Tanner thought, and yes, I guess it'll have to do.

"Nancy, please take good care of our guest 'til we arrive tomorrow. Captain, this is our best nurse on board, and what she says— well, just pretend it's me talking. Follow her orders and you'll arrive hale and hearty on d'Avigdor. 'Til then, Captain," he said as he patted the nurse on the shoulder and left the room.

"Woohoo, a festival in your honor—that's

a day you'll never forget," she said as she smiled down at Tanner and fiddled again with the settings on the auto-Doc.

"What exactly does that mean?" he asked as he took a final sip from the almost empty glass.

"It's held in the Palace festival grounds and runs all day and night too. There'll be the logging competitions for the forestry workers from Anulet, and the Adepts will have a fortune telling display. The Bacu who are close will show up with all their gypsy ways, and the Leudies will be there to trade. While this festival will be mostly local because it's so soon and that's not enough time for many more to get here, the big festivals at the spring and vernal equinoxes attract thousands of revelers and merchants and artists. And you're to be the guest of honor, which means that you'll enjoy the big feast at night and sit at the Duke's right hand, an honor to be sure." She continued to fiddle with the settings on the auto-Doc, moving up a slider here and tapping a gauge there until she was satisfied.

"I've upped the levels somewhat, Captain, which might make you a bit sleepy, and you should rest if you can. Nothing helps the autoDoc do its job better than a resting patient. I'll be right over there at my console if you need me, but do try to rest," she said as she slipped away.

He watched her get settled over at the far console and thought she must have dimmed the lights a bit as he slowly fell into a deep rest, dreaming of festivals and Pirates and cruisers full of Scotch ...

#####

Two days later in his cabin aboard the *Marwick*, Tanner thumbed for the incoming messages and was relieved to see one from Admiral McQueen. After the normal Navy icons and security codes appeared, his superior's face then filled the comm screen.

"Well, my boy. Saving the life of a Duke can have its rewards, as I'm sure you're finding out, and the fact that the Duke is also on the Council is also important to note, as he has arranged all much above me by the way. So as I understand it, you're on 'shore recuperation duty' for almost another full week, at which time perhaps you'd better come on in to update me on how your mission is coming along. That's if you can tear yourself away from the festival," he said dryly, and as he rung off, Tanner could see him shaking his head.

As he composed a simple text message answer to acknowledge this new itinerary, he again pressed down on his right foot with more weight and tried to see if there was any residual pain in the leg itself. But there was none; the Duke's auto-Doc had done a superb job and the tibia had mended truly. He sent the message with a quick finger stab and then stood to go to the gym and work that leg and the rest of his body too.

He grinned as he thought of how out of shape he'd gotten and nodded when he reminded himself of why that had happened, as he quickly changed into gym clothes and left his cabin to find the stairs to go down to the gym deck.

Taking a filled thermos cup, he moved down the hallway to the turbo-lift and waited for it to arrive as he sipped his Scotch in the cup. As he got to the officer's quarters level, he suddenly thought of the festival and its Adepts and popped by Lieutenant Sander's quarters to invite him to the gym and to query him on Adepts in general.

#####

The technician with the cleanest lab coat sat at the console in the lab and shook his head at the small group of similarly clad scientists around him. He pointed to a bar chart on the screen and then flipped his hand over as a sign of frustration.

"This should not happen as there is no physical property of Argosenium that would account for this declination of the fields generated by the neutron to proton transition. And how that is accompanied by the emission of an electron and an anti-neutrino which causes the emission of a positron is beyond our understanding of the element. This should not happen. But it appears that it has on the Hypnos."

He shook his head again and twisted around to look at the group.

"Ideas anyone?" he queried and then waited.

No one spoke. Only two days ago, the Hypnos had been towed in by one of the Barony Navy supply ships, and they had been working on the secret Argosenium mechanism here in the secure lab in the Baron's palace since. Thirty-eight straight hours,and no break for either the scientists or in determining the cause of the failure of the mechanism.

"Doctor, it might seem like the only answer, as someone smarter than I am once said, is that the answer to any issue is always the easiest," said a young man fresh from the University over on Juno only a few months ago.

"If we all recognize that when an atom is in an external magnetic field, spectral lines become split into three or more components is the phenomenon we call the Zeeman Effect. This is caused by the interaction of the magnetic field with the magnetic moment of the atom and its electrons. Hence, the only explanation is that whatever the component is that gives the Argosenium its power over the candle ceases to exist after some threshold of usage. Simple, yes?" He smiled quickly and then backed up a half a step as the head scientist rose.

"That just could be, however improbable that may be. We need to test then—A/B testing on new samples, plus any variants ..." he said as they all moved off. The only thing that was bothering him was reporting this to the Baroness ... that was always what could only be described as a ghastly experience. The shudder beneath his lab coat couldn't be seen, but it was still there as he strode down the wall of screens and consoles and equipment.

#####

Going to the festival was all new to Tanner, and as he strolled the fringes of the grounds on this summer day, there was much to see and to do.

First, there were all the buskers. Everywhere you looked, he realized, there was someone who was performing some kind of skill and hoped you were suitably impressed enough to like what you saw or heard and would drop a few credits into their basket. He saw six-armed unicyclists from Eblo, in the Alex'in hegemony, who juggled and sang at the same time, and sidewalk painters who'd do a quick sketch of you in a minute or less. There were a horde of Altos, that race from Randi who was known for being able to somehow sing in four-part harmony alone and who in a choir sounded like hundreds of singers.

Lieutenant Sanders pointed out even more of the more exotic Rim species; Tanner had seldom seen a DenKoss off its own world before, but sure enough, a tank or two went by, with one of those fishy-looking aliens sloshing about inside. He nudged Sanders and asked if perhaps one of them might have recently been on Conclusion ... and if Sanders recognized her, or it?

Sanders shrugged and said quite simply, "No, Sir!"

As they made their way past the buskers, they found themselves in the games of chance area and watched as many Nerians tried their hand at pitching balls at targets that looked far too small or watched as a giant wheel turned to mostly stop on a number that was uncovered with a bettor's credits. Tanner pointed at the game and grinned as if to ask his Adept officer if it was a straight game and the lieutenant grinned back at him.

"Not on your life, Sir. Note no Adepts play the game?" He shook his head, and Tanner realized that if a game was at all rigged for the house, then Adepts would know and not bother to play.

"But what about all those players, do they not know that?" he asked.

"Sure, but note the sign on the top," he said as he pointed.

"This game will not host any Adept players," it read.

"Um. So the real players think that an Adept would have an edge, therefore they are barred from playing. When in fact, Adepts know it's a rigged game and wouldn't bother?" he questioned.

"Right, Sir. Just another con ..." Sanders smiled as they walked on among the families and teenagers that swelled in numbers as they got closer to the competition areas.

Passing food court after outdoor food booths and even food trucks, they stopped only long enough to buy a frozen ice-cone, and as they quickly tried to keep them from melting all over their hands, they found themselves near the large water tank where hoots and cheers were coming from.

Moving along the edge of the tank, they climbed up one walkway and peered out into the tank. It was obviously a log burling contest as Tanner could see at each end of the tank on walkways contestants with numbers on their backs awaited their call to mount the log from their own end. As he swiped the cone with his tongue, he heard the announcer offer that the next match was between last year's winner, an older contestant from Anulet, and a younger challenger who'd climbed the listings and done quite well to get to this level. As he watched, each man slowly worked their way out along the top of the floating log to take their positions within the striped zone at their own end. Suddenly, a buzzer sounded and the cheering began.

One man turned 180 degrees immediately and began to step quickly to turn the log beneath his feet, while his competitor also quickly turned and began to tread backward. As the speed increased, Tanner noted that it was the challenger who'd started things off, and he increased his speed trying to run last year's champion off the log to no avail, as the older champion's feet moved like the wind. As the challenger continued to try to speed things up, somehow the past champion was able to slow the spinning somewhat and then he leapt up and turned and came down to immediately try to increase the speed himself.

That was enough for the younger man as the log burled only for a moment, and he flew off and into the water amidst cheering and catcalls from the crowd around the tank.

Tanner grinned at his lieutenant and nodded toward the champion who was holding up clasped hands over his head as the log slowed beneath his feet.

"Any way to tell that he was going to do that?" he asked.

Sander shook his head.

"Not in the least, at least not to my abilities, Captain. He was simply quoting a nursery rhyme in his head and then he turned to attack when he got to the end of a verse. I'd suspect that he had planned to do that, right when the verse ended, but it wasn't a conscious thought that I could see ... just that dang nursery rhyme over and over."

The two men left the tank area and slowly moved by the log cutting and climbing areas. As they moved through, they saw crowds at most of the various competitions, cheering and egging on the competitors. Going around the crowds was easy enough, and then they found themselves at the Issian Adept area, with various displays and tables and chairs set up for anyone to watch or to get their fortunes told. As all Adepts were Issians from Eons, they were always in black, always in robes and not shirts and pants, always with that black shawl on their head that sometimes covered their entire face or sat perched on top when they were communicating. For hundreds of years now, this religious cult had been the birth ground for the ability to see into another's mind; to be able to look inside to see what the conscious thoughts were that were out in the open.

Tanner knew that you could hide your real thoughts for a while, behind nursery rhymes like the log roller they'd met for instance. If you could consciously think of one thing, while holding your true thoughts off to the side, no Adept could find out what you were truly thinking. And he also knew that this was hard to do for any length of time. And when faced with a dangerous situation, he also knew that you just couldn't keep your thoughts away from what faced you and on nursery rhymes. It just didn't work.

Some Adepts called Masters, he knew, could sometimes get a feeling of your overall tone of mind, for instance were you happy or were you sad. And some of the very best ones could somehow measure your own mind against others they'd met and somehow come up with a generality about you and your future. But never with any guarantees or for the most part even a surety. Here at the festival, he thought, it'd be mostly done to impress the locals and not much more.

As they moved along the fringes of the various participants, Tanner saw an older woman, located at the very center of the area in

189

a roped-off area, who was looking straight at him, who never took her eyes off him as far as they made their way along the outside of the area. He nudged Sander and arched an eyebrow at him.

"Yes, Sir, she is a Master Adept and she wishes to talk to you is all that I get, but she is very, very strong, Sir. Her skills are far advanced from my own," he said quietly, as he led their way through the displays and other Adepts who were scattered throughout the area. As they got closer, they went by other Adepts who sat talking with a seated festival goer, telling their fortunes for a price or reading their minds for fun.

Coming up on the roped-off area, Sander looked at the Master Adept, then nodded, and moved the rope to the side to let them enter. As they did, the woman pushed out the chair opposite her with her foot to allow the Captain to sit, which he did. He looked at her and waited. She would do the talking, and he'd do the listening.

She stared into his eyes, her face blank and impassive. Around her head she wore the shawl of the Issian faith and at her collar the icon broach of a ringed planet. Dressed all in black, she was a normal-sized woman of Eons, short in stature. Her only really unique feature was her staring green eyes, Tanner thought as he gazed back at them. Barely wrinkled bronze-toned skin surrounded those eyes, and her eyebrows sat over her eyes like skinny caterpillars covered in sparse fur.

"Well, it's our guest of honor," she said and dipped her head as a sort of ceremonial bow to him.

So he smiled back at her, bowed down a bit further, and then sat up to stare back at her.

"And I see that our honored guest has had trying times in the past few years, times that found him unable to remember much of those years." Her gaze never wavered, drilling into his own as thoughts of the Scotch years drifted by in his head.

"And I see that your current quest is a bit delayed; you await developments that you do not control," she added and then held out her palm on the table for him to place his own within her grasp.

He did so, gently placing his hand on top of hers and looked down as her fingers slowly curled around his own palm.

"Um ... yes, and I see ... I see that your quest involves Royalty here on the RIM ..." she added as he raised his sight to again look back at her.

"Well, yes ... Ma'am. The Duke and I are, well, I would suppose that we are fairly close after our last few days together," he said with a simple smile on his face. After all, he was the Duke's guest of honor.

"Not the Duke, Captain, but someone else of Royalty holds much of your future within her hands—but be careful, Captain, if you choose incorrectly ..." She dropped her gaze with that and pulled her hand away quickly.

"But wait, what do you mean ... what can you see?" he questioned her, as he leaned forward over her small table that stood between them.

She shook her head and looked away, and it was Sander's pulling grasp that he next noticed.

"Captain ... Captain, she is through. She will speak to you no more, Sir. Come, we must leave. Sir, please ..." he said as he pulled Tanner to his feet and away from the table. Walking away, Tanner looked backward and saw that the Master Adept had now covered her head with her shawl, and at tables around hers, other Adepts were silent, watching him and Sander walk away.

They walked a bit farther, until they were able to find a seat on a bench opposite a wrestling match between two Leudies, all that bare blue flesh rolling and twisting before them, their neck snakes trying to snap at each other too. Tanner sat quietly for a moment and then turned to Sander.

"Sir, sorry, but no. I was totally unable to read anything from the Master but what she directed to me to hear. All I can say is that she believes she is totally correct—that she was unable to hide from me," he said, shaking his head.

"So, what did she mean 'her hands' Sander? The only Royalty that could be is the Baroness, and I've no idea what that meant, nor what kind of choice I'll face either," he said with little conviction. What the Master had said meant little to him, he realized, without some further explanations.

"No, Sir, actually we can't go back to see her as she will not speak to you again was the last thing I got as we walked away. I am afraid that the caution you received was all that she was willing to pass along. Course, there is one small item you may not have thought of," he added, looking at his captain.

"Um ... then I assume if you're offering same here, Lieutenant, that you know I've not thought of it. Out with it please," he said.

"Sir, she mentioned Royalty and 'her hands.' Perhaps she meant the Lady Helena, the Baroness's step-daughter?"

Tanner closed his mouth, and instead of interrupting the lieutenant, he sat and watched the wrestlers in front of him. Paying little attention to them, he nodded after a moment and half-turned to Sander.

"Yes, that too fits within the Adept's answer, but I can't imagine her playing any kind of role at all in my future. Of course, the real trick would be which one of them the Adept meant," he pondered as the sounds of a referee's count just ahead of them began in a loud voice. As the cheers and catcalls of the crowd rang out, the two sat and watched another whole match before Tanner shrugged and stood to leave the area.

"Come on, Lieutenant, back to the ship and let's dress for the big dinner tonight, dress whites all around," he said as they began the long walk back to the *Marwick* picking their way through the even bigger crowds to get ready for later this evenings feast.

As they moved through the festival grounds, a pair of eyes from a small tent near the Adept area followed them as they went by; green eyes that never wavered until they were out of sight …

"Come, Tanner, one more, I insist," the Duke said, as he held out the new bottle of single-malt Scotch above Tanner's now empty glass as the steward retired from the room.

Tanner shook his head and noted that it felt much much larger than he ever wanted it to feel again and held his hand over the top.

"Sorry, David ... just couldn't, don't need any more at all ... got far too much aboard as it is ..." he said slowly to avoid slurring his words.

The feast had gone well, and he and the rest of the Duke's party on the dais had enjoyed roast oved and sirloins of beef and boar ribs from the royal farms here on d'Avigdor. There had been some speeches, and he'd had to accept a nice medal from the Duke and a scroll that made him an honorary member for life of the Duke's hunting lodge on Anulet. He'd kept his remarks short and thanked the Duke graciously for providing the hunting education that allowed him to save his host. Once that was done, the stewards had brought out bottle after bottle of various local and galactic favorites, and his officers had really partied well as only Navy men can do. The Duke seemed not only to not mind, but often went over to their tables and sat with them for a period of time, toasting and truly being just another Navy man at a party.

Later, they'd been entertained by dancing troupes of Alex'in; more than fifty of these insect-looking aliens had danced and fluttered in the royal banquet room for almost an hour. Then a choir of Altos had sung deep tenor and bass quatrains while Quarans had then cavorted and jumped almost to the ceiling in their own acrobatic manner. Off to one side, an orchestra provided much music throughout the evening and now into the late hours heading toward dawn. The Duke had let everyone go when they had pleased, and now the room contained only the two of them and that new bottle of scotch. So far, Tanner had only had to have one drink throughout the night, trying to not succumb to the temptation of his favorite liquor in all the worlds.

"Nonsense, Tanner. Gotta have one more, let's call it a night-cap, and then we'll retire," he said as he poured a bit sloppily a good three inches of Scotch into both glasses.

"Fine ... now, where were we," he said as he sipped the fresh drink.

"We were ... were ... we were talking about how much of your time is spent in meetings to ... ah ... to do what?" Tanner queried.

"Um ... um ... to manage my kingdom." The Duke smiled as he suddenly remembered where the conversation had been left off before that new bottle of Scotch had been brought in.

"Sure, that's where we were. It's tough to know what to do in all cases, but I learned most of what I know by being my father's heir. I try to do what I think he would do, and in most cases it's worked out very well. Our citizens are happy, our worlds flourish, and for the most part, we've no real problems on the horizon," he said proudly and only once did he stammer as his alcohol-laden brain tried to keep up with his mouth.

Tanner nodded in agreement.

"Right, David ... right. Uh ... say what was one of those 'cases' where things didn't go so well,?" he questioned, wondering what the Duke might have had trouble with. After all, this Duke ran six worlds in his Duchy where his word was law—what could cause him any troubles?

"Well, ITO, of course. We found her, tucked along the edge of the Nerian nebulae, in a pocket of old star matter and dust that hid her from mostly everyone else—including the damn Baron," he said with what might be called steel in his voice. "Yes, Tanner, we found the planet. We approached them with standard first contact procedures too and quickly learned that the planet held not a sentient on it ... but that our sensors quickly detected large deposits of Lawrencium close to the surface. We began to arrange for colonists to go and to mine that rare earth metal for us, as I readied for our announcement of first claim to present to the Rim Council. But we were stymied by the Baron when he quickly noted that he already had established a colony on the other side of the globe about three weeks earlier than our own. It wasn't true, we felt, but we couldn't prove otherwise against their Adepts and colonists, so we lost out on one of the richest finds of Lawrencium anywhere out here on the Rim," he said as he took a short swig from his glass.

Tanner nodded and took a minute sip from his own glass.

"I see, so it was a matter of a few weeks at best. Too bad, because as I understand it, the Lawrencium they have offered for assay has been high in percentages and quality too." He shook his head, a world lost for a few weeks. He sipped his Scotch.

"Right again. The loss of riches, because we were unable to prove the Baron had lied," the Duke said, tossing back another mouthful.

"Was that the only case where things didn't go well?" he said.

"That's the big one, course, there's others too. Like we lost a whole ducal ship of colonists to the Pirates last month, passengers, crew, the works! Off Alex'in, skirting Pentyaan space, of course. She'd filled up on Skogg with big construction equipment and all, some drilling rigs and some ore moving equipment and then she was gone. 110 souls in total, and one of my father's original frigates too, the Priam—all lost —and so far, my Navy can not find a trace of them or her." He shook his head.

"But until I know what happened, she's not being claimed as lost nor the crew or colonists missing as yet. We're still searching and we will find them soon ..." he said, his voice trailing off as he looked across the huge banquet room at nothing in particular.

Tanner nodded and swirled the liquid in his glass. More missing colonists and this time crew and ship as well. And nothing had been sent out to the rest of the Rim about this loss. The Duke had held this information very close to his chest, allowing no one to learn about this event.

Tanner nodded again and swept the glass up and the Scotch down his throat in an instant. Standing, he pitched the glass as far as he could toward the far wall and turned to the Duke as he heard the sounds of the smashed glass.

"Your Highness, permission to retire— I'm in need of rest, David," he said slowly and succinctly. As he did, the Duke grinned up at him as he too rose and hurled his own glass after Tanner's.

"Well done, Tanner. And yes, see you tomorrow," he said and looked for the helping arms of two stewards that had suddenly appeared and began to slowly move him toward the inner chambers doors.

As Tanner strode down the long banquet hall, he had much to think about and pondered as he walked what had become of the Duke's ship and its colonists and crew. A question he knew that would have an answer, just not one readily available.

Chapter Eight

Landers Station was what anyone with a sense of aesthetics would call ugly. As the low-orbit station that hung above ITO, she'd been built at the Barony's shipbuilding yards on Neres almost three years ago. Moved here when the colony had registered with the Council only a few months ago, she'd been added to and then added to again. Wings of quarters and warehouses for materials angled off her like branches off a tree. In some areas, she was hundreds of feet thick with bulkheads and interior space, and in others, it was a spiderweb of single passageways and life-support plenums.

Much of the traffic to the station was incoming empty transports that were meant to pick up ore and ship it back to Neres for smelting and refining. As there was now a quarantine on the planet itself, those transports had stacked up awaiting the cargo pipeline to begin to flow again soon. Colonists also were held on the station awaiting tenders down to the planet when that quarantine was lifted, whenever that might be, as no one really knew, it seemed.

"At least that's what their comm officer said, Sir," Lieutenant Rizzo reported after chatting with Landers Station. He turned toward Tanner and had a questioning look on his face.

"Sir, shouldn't they always know exactly when a quarantine is over?" he asked.

Tanner nodded.

"Yes, normally that's true, Lieutenant. And especially for the Natrium Flu, as its length of incubation is well documented. But as I see here in the bulletins we received last night on our way in, the problem seems to be with the colonists themselves. Due to the heavy earth metals and their high concentrations near the surface, it seems to have somewhat changed the normal period of incubation for the influenza. Which means that they're going on a case-by-case basis down there—which in turn means quarantine exists 'til their medical staff can lift it. So until then, Landers Station is as close as anyone can get. Ansible back and let's see if we can get a berth or we'll have to use a shuttle," he said, and he turned back toward the front display with the station calmly positioned in front of them.

"Lieutenant Greeley, any idea on the number of those transports stacked up over there? Are there others we can't see being held off somewhere else?" he said as he mentally counted the ore carriers he could see.

"Sir, there's only fourteen there by sensor

count. And I did a quick scour, and there's no more to report being held anywhere else, Sir," he added as he looked down at his display.

"Not a lot of transports for when the quarantine comes off, I think," Tanner said, and he drank another swig of his coffee.

As he pondered that for another minute or two, word came in that they'd have to shuttle down to the station as all berths had been taken up or reserved for Barony use. He grunted with that and arranged his away team and shuttle pilot, and they moved down through the Marwick to the shuttle bay.

Moments later, under his command, the shuttle pilot did a complete circle around the station first, noting nothing really surprising in their circuit. There was the occasional flare from a welding bot doing maintenance on the station's surface while still others floated near cargo bays doing regular maintenance work and cleanup of escaped rock and ore that floated near the cargo bays. As they came round the station to the sunlight side, they made their way to their assigned shuttle bay and docked inside quite neatly and quickly. Working their way through the station's own customs and medical officers, they were soon in the main corridor and moving inward toward the administrative elevators that would take them up to the station master where they'd pay their respects.

"Remember, fellows, watch everything and note everything. And you, Sander, you put out your 'feelers' and take in as much as possible," Tanner said to his away team. His XO Templeton and Lieutenant Greeley nodded, and Lieutenant Sander smiled back at him. They knew they were there on the station to find out as much as they could and to just act like Navy men everywhere. Tanner had no doubts that wouldn't be hard for any of them, as they left the lift and moved down the corridor to the Administration Offices.

Turning inward, Tanner and his XO went into the offices as Greeley and Anders walked on toward the center mall area. The administrator's receptionist smiled up at them and motioned with her hand to enter.

"Morning, Captain, XO. Administrator Cooper will see you right away," she said as they marched by her small desk and into the office to the left.

And what an office, Tanner thought. Enormous windows opened up on a view scape of ITO below, a world swirled with blues and greens and speckled with clouds. Closer to the station were arms of the station and the held berthed ships and shuttles. Even a Barony Navy cruiser was docked, it's blue and red crown symbol quite evident in the steady sunlight. Smaller bots under power moved around the cruiser doing regular maintenance chores while again the flash of welders could be seen occasionally.

"Captain," the small man in the chair said, as he turned away from the view to face his guests, "so nice to have you here. We received news of your quest to visit us and will make the station wide open to you and your men." The man rose and rounded his desk to offer his hand, which the XO and Tanner took, and then they settled into the chairs in front of the large desk. As the administrator returned to his chair, Tanner noted a rock, an ore sample most likely, was proudly displayed on a wooden pedestal on the desk. It's faint purple color and specks of something silver caught the light in the office. It seemed to glow, he thought.

"Administrator Cooper, we're pleased to be here and thank both you and the Baroness for your hospitality. But to be perfectly frank with you, this is not a quest at all. We're just looking for a few ex-naval men who're rumored to be on ITO—or maybe here on Landers Station. It's really no big deal. We're just 'following orders,' I'm sure you understand," Tanner said. Their cover story of looking for ex-Rim Navy men had seemed a likely one, and his XO had contributed blaming it on their superiors would surely ring true to this bureaucrat. The administrator took the bait right away.

"Always the way, eh fellows! The boss sends you on another of her—or their—wild goose chases. No real reason behind it, just do it. Yes, I commiserate with you both. It's no fun just 'following orders' and I should know," he said as he pointed at the stack of files and paperwork on his desk. "About all I really do here is shuffle paperwork mostly and for real reason." He sighed and leaned back in his chair, half turning toward the huge window behind him.

"This place is pretty self-sufficient. We simply send down colonists and bring up ore; the ore moves back to Neres via those transports, and then they return with more colonists. Not as many as we'd like, mind you … but the colony grows a bit each month. And I'm the guy who signs for everything." His voice was a bit exasperated, but even Tanner could understand being stuck in a bureaucrat hell.

"Same for us in this case, Administrator. We just have to look for a couple of ex-Navy men who're wanted back on Juno in time for the next Rim Council meeting. Seems someone wants to talk to them before that, which only gives us about two more days of looking."

Tanner pushed back his chair slightly and got to his feet as did his XO.

"So, we'll be off. We thank you for your

hospitality, and I will make sure that our men behave themselves, and we will depart sometime tomorrow—most likely by mid-afternoon," Tanner said as the administrator jumped to his feet.

"Right, Captain. If you have any troubles at all, just have whomever message me immediately, and I'll speak to them. Can't have a Baronial guest receive any troubles here at all ... you can count on me, Captain," he said as he waved goodbye, framed in the window behind him with ITO.

Tanner nodded and he and the XO left the offices quickly and turned toward the large center mall area ahead and to the right. As they walked, Tanner shook his head at the XO, who was going to make a comment it seemed, and pulled out his PDA. Quickly, he wrote "Most likely we're being recorded," and the XO nodded after reading the note. Tanner erased the note and they walked on. Even though the administrator had been more than friendly, Tanner thought, he was still in the employ of the Baroness, and for a Rim Navy man that meant caution for openers. Hospitality, yes— but trusting, no.

At the center mall, the two stopped and looked at the large cavernous space ahead and above them. This area was the center of the station, and as such, was the home for most of the entertainment spots, the hotels, the shops, and stores. They even had a zoo, Tanner noted. Throngs of colonists mingled with station personnel; he saw a few station guards about, in their midnight black and royal blue uniforms, the norm for all Barony forces. Over on the far left were some sidewalk cafés where one could sit and people watch, which is where they headed first. Grabbing a small table, they ordered mineral waters, and while the waiter went inside to find their drinks, they watched the stream of people and families as they walked by.

"No one seems to be in a hurry, nor even a bit agitated that the quarantine has stopped their progress down to ITO," Commander Templeton said dryly. "In fact, it's like they're all on vacation," he added.

"Excuse me, but you're about right on that point, Commander," a man sitting with his family at the table next to them interrupted. He smiled at the two Rim officers and nodded his head.

"Sorry to interrupt, but we're so close here and I thought that I'd clear up any misunderstandings you might have. My name is Donny Turner and this is my wife, Judy, and our daughter, Amanda. Amanda is fourteen today ... so we're out for a trip to the zoo and then a nice dinner." His wife grinned at them, and the daughter smiled shyly as she used her long spoon to get right to the bottom of her ice cream sundae glass. Teenager and she'll grow to be a pretty woman, Tanner thought as he noticed the deep dimple in her right cheek. He smiled back at them all.

"Well, Donny, Judy, and Amanda. Nice to meet you all. Now tell me, you're colonists, correct?"

"Correct, Captain. We will be moving down to Emmanuel when the quarantine is lifted. I will become the Assistant Head Assay Chief, and Judy will work in the offices at the new college there. Amanda will be beginning her final few years of school at the New Barony High School. And while we await that final move, we are all treated as guests of the Baroness—we pay for nothing here on Landers Station. Now that's what we call a true vacation," he said as he finished off his glass of what looked like lemonade and ordered another one.

"So while you await the final leg of your journey, everything is paid for here on Landers?" the XO queried.

"We all get one of these," Amanda said, as she pulled a small card from her breast pocket. She offered it to the XO who took it and looked it over.

"We use it to 'pay' for everything, but we

don't use our own money. We use the Baroness's money, we suppose," she said as her dimple deepened. Twinkling birthday eyes and that dimple; Tanner suddenly wished to be twenty-five years younger as he smiled at them all.

"That's a real nice thing to have done. Next time we see the Baroness, I'll comment on how nice that was," he said as he looked over the card before handing it back to her. It looked like an ID card with Amanda's name, her colonist number, and date of birth, which was today, he noted, along with that black magnetic strip that carried other information which he couldn't see, of course.

"So, any idea on how long this quarantine might last?" he asked with no hint of caution in his voice.

Judy replied, "Not really. All we know is that it is supposed to be over soon. But we've been here almost two weeks, and we've heard that same thing every day." Her head shook negatively, and she gestured at the throngs of people around her.

"Colonists keep coming, so we assume that it really will be any day now. All we can do is to wait ..."

"And go to the zoo!" Amanda said as she grinned and stood to her feet.

"Come on Dad, Mom, let's go! I want to

see the Jael feeding again," she said as she shook her Mom's arm and pulled her toward the edge of the street just past their table.

"Well, Captain, Commander, it seems that we're on our way. So nice to meet you, and if you're ever in Emmanuel, please look us up. We will be living in the first yellow house past the bridge going east out of the city, we understand. And we'd love to say hello again." Donny and Judy joined Amanda in the street and moved along with the throngs of people in center mall.

"Want to drop by that Jael feeding session?" the XO said a bit dryly, a lift of one eyebrow accompanying his question.

Tanner shuddered.

"Not on your life! Was almost dinner myself, and that's as close as I'll ever get to one of those beasts," he muttered as he shook his head.

"Message Anders and Greeley and let's get back to the ship. Shifted shore leave to begin in one hour for all except for a skeleton duty crew," Tanner said to his XO, as he stood to join the flow and return to the ship.

Later in his quarters, Tanner noted in his own log that the colonists all seemed to be happy awaiting the end of quarantine, the Baroness paid for their upkeep while the quarantine lasted, and Lieutenant Anders had found no dissenting viewpoints at all. Even the Landers Station personnel had shown that the Rim Navy crew was to be treated with respect as the Baroness's invitees.

On the whole, Tanner thought, everything here was above-board and the quarantine would be lifted when it would be lifted—until then it posed no one any problems. He glanced out his own porthole at ITO that lay below, now darkened in twilight. Shore leave sometimes posed a problem for their hosts, but he didn't expect any troubles from the Landers Station guards. My crewmen will be well treated. He turned back to reports and provisioning tallies that needed his attention. He sighed. Being the captain was not all fun. He made the note to leave tomorrow by noon to get a bit of a jump on the thirty-two-day trip back to Juno. Time to go back to Juno. He picked up his stylus, began to check additions, and poured another Scotch.

#####

"Well, Captain, what else do you have to say for yourself?" Colonel McQueen held up a hand to stop Tanner from replying. He'd just listened to the captain's report on his mission and the few clues that Tanner had been able to gather on the Pirates.

"You get made captain, a good thing, I

thought. Your mission was to go out and find
the location of the Pirates, and other than an
Adept officer's pre-cog thought that there may
be a Pirate called Rhys ... you come home
empty. No Pirates. No location and to top it all
off, you get drunk AGAIN and alienate the
Baroness's step-daughter, the Right Honorable
Lady August, you almost get the Duke
D'Avigdor killed in a hunting party, and now,
you suddenly realize that you've no idea where
the Pirates are, let alone how to stop them. Do I
have that just about right, Captain," the Colonel
said, his fingers tapping on his desk and his
eyes boring into Tanners.

Tanner stood at ease but not really.
What'n hell is the issue?

"Sir, with permission, I would be the first
to say that yes, my mission goals are far from
complete, but due to the ... uh ... mitigating
circumstances—"

"And exactly how does pissing off the
Baroness's step-daughter," snapped the
Admiral, "qualify as a mitigating anything? Do
you have any idea on just what kind of an idiot I
look like to the Baroness when her daughter
files that kind of a report AND the Baroness has
demanded that the report be a part of the next
Council Agenda? And it will be ... and so in less
than a month, I need answers, Captain ...
answers." The admiral shrugged, as if to ward

off the knowledge he didn't have and looked at Tanner for an answer. And Tanner had none, yet.

"Admiral, I do realize the kind of pressure that you're under, and yes, I also realize that I must—I will find those Pirates, and yes, I also know that this must be done before the next Council meeting. So my promise to you is just that. In the next few weeks between now and the Council meeting here on Juno, I will find the Pirates ... and bring them to justice. You have my word on that, Sir ... and you can count on that, Sir." Tanner snapped to attention and his eyes drilled straight into the wall above the admiral's head.

The admiral sat still for a moment, quietly frozen like a Jael who was stalking his prey, seeming in deep thought. He fiddled with his desk mat's corners and geometrically lined up the mat with the edge of his desk ... and then seemed to have made a decision.

"Tanner ... Captain Scott ... I believe you. And I will hold you to your word. I need the Pirates in hand by the next quarterly Council meeting, and there can be no equivocation on this time line or matter at all. Failure to fulfill your mission will mean major sanctions against your standing here in the Rim Navy, I'm afraid. And my boy, this will not be to my liking, but I will be required to enforce that termination—

214

the Council and the Baroness will see to it! Get out there and find them! Dismissed," he added in a softer tone and then reached for a file folder on his desk as he half-turned away from the rigid captain in front of him.

Waiting for the elevator, Tanner had visions of life here on the Rim without being a Navy man; of maybe trying to find a home out on Bottle perhaps with a native girl or even living on the Duke's dime on Anulet at the ducal hunting lodge ... and shook his head. There would be no life here for him, he knew, without the Navy and that meant that he had to work on finding the Pirates. And finding them fast. The only way to defuse the Baroness and her daughter, pretty as both of them were, was to hand over the Pirates.

#####

"Sir, we're approaching Eons, and we're about—"

"Attention, *RN Marwick*, this is Eons Orbital Control, please identify yourselves ..." came the standard Ansible directive from the ever-patrolling ship in high-orbit around the planet.

Eons was the one world that lay truly outside of the galaxy here in this part of the Rim. It was slightly below the plane of galaxy from galactic north and with a blue giant star almost twice the size of Rigel. It held its position only because its star was so immense, so large that its closeness as second planet in that system meant that it moved around its star quickly with a year there being only 103 earth days in length. Dessau, the capital of the planet, was also home of the Rim Naval Academy and was one of the planet's claims of fame, but not the one that truly was at the crux of Eons reputation.

The reason that Eons was known throughout the Rim was that it was also home for the Issians ... a religious group that bred the Adepts and brought them to maturity here on the Rim. Issians were well known, of course, throughout the Rim but not toward the galaxy center with any real penetration as they tended to maintain their well-being only here, close to the inky blackness that lay just past Eons. And other than the close links that they held with the Rim Navy via their Adepts becoming officers, they truly held to themselves, only occasionally forming close-knit closed groupings on few other planets at all. Most Issians lived on Eons which was the way of the Rim, and that's what most people expected.

"Comm, call over to Orbital Control and let them know we're going to touch down at the port on Dessau, and we'd like to get in and supplied quickly, if possible, under Code Red

A-7. And get them to acknowledge right away too, Comm," Tanner said in a rush then to his communications officer, looking for speed on this landing.

As the Comm officer quickly snapped their requests down to planet authorities, Tanner watched the display screen awaiting the green highlights that would show permissions had been fulfilled and that they could land ... and was still waiting when Lieutenant Elliot sighed and clicked on the audio signal.

"Yes, thank you *RN Marwick*, but as no one here knows what a 'Code Red A-7' means ... uh ... sorry, Sir, we're still trying to find an academy officer to ... uh ... one moment, Sir, please ..." The cadet's voice faded at that point.

"Sir, the Eons Orbital Control station is populated with Rim academy cadets, who ... um ... have not yet, I'd suppose, had any training on the various Rim Navy landing codes, well, I mean the special use ones," Elliot said in a explanatory tone. "Guess they'll ask for help on that one and then," he finished with an aside.

Tanner nodded, knowing that the lieutenant had only been on active duty for less than a year, and yes, he'd surmised the same thing. Cadets needed to learn, but that time line he had was getting shorter.

"Permission granted, *RN Marwick*," said the cadet on Comm duty on the Orbital Control station, as the perms on screen went green. Tanner thought to give that cadet an A and motioned for the Helm to take her down.

As they stood on their tail, the thrust from impulse engines balanced their descent, and they dropped steadily toward Eons and the landing pad below. Other ships slowly rose as they touched down, other Navy ships, a Barony cruiser and frigate, and even an Alex'in hegemony sphere too, Tanner noted, but he had no time to dwell on it.

Tanner finished up his logs and nodded to the XO about sending in the port chandlers quickly and getting squared away while he rose and left the bridge with Lieutenant Sander. They made their way down to the surface and the waiting group. Once they'd signed off and made their Customs/Health declarations and nodded to the Navy base commander and made their excuses, he and Lieutenant Sander moved quickly to a queue of robo-cabs and moved off with some speed.

"Right, Lieutenant ... let's just go over this one more time, and no, I don't need to hear all of those cautions every time I make a qualified guess, okay with you?" Tanner said, as he settled back into the corner of the rear cab seating. "We okay with that?"

Sander nodded. "I'm good to go, Sir!"

"Okay, first task then is to find the

Master Adept from the festival back on d'Avigdor, the one who read my fortune and let us know about those 'Royal female hands.' She, if found, may just be a link to more than my future with a Royal, but may also know about the Pirates, correct?" Tanner looked pointedly at Lieutenant Sander and awaited his agreement.

"Um ... Sir, as I pointed out before," Sander said as he held up both palms to his captain in supplication, trying to get a word in quickly before the interruption, "we really, in my opinion, are grasping at straws on this quest. We do know that this Master is here, but whether or not she will even see you, let alone be able to 'see' anything else that may help us, is the point of the matter, Sir," Sander added quickly, "and that's why this may be a lost cause here on Eons ... Sir ... um ..."

Tanner nodded. He knew the lieutenant was making solid sense, but he also knew that the Master Adept had seen something ... and he wanted to find out as much as he could before he was left with the only other slim chance that he had to find the Pirates, one that he didn't even want to countenance. Not yet, in any case.

"Well stated, Lieutenant, but we go on and I do thank you for the aid so far in even finding the Master," Tanner said.

"But as I indicated, Sir, she may not even

allow us to speak to her … remember, this is her planet, her city, and her temple that we must encroach upon. And my own abilities do not allow me to see ahead at all, especially here on Eons with all the Adepts here. It's like having 100 choirs of Altos in your brain, all singing a different song and all in four-part harmony. Only a Master Adept can make sense of this environment and even then only the best of the best. But … we will try, yes?" Sander said, and then he too sat back in the other corner of the robo-cab plas-seat, his eyes darting sideways to look at his captain.

Tanner nodded and looked out the window at the city of Dessau as it passed by, smooth architecture and stunning towers near the landing fields that slowly gave way to bustle of the city core, business districts, and open air marketplaces. After about another mile or two and smaller low rise buildings, the city began to thin out. A few parks went by, then what looked like dry sparse open fields, and up ahead, the squat gray stone buildings of the Rim Navy Academy appeared, and they cruised right on by as they didn't have time this trip to Eons to drop in and make nice.

Ahead, there was a sloping level down to a river, and once across the bridge, they climbed the opposite shoreline and worked their way up and over top of a ridge and then another. Eons had trees but there were none here, only grasslands that poor rainfall had made it slowly brown and sparse. But the grasslands were not what demanded his attention; it was the walled village that lay ahead with its large central temple and tall tower that loomed above the brown brick walls. Gates were occasionally spaced around the exterior walls, but the road led only through one of them, and at that portal, there was a barricade that would stop them, and it did...

#####

The person who appeared from within the walled village itself ambled out to the robo-cab and moved to the rear window where Tanner sat. The Issian wore a black robe with hood though it was not covering the head, and what Tanner thought was a veil or a bib of some kind over his face—least Tanner thought it was a man. But he was wrong, as he saw the greeter drop her veil and smile wanly to them.

"Welcome, Navy officers. We welcome you to our village. You are welcome, but you will need to remember that you will need to leave before sundown today. No strangers are ever allowed to remain here after sundown, not even those of us who have left our society and have found other pastimes," the woman said in a dry throaty voice as she bent and looked over at

Lieutenant Sander.

"We would like to thank you, Mistress," Sander said quietly, "and we will leave the village before sundown. You can be assured of that." He glanced at Tanner and laid his hand on Tanner's arm.

"May we ask, Mistress, please if—"

"Yes, Lieutenant, please direct yourselves into the village straight ahead and proceed directly to the temple. You will be met there, right there, once again. And we thank you as always with our thanks." She made a quick movement with her hand and arm and the barricade rose, and they slowly moved into the walled village.

Ahead and to each side lay low single-story row homes, all the same shade of brown. Like milk chocolate, Tanner thought, a village of milk chocolate. The cab slowly moved down the road toward the temple that lay a few hundred yards ahead. People who were walking moved slowly out of the way. All the adults from what Tanner could tell wore that black, but the children were dressed more in kids' clothing, jeans and overalls and skirts, some even in bright colors. Some of the kids waved ... and one or two of the little boys tried to snap a salute to him, and he grinned back at them each time.

"Seems like we were expected, as well as greeted pretty nicely, I think, Bram ... you?"

Tanner said.

"Um ... yes, to be expected, really, Sir ... they knew that we were coming via the Ansible message we sent through on our way here is all," Sander said and made ready to leave the cab as they pulled up at the temple, a large dark brown building that rose at least 100 feet above the street.

Bittersweet chocolate, Tanner thought as they left the cab and made their way up the wide front steps to the tall two-story doors that were closed. He looked for a bell or a door knocker or anyway to "ring" through to the occupants, and as he gawked at the frames and door sill, the left hand door opened slowly with no one in sight. They entered and slowly walked through an anteroom area to what Tanner thought was a congregational room ... large, and wide and with pews of a type of wood he'd never seen before with green lines of speckled grain over a dull beige core.

Ahead down the long center aisle was a black-robed man, veil off, Issian, awaiting them, and as they approached, he gestured for them to move down the aisle toward him up at the front. As they walked, on one pew about halfway down the left-hand side sat one Issian in robes. Quietly ruminating on his god, Tanner thought. As they passed that black-robed figure, Tanner looked at the face of that Issian and could not even see the eyes as the veil covered his whole face. Approaching the first of the rows of pews, they slowed as the Issian ahead stepped forward to meet them.

"Welcome again, our Navy friends. We welcome you to our village and our temple. May I offer you some water, if you have a thirst?" he said as he gestured toward a small side table with a pitcher and some plain ceramic glasses. Just as Tanner was about to decline nicely, he once again felt the lieutenant's hand on his arm.

"Um ... yes, thank you. That would be very kind," Tanner said, and as he tried to walk over to that table, Sander's grip firmed up even more ... holding him there.

"Our pleasure, then friends ... please wait moments, please." The Issian quickly poured a single glass and handed it to Tanner, who glanced questioningly at his lieutenant, who just shook his head.

Tanner drank a quick mouthful or two of the warmish tepid water and then held the glass out to the Issian, who accepted it gratefully and then moved and gestured toward the side door on the left, but he held out his arm to stop Sander from moving. Tanner looked back after only a couple of steps, but Sander just nodded and went back to sit alone in one of those pews, and Tanner then turned to trod the carpet quietly. By the time he got to that door, it opened and led him into a small sitting room where there sat another robed and veiled Issian.

Tanner sat directly opposite the Issian whom he assumed was the Master Adept that they had been seeking and looked at her with some pointedness. He cleared his throat and then was stopped by a hand held up by the black-robed figure, and he waited. And waited. And waited still.

From somewhere behind him, Tanner heard a voice, and he half-turned to see another black-robed, veiled Issian who walked over to the sofa settings and sat beside the already seated Issian, and then both of them dropped their veils. The Master Adept had been the second Issian to have just entered the room, and the original person was not an Issian at all but the Right Honorable Lady St. August, the step-daughter of the Baroness, who he saw looked both a bit irritated and annoyed and still very closed off to him.

Tanner sat shocked and opened and closed his mouth a few times before he could even shed his surprise, and the Master Adept spoke after a moment.

"Captain, your surprise is noted. We thank you for that, but you should not talk but listen instead. We want your help and the Lady's help too, and for that help to we Issians, we will explain what you need to know, but only

to the degree that we have seen your future ..."
She spoke clearly, Tanner thought as he spoke
up quickly.

"Yes, Master Adept, and now I also see
who you meant owned those 'Royal female
hands'— this Lady St. August, it appears," he
said quickly to try to acknowledge her input
from the festival.

"As I said, Captain ... you need to listen.
The hands I spoke of belong not to this Lady,
but to her step-mother, the Baroness of Neres.
It is her hands that hold your future, and not
this woman." She said this with a teensy degree
of shortness, Tanner thought and bowed his
head quickly to acknowledge his mistake.

She continued with ease.

"You are here to learn what you need to
know to be able to help not only us, the Issians
here at the RIM but all RIM peoples and
especially the hostages gathered by the Pirates
and now held in servitude on ITO. They have
been captured by these Pirates, under the care
and control of the Baroness, to use as miners on
ITO to mine in secret a new element that allows
these Pirates to somehow capture other ships.
And rob these other ships. Why the Baroness
needs to build her treasury—of that we know
little as that is beyond our abilities ..." She left
off for a second as she shook her head.

Tanner sat shocked, his eyes round with

surprise.

"Yet our abilities have helped us learn all of this so far from our other Masters and our only Adept on ITO as well, a youngster but one of great talent, it appears. And we wanted to impart this knowledge to you, as the one who can help rid the Rim of these Pirates and perhaps more," she said as she glanced sideways to the Lady, who just looked between the Master and Tanner and then spoke for the first time.

"And again, Mistress, I reiterate, what in God's name makes you think that this ... this drunk can be counted on to not only help, but to defeat the Pirates, seeing as he'll probably just get drunk and miss the whole thing!" She voiced her displeasure and her contempt well, Tanner thought, and she went on. Drunk? He'd not had a drink in almost half a day. He shook his head.

"Further, I have been sitting here for hours awaiting what I thought would be our hero to come in, and I find that you Issians are going to depend upon this ... this ... washed-up has-been to defend the RIM and help those poor Issian hostages in ITO's mines? What kind of nonsense is this, I must ask," she huffed and dragged the hood back and away from her long blonde hair. Her eyes flashed and she tossed her head with anger. Tanner noted she was one fiery yet truly beautiful woman.

"Lady St. August," the Master Adept said, "you are upset which is fine, but surely you would have to agree that with our skills as Adepts, our abilities to 'see' into the future with a great degree of certainty and our ability though little known to be able to 'link' between worlds from one Master to another has shown us that this is the man to do this for all of us," the Adept said with a hint of steel showing in her tone and timbre of voice.

"We asked you to come here, accompanied by your own Adept who waits without, Lady St. August, to enable you to learn what we know, what we will do to help you and this Navy Captain both rescue the hostages— some as you realize are Issian citizens, and that is of paramount importance to us; we want our people freed, and you can help with that ... if you agree ... to hear me out ..." Her voice trailed off as she looked at the woman beside her.

Directing her gaze only onto the Adept, she stared for a minute of silence, then one more minute ... then she looked over at Tanner and then back at the Adept. And she nodded.

"Fine, I understand what you have said, and yes, I do agree that you ... you ... Issians are best suited to do this ... or rather to help with this ... but this man does not get my vote to help, not now and not ever. No matter what Adept Gillian has told me, no matter what

228

'persuasion' she worked on me, my mind is firm on that point," she said forcefully.

She sat back and stonily followed the rest of the conversation between the Adept and Tanner. When asked for an opinion, she gave it with what Tanner thought was a begrudging tone, but she did come up with an idea to help with ITO, and yes, she even offered up a small palm branch when it came to how this would be handled at the upcoming quarterly Council meeting and even nodded consent a couple of times when asked for a "Royal" touch on some items.

The Master Adept then nodded to both of them and spoke clearly and succinctly to them both. "We thank you for your help on this and wish you the best in your endeavors. We know you both mean well, and yes, we will be watching for your success in this, and Captain, please be careful with the Pirates. We know that they are definitely the antithesis of everything we hold dear and will need a firm hand to defeat them. We thank you, and we bid you good fortune ... please rejoin your Adepts and let's get our Issians back here ... to their home!" she added carefully and rose as she put back on her veil and swept out of the room with purpose.

Tanner looked over at the Lady St. August and smiled.

"Guess we're gonna be seeing a bit of

each other in the next little while," he said and waited for her answer, which appeared to be taking some time for her to come up with ... but eventually she spoke.

"Captain, we are not friends. We will work with you in this undertaking, and yes, even later on Juno. But we are not friends, as I despise men like you. But maybe—just maybe—you are the man who can defeat these Pirates. We will rendezvous then at ITO on the chosen day, and we will not brook any tardiness NOR any drunkenness either, Captain ... so until then. We will leave now," she offered at the end, and again, veil now swung across her face, she moved off toward the same door that the Master Adept had left via and Tanner was alone.

He sat for a moment, then left the room, and gathered up his lieutenant. Once back inside the robo-cab, he held up his hand to Sander for quiet as he tried to digest what he'd just learned from this meeting as the cab left the village and they climbed the hills on the road back to Dessau with one stop first, Tanner demanded. One stop and then a big, big Scotch. Maybe two.

Ahead was the RIM Navy Academy road into the grounds, and Tanner turned to Sander at that point to quietly let him know only what he needed to help further the mission. Sander nodded and listened and asked not a single question. And they entered the Academy to pull up in front of Kinsolving Hall.

Pushing up the stairs, two at a time, with Sander in close behind him, Tanner reached the doors just as they were challenged by the cadets on guard at the portal entrance.

"Sir, please advance and be recognized," the cadet officer brayed out loudly, his hand stacked up over his sidearm. He looked directly at Tanner, his eyes flicking at the silver eagles and then back to Tanner's face. "Sir, Captain, Sir, I mean ..."

Tanner said quite pointedly and succinctly to the cadet whose job was to challenge all visitors, "Captain Tanner Scott, *RN Marwick*, here to see the academy rear admiral, cadet," and he awaited confirmation as the conversation was relayed into the bowels of the Hall, and the cadet received back the approved status via his ear-piece.

"Sir, permission granted. Please follow Cadet Simmons to the rear admiral's offices, second floor, Delta wing, Sir ..." he said, and he almost smiled, Tanner noticed.

"Well done, Cadet. And thank the duty officer for me as well. Let's go, Simmons," he said as they moved within the front doors and down the hallway to the left. Ahead of them, the hallway stretched out for more than fifty yards, wide with agate green terrazzo floors and large photos on each wall that hung from mid-chest height up to well over the heads of the cadets that were swarming the hall, all fussily dressed in khakis and carrying books and backpacks and noisily chatting and arguing as they held up the group.

"Bullshit, Smathers," one cadet was haranguing another, "there is no way that a pulse cannon can pierce in that far ... even unshielded, the furthest a ball will penetrate is a bit less than twenty feet." He slid a page of a textbook under the nose of a taller cadet to his left. "That's what the book says," he parroted, "and that's what they'll test us on—"

"Ten-shun!" Tanner barked, and the corridor froze after all present came to full attention no matter which way the cadets were walking in the hall. Their guide, Cadet Simmons, took only a second to respond, but then barked out, "Captain in the Hall," and then froze at full attention too.

Tanner smiled to himself and then strode up to the cadet who had been quoting his textbook. He reached down to the cadet's side seams, took the book, peered at the page that had been proffered as the proof on the pulse cannon piercing depth measure, and then smiled.

"Cadet, this book is out of date. On that measure, I can attest that the piercing depth of a pulse cannon is at least twenty-four feet. And I know that for a fact, having suffered same just a few months ago." He looked at the cadet with interest.

"Sir, thank you ... uh, Sir. But this book, this text was written just a few years ago, by Admiral Childs, our academy commander ... so, Sir, while I judge that you may be mistak—"

"Ten-shun, Cadet," their cadet guide barked.

"Cadet, this is Captain Scott, now of the *RN Marwick*—but previously of the *RN Kerry*. Do you remember what happened to the *Kerry*, Cadet ... uh ... Cadet Radisson?" their guide said, recognizing the cadet they were grilling in the Hall.

"Sir, yes, Sir!" Radisson barked back, "The *Kerry* was attacked by Pirates, and yes, there was damage, Sir, and loss of life too, Sir." A drop of sweat appeared on his now furrowed brow. His voice shook only slightly and his color had lightened only a touch, Tanner saw and then decided to end this now.

"Cadet ... uh ... Cadet Radisson. We lost at least two dozen feet of deck on the Kerry. As well as Navy men. You're right in that you're quoting the text, but that's not enough these days. You must always consider that change is surely as much a part of weapons and their firepower as it is in all things. Dismissed," Tanner added, and all around him, cadets slowly began to continue down the hallway and moved around their little five-some like water around a rock ... eddies and ebbs and currents moved about them.

"Sir, this way, please," cadet Simmons said, "the admiral awaits us, Sir," and he pushed by Radisson and his cadet friend who stared at Tanner and Sander, mouths open and faces slack.

"Cadet Radisson? See me next year, son ... I like your style," Tanner said as he moved past the two cadets and once again in tow behind their cadet guide.

Above the ground floor, after the long stairwell hung with a host of photos, they met the second floor and were ushered up to the admiral's offices. At the doorway, Cadet Simmons opened the door and did not follow them in ... but left after closing the door behind them. Within those offices, all was painted white, walls, ceiling, and doors, stark white on white with almost no personalization, except for one wall. On that wall hung rows of photos, not too many Tanner noted, but still a grouping, and above them were the words "Academy Alumni of Valor" in the RIM Navy colors of blue

and gold. Nothing else was written there, and
nothing else ever would be as these were all
photos of alumni who had died while Navy
officers, Tanner suddenly realized. He searched
and found his ex-captain and crew members
from the *Kerry*, alone on the lowest row, and he
suddenly went white and slowed, his mind
working on that loss and his heart suddenly in
his throat. He wanted that Scotch now more
than ever. To lose himself in a bottle. To end
these feelings of loss by helping him cope by
getting sloshed. Sloshed. He shook his head.

Valor, he repeated ... and the Pirates are
to blame ... God, let me find them ... let me be
the one! His thoughts were interrupted by a
short cough.

"Haw ... er ... Captain Scott ... and
Lieutenant Sander, do I have that correct, Sirs?"
the master sergeant said from behind his desk.
He did not rise. Nor would he much follow Navy
etiquette, so I won't challenge him ... I've
already made enough of a disposition here, and
still got some distance to go too ...

"Sergeant, yes, you have us correctly
identified. Scott and Sander to see the admiral,"
Bram said, and they waited while the admiral's
adjutant used their comm to call in and then
pointed off to a few chairs, as this would be a
minute or two, the visitors surmised.

Tanner looked at Bram and smiled.

"So, was I that much 'out of line' correcting that cadet, Bram?" he said contritely, his voice soft so they would not be overheard.

"Sir, not a bit. The pulse cannon specs that he was quoting though were exactly the same that I was taught, and that book was written by the admiral we're waiting to see." His voice too was soft but his points were spot-on, Tanner knew, and he took his time before he answered.

"Bram, the pulse cannon specs were out of date. The *Kerry* was only four years out of dock. She was made as well as any Navy frigate and we lost men. I lost my captain, so it ... it behooved me to speak up. So, while I did not want to berate that cadet, I had to say what I had to say when faced with that untruth! And I would again," Tanner said, his hand clasped in front of his chest missing the feel of a glass half-full and his voice still quiet but firm. His eyes were steady on Sander, and he looked away after a moment to see the admiral's sergeant about to interrupt.

"Uh, Sirs? Admiral will see you now," he said as he rose and opened up the large plain white door whose only adornment was the Rim Navy crest ... and they went into the academy commander's office.

They were met just in front of a large desk of ebony with a large communal sitting wing off to one side. The admiral greeted them quietly but surely according to etiquette, Navy etiquette at that.

"Sir," Tanner said as he saluted and came to attention, mirrored by his lieutenant, and they had that salute returned just as snappy as their own had been, as the admiral rose and rounded his desk and said, "at ease," and reached to shake each officer's hand.

"Captain Scott and Lieutenant Sander, welcome to the Academy. Please be seated here and let's get to it, shall we," the Admiral said as he also sat at that seating wing and slowly sorted his cuffs as his dress khakis looked a bit bigger than he'd needed. Wonder why that might be, but that can wait too, Tanner thought and then came right to the point.

"Sir, we first of all would like to thank you for agreeing to see us without a previously arranged time. Our apologies on that, Sir," Tanner offered up a small apology first, trying to appease the admiral should their not checking in earlier in the day have somehow been "off target" for the admiral's Navy sensibilities. He looked at the admiral who still played with a cuff as he twisted it up higher on his forearm, looking to anchor it away from sliding down and covering almost all of his palm. Across the desk sat a large side table stacked with piles of paper and a clock, and old fashioned maritime clock under a glass bell that chimed the quarter hour softly just then.

"Not a problem, Captain. Of course, we knew you were there, as we too receive full notice of all landings and/or leavings over at Dessau landing port, so we knew you had arrived. And yes, your landing team did fulfill their duty of registering the reason for your visit as being to speak to someone over at the Issian village, so we knew that perhaps you would not even stop here at all. So we were a bit surprised then only in that you did show up. Nothing is amiss, may I ask, Captain?" His cuff now unattended, he stroked his white goatee slightly as he looked askance with a raised eyebrow to the captain. His pose was relaxed, but Tanner judged that his attention was growing. It's time, he thought.

"Sir, we have a special ... uh ... a special request to make of you, and this is an instrumental part of our mission, one that I can only share in part with you. We, Sir, have been charged by the RIM Navy Admiral McQueen, to find the Pirates—and Sir, we would like a bit of help from you ... and the Academy. Sir. If possible, Sir," Tanner stated, not as well as he had hoped, but then again asking a Navy officer, an officer who was his superior by a big jump to break Navy Regs, was always going to be a mouthful. Least in my world, Tanner thought.

"And exactly what would that request be," the Admiral said, leaning forward to listen to what might be coming.

"Sir," Tanner said, "we need a mutiny to occur on an Academy training frigate with the mutineers running to ITO to set down while the *Marwick* gets the job of bringing them to justice, or a reasonable facsimile of same." Tanner got it all out in a rush, his voice cracking only once on the early word "mutiny," and he waited with bated breath as the Admiral sat very still and just looked back at him. And he sat and didn't move ... and then he sighed and nodded.

"Fine, Captain. I take it that all academy cadets will be acting only as some kind of undercover agents in this; that all officers who are mutinied against as well as the mutineers will be 'in' on the mission and there will be no—and I insist on NO repercussions for this on any of the mission officers. That is my only proviso, Captain, will that be agreeable?

"Sir, not at this time—er, what I mean, Sir, is that yes, we agree in theory, but we need —the mission needs the mutiny to be a real one. We need for the faculty and senior cadets, all the officers, to be under the real assumption that the mutiny is real ... anything else may just be seen through too easily by the rest of the Rim inhabitants, and that can put the whole mission to find the Pirates in jeopardy, Sir. That is a needed item ... Sir ..." Tanner added, trying to be as honest as he could to the admiral yet still trying not to indicate who actually had been a part of the planning of the mission.

There was no way he could ever offer that up ... so he sat and waited for the admiral who appeared to be pondering Tanner's counter proviso. And they waited for about a minute as the admiral looked out one of his white-framed windows out and down to the quad below where drill cadet sergeants were making their squads go through their paces in close order drill. And then the admiral cleared his throat.

"Agreed, Captain. This will be a live mutiny, but I will hold you responsible personally if anyone is injured during the mutiny itself, Captain. I can organize same and use trusted cadets to pull this off. As well, I have some rather ... er ... 'mild mannered' faculty who just might need a bit of a shaking up to put out on a training cruise ... so, let's see ... yes, I can arrange this, Captain. But you are still responsible ... and I intend to log this as well, Captain. Do we have an agreement here?" he said, his eyes locking onto Tanner's as he leaned forward once again.

Tanner thought for only a moment and then grinned hugely at the admiral.

"Sir, yes, Sir," he barked back at the

admiral and nodded to cement their deal. The admiral would arrange for the mutiny of an Academy frigate near ITO, and then as the Marwick would be close at hand, the admiral would then contact them to go into ITO to quell the mutiny. And RIM Navy Regs quite clearly stated in no uncertain terms that any ship trying to either quell a mutiny or trying to arrest the mutineers had to do that with all haste; nothing was allowed to get in their way except, of course, the quarantine. But with the help of Lady St. August, they would circumvent that blockade and gain the surface on their mutiny quelling mission. This could work, Tanner thought as he smiled. Our mission now has a degree of success ... if the Admiral could pull off his end. A big word, that "if," Tanner knew ... but Admiral Childs was a force to be reckoned with as he was Admiral McQueen's predecessor, having run the whole Rim Navy for almost twenty years.

As they sat and worked out the details, Tanner learned that he had nothing to worry about as the admiral found holes and plugged them in their mission plan. He sought answers too and forced Tanner and Sander to stop ad-libbing some of the issues that they might face and come up with a full set of "best practices" to count upon instead. The admiral helped big time, Tanner thought as they put the finishing touches on the mission and they rose to take their leave.

The admiral shook both officers' hands and returned back to behind his desk as his adjutant suddenly appeared as the door opened, and he paused as they half-turned back to the office door.

"One thing, Captain," he said, his hand once again playing with his cuff. "The textbook answer of twenty feet was accurate at time of printing. But that spec has already been updated, and the printing proofs are over there," he said as he pointed to his side table that held a few stacks of manuscripts, books it appeared that were being vetted for content.

The admiral shrugged. "Being not up to date is an issue all higher educational institutes face ... but we are trying to correct our facts, Captain ... even at the cost of lives ... Navy lives, Captain!" he finished with his voice low and almost melancholy in tone.

"Gentlemen," he added as they saluted, "Godspeed." He saluted smartly back to them, and they turned and left his office.

Out in the robo-cab minutes later, turning down the main road out of the Academy, Tanner watched the cadets count their marching cadence as they moved by, while their the drill sergeant cadets moved between the ranks, cajoling and persuading them for more and more effort, more spunk, more spirit. A lifetime ago, I was a cadet too, Tanner thought and wondered on that topic on the return trip to the Marwick.

Chapter Nine

"I am sorry that you may think that such duties, fully valid RIM Navy duties, mind you, are somehow beneath you," Admiral McQueen said quietly on screen. "This is not," he said as he shrugged, "a simple duty that can be forsaken, Captain."

Tanner squirmed on his seat in his ready room as the Ansible comm screen played back the message sent to him on the admiral's personal secure channel.

"We must all do things that we think are unimportant, and while I'm sure that you're not happy with policing the latest Jump Games on Neria, that's what you will do. I also am sure that you're shaking your head with what may be negativity, but once again, Captain, that's your lot for the next few days."

"You and the *Marwick* are to proceed to the Neria Station; assume the role of the RIM Navy liaison and watch, police if needed, and generally ensure that this 'sporting event' runs without any kind of a hitch to the Rim. Council members, I'm told, may even be there, as well as the Caliph himself, Sharia Al Dotsa, who is a friend to the Navy and will undoubtedly meet with you, and you are to be the perfect Rim

Navy officer, as are your crew on station leave. Those are your orders. You may certainly now yell at the screen and me vicariously, but those are your orders. Follow them, Captain Scott. Admiral out." He faded from the comm screen.

Tanner sat for a moment and then just shook his head. At least, he thought, Neria was toward ITO, about a nine-day trip out of the way by FTL, and he'd be closer to where the final confrontation with the Pirates would happen ... at least. He also sighed once and then swung around to his ready room view port and the flow of stars. Change heading would be first, he thought and sighed once again as he returned to the bridge to proceed to Neria Station.

On the cerulean blue love seat with the fuchsia pillows, the Baroness lounged back and stretched as she passed the time in her private study. She was a tad tired due to the extra time she'd spent with her personal trainer almost all morning. Her quads felt tight, but they hadn't even been worked on as much as her delts as today had been upper body intensive work.

The recent leaving of her head scientist with the news that Argosenium broke down after approximately nine days of use was bothersome. The costs alone to get the frigate outfitted with the Tachyon over-drive and then mounting the specialized Argosenium mechanism had been eye-popping.

And if the costs had a return of only nine days of effective life in the field, then that was a problem. More new Argosenium would need to be mined, refined, and then centrifuged for purity before it could even be added to the drive mechanism again at more costs. And that meant that more and more hostages would need to be taken to mine the ore as they died in mounting numbers.

Life she realized was expensive. Costs of mining were high. Costs of having hostage miners were high. Everything was expensive and the hunt to build revenues was always on her mind. The other mines on ITO produced rare earths and other Bohr metals too that were so very profitable for the Barony. The Argosenium had been a surprise and one that was so, so costly.

If only the captured spoils were much better. Diamonds and specialty ores were well worth the effort to pirate, but the simple fact was that most of the ultra-expensive cargo shipments went under anonymous bills of lading. If no one knew what was in a container, no one would bother stealing it was the rationale, she thought. Damn them. We need treasury funds and the costs are so so high.

She took another small sip of her recombinant juice drink to try to rehydrate her quads, and after that sip, she sat back again. "If costs are higher than what you want, you need to rethink the program," she remembered from years ago.

She supposed that to limit and defray costs, one could consider closing down tunnel number two up at the Argosenium mine.

And all the pieces and parts that went with that mine.

All the costs she repeated to herself and half-smiled as she re-crossed her legs to ease her quads.

Each and every one of them ... perhaps ...

#####

"Okay, Jocko, one more and then let's knock off for lunch time, okay?" the gray-suited trainer asked the thin man beside him.

Jocko nodded, his face as usual showing no emotion. Beneath his shock of black hair, the sorrel-colored face of an ex-Neria Prime miner gave away nothing; it was too stiff and leather like to ever offer a smile. At 155 pounds and 6 feet 8 inches tall, he was about the right size for an inner planet miner ... and he had the skin to prove it. Gave me my edge, Jocko thought, and that is what is important. Not what I left behind, nor what I could have been ... but what

I am. A champion vacuum jumper, soon to be a citizen member of the Nerian caliphate my own self. He smiled at that and then turned toward the shimmering green force-field jump-curtain.

He walked back to the jump-curtain line and looked out across the gap to the finish line catch-curtain, seventy-five yards away. Stars lit the black inkiness around him, and as this was on the dorsal side of the station, even Nerian, the planet that this station orbited around, could not be seen ... just the blackness of the RIM and the catch-curtain across the vacuum track of outer space.

He nodded to no one and then turned around to walk back to the start point which was ten yards distant. Here in the residential wing, this specialized training camp had been set up especially for him by the Nerian caliphate Family. As their monthly champion for the past eight months, he was expected to train every day for at least four hours a day, jumping, then looking at the jump stats, and then jumping again. The addition of this training camp had been something new in the last few weeks, but he admitted it was very handy to train under actual conditions. And with it being located deep inside one of the residential wings, it was hidden from all others who weren't to know. The Caliphate must win, and if I can win just this one more monthly VacJump, I'm "in" myself, Jocko thought as he knelt in the push blocks that lay exactly ten yards from the jump-curtain and then slowly tuned out the station around him. He looked down to his waist to check his exit-pod and noted it was at half-full, knew that'd be enough O2, and got set in the blocks.

His deep breathing began with long, very, very deep breaths that would pump his blood full of oxygen, again, and again, and again. The time limit was no longer than sixty seconds as to how long a vac jumper could build up their oxygen or when they had to jump. Some jumpers took only a few quick snorts of air then waited to propel themselves at the jump-curtain, while others took the full minute, trying to build up the O2 that they'd need. Then they'd go out there with all the rest of the competitors to test their enduranceuntil they felt the point was reached to hit their exit-pod button to move them to the exit force-field and out of the jump. Such were Jump Games and the rules were simple. The one who outlasted all others out in the arena won. And that was it, Jocko knew ... all he had to do was to outlast them all.

Jocko knew that for this training round, he would be out there for around nine seconds or so, nothing to really worry about, but he still used up almost fifty seconds of breathing buildup time. Then at the bell, he began his sprint to the jump-curtain, exhaling every bit of air from his lungs as he built up speed.

When he hit the curtain, his lungs were empty, and it was like the first time all over again. He was back on Neria Prime, the close in world of the system where he had spent almost twenty years mining the iron pits; he remembered the mining bubble explosion right behind him as he fled across the shale and red sands toward the truck ... no air-pack ... alone under the sun ... his skin drying so quickly he could hear it begin to crackle as he sprinted to the force field doorway. He had made it too, and now almost two years later, here at the Nerian Station, 33,000 miles above the system's capital planet, he sailed weightless in the vacuum, the stars ignored ... his past now ignored ... with only that green catch-curtain ahead as his focus. His leather-like skin now didn't even blister like some of his past competitors did, nor did his eyes bug out; instead his toughened body starred slowly to the left along his axis as the curtain came up—and he was through and safe once more.

He ran off his speed for a few quick steps and then turned and jogged back around the training gap to the start area on the other side, mentally checking off that yes, everything had again come through a vacuum jump with no side effects. If only all had back on Nerian Prime, he thought, but then shook that off and finished his job at the comm station with the trainer.

"So, let's take a look-see, alright?" the trainer said.

Jocko nodded, and they both watched a slow-motion replay of his start, jump, his catch-curtain entry, and then landing and finish.

The trainer nodded at Jocko.

"Other than that little veer to the left that your body does 'cause you push off with your right foot so hard, another perfect jump, Jocko. At 75 yards, your vacuum time was only a bit more than 9 seconds, so well short of the 15-second barrier, and besides you have already done 100 yards, so no worries there at all. In fact, nothing to do now, but go for lunch," he said as he closed down the comm station and looked across at the russet-colored man.

"Right, let's get back together say at 1400, okay with that?" Jocko said, not even bothering to wait for an answer as he walked away to towel off the bit of sweat that always covered his body after a vacuum jump as water always came out through a jumper's pores. He walked off, not thinking about the earlier vacuum jumps, or training, or even becoming a Nerian caliphate citizen member ... but of Neria Prime and times lost ...

Around the Nerian Station were docked and moored ships from many of the RIM Confederacy worlds all gathered for tomorrow's RIM Vacuum Jump Games. There were DenKoss water ships and Leudi cargo freighters, and choir ships from Randi docked beside hunting ships from the Duchy of d'Avigdor, while four or five Barony of Neres cruisers sat out at the fringe of the gathering ships, all docked and gantryed together. Chandler tenders were busy ferrying out supplies, and repair droids were blinking their notice lights as they swarmed out to the various maintenance tickets they were programmed to service. Lying at high-orbit, the Station was a mass of modular wings and units and had been pieced together over the last forty years in the belief that what happened here on the Station would never happen below on the world that owned it.

The Caliph himself, Sharia Al Dotsa, believed as did all of his citizen members that their nine-world Caliphate would be better served by putting vices of the flesh, of the mind, and of the soul off planet, and hence the growth and huge current size of the Nerian Station in high-orbit. The Station, of course, was still patrolled by the Nerian Ramat, the army of the

Caliphate, in their crisp brown khaki uniforms and their polished indigo blue boots. Even now, their small indigo blue shuttles flitted among the off-world moored craft, ferrying their own Customs/Health officers from ship to ship. Many of them were gathered still at the home-craft only docks, awaiting further orders, and many still were moving off to find other newly arrived ships.

Tanner turned back from the forward view screen to make his initials in the log screen in the right-hand side armrest of his captain's chair and counted themselves as just such a newcomer.

"Sir," Lieutenant Bates the *Marwick* Ansible officer of the day said, "Permission to board for Nerian Customs/Health request from port aft mooring station ..." and awaited Tanner's wishes. Bates was a good Ansible officer, Tanner knew, but surely, he could have handled this himself, he thought.

"Um ... anything special about that request, Lieutenant?" Tanner queried, his voice quiet in the normal Bridge hubbub of a mooring at a space station. Helm was busy with final vectors to arrange for gantry issuing, and while Tactical had no duties, Tanner could see that Lieutenant Rizzo was running diagnostics.

"Sir, not really ... but I did think that what with this being the Nerian Caliphate and all, that I'd at least check their boarding officers. And Sir, one of them is a Nerian Caliphate Royal, least that's what his blue robe says and his ID states ..." he finished off, his voice just as quiet as his captain's had been.

"Odd, a bit, I suspect," Tanner said but then nodded back to allow them to board. "Keep me apprised, Lieutenant, of where they go and whom they talk to—all the while let's not let them know we've got ship's surveillance on them, shall we?" he said and watched as Lieutenant Rizzo now with a surveillance program to quickly setup coordinated with his Ansible officer.

"Helm, we all done?" Tanner asked as he stood to quickly go to his ready room just off to starboard. His Helm officer nodded and then confirmed that yes, all was done mooring wise, the gantries were rolling up to their aft boarding ports, and the Station chandlers were awaiting supply orders. Tanner nodded to his XO, and Templeton took over the work needed to get that started. Tanner retired to his ready room.

On screen on the ship's computer terminal, he quickly logged in and notified Lieutenant Rizzo that a sub-feed of the Caliphate Royal's surveillance should be sent here to this screen, and in a moment he was looking down at the *Marwick* aft boarding port. He noted the usual exchange of credentials from the Customs and Health officers in brown khakis to his Lieutenant Greeley who was today's Deck officer. Tanner looked behind them to see what this fuss was all about, and he whistled to himself.

The Caliphate Royal was tall, more than six and a half feet, he judged, and clad as usual in the royal Caliphate indigo blue robe and shawl, an ajrak colored with fields of brown and the indigo blue in diamonds among the design. No one but a Royal could wear that style or color, Tanner had heard, but he had never actually seen one before. "I wonder," he said as he watched the boarding team make all the needed exchanges and questions were asked and answered. The Caliphate Royal just nodded assent when asked a question or two by the Marwick lieutenant and offered up nothing more. Not a bit of trouble, Tanner thought, and he was about to turn off the surveillance feed when he heard the Royal address Lieutenant Greeley directly.

"Kind Sir," the Caliphate Royal said, "I am Nusayr al-Rashid, the new ruler of Olbia, one of the Caliphate realm worlds, and I wondered if it might be possible to meet with your Captain? Captain Scott, I believe, but only for a short time?" he said, his voice as polished as the indigo boots he wore. He simply stared at the lieutenant and said nothing more.

Lieutenant Greeley, however, was a bit flustered by this odd request and showed it to a degree.

"Sir, I can certainly ask—I mean, yes, of course, I will ask but I can offer, Sir, that as we've just moored here off your Station that the captain is normally very busy, tied up in fact with all the various command duties that accompany such a docking. But please, if you just give me a moment ..." he said as he quickly punched in an inter-ship comm link and spoke quietly to the daily Comm officer. Tanner jumped in quickly and affirmed that the Nerian Royal was to be taken to the conference room on Deck One and offered full ship's hospitality while Tanner moved to the central axis turbo-lift to drop to Deck One to meet this strange Royal.

"Wonder what he wants, and more, what he needs," he voiced to himself as the lift moved down the thirty decks. Tanner moved over to the conference doors and saluted the visitor's guard, a CPO in the *Marwick* Provost Corps and was saluted in return.

Inside the conference room, the Royal sat casually in one of the comfy sofas that was placed over at the far wall of the room. Tanner joined him and sat opposite taking his cues from this Royal and looked and waited. Moreover, he did not wait long.

"Your admiral, Admiral McQueen, has asked me to relay a message to you. Personally," he said, "I think that this is very different, but we owe the admiral—the Caliphate does, I mean, and as such, the Caliph Sharia Al Dotsa, my first cousin, has charged me with this message, Captain Scott." He half-turned to look out of the starboard side windows and watched as another brown and indigo blue shuttle cruised by slowly ... aiming at a group of off-station moored ships up against the curve of the galaxy and the glow from within.

Tanner waited as he thought that this was a very strange messenger to carry such a seemingly secretive message from the admiral, but he sat and awaited same.

"Your admiral has sent just this, Captain," the Caliphate Royal said very clearly and succinctly.

"'Beware the Barony,' and that, I'm afraid is the sum total of the message, Captain."

"Sum total?" Tanner inquired, his voice rising at the end of that phrase.

"All is what I meant, Captain. I have repeated the full three words that I was given and have left nothing out. That is what the message was in its entirety, Captain. On that and our sacred scrolls, I swear," the Caliph's son added and bowed his head as all Caliphate citizens did when they swore on their most religious artifacts, their sacred scrolls.

Tanner nodded. He looked away out the conference room windows for a full minute, trying to determine why the admiral had sent such a message, when in his opinion, only he had any idea of what was to occur in the next few days. He nodded once again to the message bearer and looked the taller man in the face.

"Was there anything else, any time line or anything at all given with that message?" he inquired once again.

The Caliph's son shook his head in the negative sense and rose at the same time, the blue hem of his ajrak swirling around his ankles.

"Not at all, Captain. The message relayed was all that there is ... and I must now go, kind Sir. Perhaps I will see you at our Jump Games tomorrow, or you may one day visit me on Olbia," he added very politely as he bowed deeply and swept away through the now opening door and to the landing ports, his Provost guard now trailing behind him.

His message had been timely, Tanner thought, but in fact he was already aware of the Baroness and her Pirates ... but as to how the admiral had found that out, he had as yet no inkling of that.

Or was that it? Maybe the admiral was referring to the Jump Games themselves ... and while he knew that the Barony had entrants in the games, surely there could be no way to "rig" a vacuum jump to win. Either the jumper made a successful jump, or they didn't ... and died trying. So ... why the warning Tanner wondered as the admiral knew nothing about the upcoming confrontation with the Pirates.

He pondered on that for a minute or two more as he watched the Caliphate shuttle appear from the port side of the ship and slowly move off and back toward the Station areas that it was directed to. Behind the Station lay the bulk of the galaxy, foaming with light and dust clouds, but here at the edge of the RIM, all was bordered by the blackness of inter-galactic space. Beyond the RIM lay misty small galaxies at great distances, big enough to be impossible to try to breach using the current FTL drives that powered all inner-galactic travel. And even though there were a few stars that lay against that black cloud, Tanner knew that they were the very edge of the Rim itself, and as Confederacy members, he would be visiting them too in the future. But not today ... today it was a simple police action for the Jump Games. Least of our worries, he thought, but still needed. Bloody hell, he added to that realization and moved back toward the turbo-lift and the bridge.

#####

Most of the ship's officers were asleep this night as the *CS Valiant* ran her training course off the world of Roor, about midway between the Duchy and the Barony. This narrow strip of space owned by neither world system was only five light-years thick, yet held more than a dozen worlds with allegiance to neither the Duke nor the Baroness.

Called the Free Channel by many, these were the worlds that were courted at some length by both of the two powers lying to either side. Yet most had deferred any choice to be made by playing one against the other, Cadet Ensign Radisson knew, more perhaps as he was a Roorian and felt almost at home back in the Free Channel area.

Add in the Free Channel cloud nebula that was more than a light-year thick, with its swirling red, magenta, ochre, and orange wisps, this supernova remnant partially blocked the Free Channel space as it remained like a sentinel between these two powers.

As Comm officer, he was on duty at his station while the clock above the ship's front screen slowly climbed the minutes left to a full twenty-three hundred hours. Almost time to call them, he thought.

Around him on the cruiser's Bridge were three other cadets, all acting ensigns like himself, and the lone ship's officer, Lieutenant Brent, sitting and almost dozing in the captain's chair. His fellow ensigns were all making like they were bored, trying to find something to do. If they were like me, Radisson thought, they'd be sweating under their tunics. Fraser was over on Tactical, like he was paying attention, but he tilted his head as he glanced at Radisson too often with a look to the clock on every other head tilt. Jorgenson was acting helmsman tonight, and he fiddled with his TachyonDrive thrust settings, trying to coax just one more notch out of the engine. And Smith, over on the Ansible, was listening to God knows what, but his eyes never left the clock that now said three minutes more.

At a moment after the clock signaled via the chimes that it was twenty-three hundred hours, the turbo lift doors opened and Cadet Ensign Rand appeared with a tray of coffees and snacks for the Bridge crew who still had more than three hours left on their duty shift. As he carefully walked to the Tactical station, behind and to port of the captain's chair, he placed the tray with its mugs and closed boxes carefully on the display table.

"Compliments of the bakers down in the galley, lads," Rand said, nodding at each of the cadets who came over to pick up their mug and box.

"Not a lotta fresh-baked smell," sniffed Lieutenant Brent, as he slowly straightened out in the captain's chair and gestured to Ensign Rand. "Maybe those cadets need some more time on Donuts 101," he said with a grin.

"Not to worry, Lieutenant, as they didn't send one up for you anyways," Cadet Rand said as he walked the mug of steaming coffee over to the captain's chair and placed it gently on the armrest.

The lieutenant shrugged and reached for his mug as Cadet Radisson then spoke up.

"Not to worry, Lieutenant, you can have mine," Radisson said as he arose from the Comm station and walked over to the captain's chair. As he walked, he opened up the closed box pulled a sidearm from within, and pointed it directly at the lieutenant, stopping directly in front of the surprised officer.

"What in hell do you think you're doing, Cadet?"

"Just sit tight, Lieutenant. I must ask you not to move, nor to bother trying to ring an alarm," Radisson said, as Cadet Smith nodded to him.

"All your chair functions have been severed, and I'm sorry to say that you are our first prisoner, uh, Sir. This is a mutiny," he added, his voice surprisingly strong.

Around him, the other cadets also pulled

out their recently acquired sidearms and moved away from their assigned stations. Jorgenson moved to the turbo-lift while Fraser and Smith flanked the captain's chair.

"Mutiny?" Lieutenant Brent said with a large dose of incredulousness in his voice.

"There has never been a mutiny on any Academy ship. There's no place to go out here, no place to hide, and the whole damn Rim Navy will be on your tail in less than a day. Mutiny? What, were the donuts not so good, Cadets?" he said as he began to rise.

It was at that point from behind him that Fraser keyed his stunner and the lieutenant immediately slouched back, knocked out from the sidearm and asleep for at least a half-hour.

"Right," Radisson said, "we're on the time line and A-okay so far." The doors to the turbo-lift opened and five more cadets came onto the bridge. One looked at Radisson, who nodded, and that cadet left in the lift immediately, only to return moments later with the Academy faculty, the ship's Captain Grant.

"Cadet, all in order here," he said, as he glanced at the now supine lieutenant, legs akimbo and one arm dropped across the left side of his chair.

"Sir, yes, Sir!" Radisson piped up.

"Fine, Cadets Fraser and Smith, ready for the next steps?" he said as he crossed over to the Comm station with them. Below them on the display panel, Fraser popped up the previously programmed screens, and all crowded around as the doors of all the real ship's officers were first buzzed by a cadet waiting at their doors. Moments later they began to open, and each of them was quickly stunned by the assigned cadet. Most fell back toward the interior of their quarters, but Radisson noted that one of the officers, Lieutenant Baines, he thought, fell against the bulkhead and seemed to scrape his temple, but that was a small price to pay.

"Right, Cadets, down to the shuttle bay on the double. Cadets, let's see if you can manhandle Lieutenant Brent. Um ... Fraser, give them a hand, please," he said as four cadets lifted up the lieutenant and crowded into the turbo-lift as they dropped down to Deck Four and the shuttle bay over to port.

As they proceeded toward the bay doors, they were met with more than a dozen of the on-board cadets, all encumbered with a stunned ship's officer, all moving toward the shuttle.

At the loading doors, Captain Grant looked over the disposition of each of the stunned officers and arranged them all to be most comfortable. He also overlooked Fraser, who was in the process of removing three of the vital boards from the shuttle's navigational computer, rendering it still space-worthy but not able to navigate with computer precision. As he checked and then double-checked all of the final items, he nodded to Radisson and then approached his colleagues, the only other Academy faculty officers on the CS Valiant.

"Right, men, we've about ten minutes only ... so time to take that nap." He received nods and then waited until each of the faculty was supine before giving them the lightest stun setting and they quickly lapsed out.

"Okay, just me, and then you're to follow the plan exactly, Cadet Radisson, understood? You know the time-line. You know what's expected of you as well. No variations, no ad-libs, not a single change to be contemplated. Understood, Cadet? Cadets?" he stated in a forceful manner as he looked around him as he sat on the deck before them.

"Sir, yes, Sir!" they all chimed back as they nodded back to him.

"Right, well, stun me, ship us out, and then make tracks to your rendezvous. Godspeed, mutineers," he added with a wry grin and was stunned where he sat. Falling back slightly, he increased the stunned body count to nine, with five ship's officers and the four Academy faculty officers all splayed out around him.

Fraser stepped away from the shuttle

helm.

"Delayed takeoff in thirty seconds, as per plan," he added. The cadets filed out and stood to the side of the bay as the boarding portal closed. Moments later, the shuttle seemed to quiver for a few seconds and then moved out and through the force-field curtain that held back the vacuum of space, and the shuttle's engines blazed as its Inertial Drive kicked in and it moved off at sub-light.

"Bridge duty Cadets, follow me," Radisson said, and they all dropped off their stunners with the armory cadet who'd stationed himself at the shuttle bay doors.

"Say, maybe I can keep mine," Jorgenson said, "in case our cadet captain sticks me with lousy duty shifts," he joked as he held up the line leaving the bay for a moment.

Radisson just stared at him for a moment.

"No changes to plan, eh, Jorg?" he quipped back.

He was met with a nod and a smile from his fellow mutineer.

"Right, as our captain likes to say, 'no ad-libs either.'" Jorgenson laughed and dropped his stunner onto the armory cart and moved back starboard toward the turbo-lift and the Bridge.

Minutes later as Radisson sat for the first

time ever in a cruiser's captain's chair, he gave the orders to Jorgenson to plot a course to ITO. As the *CS Valiant* gathered herself for the jump to light-speed and the quarantined planet ahead, he wondered if all the intel was correct too, as he knew there was only a very slow and painful cure for the Natrium Flu.

Aboard the cruiser *Sterling*, the ship's Adept sat on her bed, in Siddhasana pose, awaiting the communal meeting that would cross over almost fifty light-years of distance in real-time. Gillian knew that Michelle needed to find the spot to be in to do this, but that could take time, so she waited.

The message would be an easy one to deliver but a hard one to make happen, she knew. Telling anyone what was expected of them was a difficult task, but in this case, it may even be a sentence of death. The Pirates' hostages were for the most part treated cruelly and harshly, but only a few had been sacrificed by their captors ... the ones who'd fought back or quit working the mine on ITO.

Gillian was about to tell Michelle she was to lead a miner's revolt, which was a difficult task for anyone, but Gillian knew that Adepts learned at an early age to comply and to follow the leadership of the Grand Master Adept, under whose name Gillian was now relaying these directions. Michelle was also the aunt of the young Adept, Roison, who at eleven was still short by more than a year from puberty and full Adept powers. She would be needed to help protect the miners from the Adept guard leader. She would fail, all believed, but she had to try. Such was the way of the Adept order and such it would always be.

Gillian stretched out her left leg breaking the yoga pose for a moment to massage her spasmed calf and then reposed back into the entwined leg pose, breathed deeply, and waited for Michelle to appear in her consciousness.

#####

Jump Games Day on Neria Station was as to be expected, a day of total confusion for just about everyone who worked the event. The various Station residential and cargo wings, Station modules, and yes, even force-field umbrella'd barges were all arranged around the vacuum arena itself. Today's competition, the annual championship after eleven monthly competitions, was the culmination of the year and would see the most in attendants, competitors, and wagering too. Thousands would attend today as this day someone would be crowned the Jump Games Annual Champion, and that meant automatic citizenry in the Caliphate and membership as a part of the Royal team alumni. All of the competitors wanted this spot as such rank enabled a life of ease while wearing the Royal indigo robes.

People thronged throughout the walkways, the malls, and corridors, and yes, almost fought for prime viewing stations at various window ports and scene-scapes that overlooked the almost totally surrounded arena area where the competition would occur. It was a festive air with everyone excited, and sometimes loud conversations on their own choices of entrants peaked while still others flaunted their own champions. Vac jumpers were well known throughout the Rim, and each colony, duchy, barony, caliphate, and world had its own champions. And today, they met on Nerian Station to compete for the Annual RIM Championships.

The local Caliphate casinos were there and supported by many other off-world betting conglomerates too; all were jammed along the center mall of the Station, as well as spotted throughout the various viewing stands and even out on some of the barges that surrounded the arena.

Games headquarters was stationed off to the side of the arena, and it was here that RIM Navy stationed their own presence with more than forty officers and CPOs, including a dozen

more of the *Marwick's* provost guards with
their yellow Sam Browne belts and crossed,
knurled lanyards. Positioned outside of the
entrance to the headquarters, these provost
guards were there to show the celebrants that
the Rim Navy was in charge of the event
policing even though the Caliphate troops were
interspersed throughout the whole Station.

Inside the Games Headquarters, past the
general area, Competitor's login area, and the
Judges Only area, was a section that was used
as the Competitor's staging lounge, and it was
here that voices were raised. Lieutenant
Framingham, assigned the duty to watch over
that lounge, finally spoke up as he moved
between the Baronial Navy Corporal and an
Alto from Randi and barked for quiet.

"Sirs! No one here," he stated once the
two had stopped yelling and now only glared at
each other, "cares about who thinks who should
or should not be able to compete. Judges have
ruled already. Anyone who thinks different is
wrong," he said, his voice now commanding the
argument.

"You don't understand, uh ...
Lieutenant," the Alto trilled, his voice almost
musical with his anger, "no one can enter the
Open Pro class who's not jumped at least once
before in the Amateur class. That's the rules,
that's the rules," he said, his face now pointed

directly at the corporal held back from him by the lieutenant's body.

"Not a problem, as I've said now for ten times," the Barony Corporal stated. My brother was entered in the Amateur class eight months ago and had to pull out after only one jump ... but that qualifies his 'must haves,' and we've already proved that to the Judges earlier this morning."

Lieutenant Framingham looked at the corporal in his red and blue Barony uniform that always, to him at least, looked just a bit gaudy. The nameplate read, "Corporal B. Doering," and his dearth of campaign badges showed him as either a new enlistee or a paper pusher from the Barony capital world. He nodded to the corporal in agreement.

"Exactly, Corporal. Judges rule and we follow those rulings and that's how it is. This man ... er ... well, his brother, I mean, was passed into the Open Pro class and that's final." He turned his back now on the corporal and faced the Alto directly.

"Do you have anything else to complain about, Sir?"

The Alto was taken aback but swallowed his anger as he shook his head negatively, as his hair combs flopped back and forth.

The lieutenant nodded and pushed away from the men, who also faded into opposite corners of the room. He noticed that the Alto was a part of the Alto team, Randians all in their event finery, and noticed that the humanoid reported back to the team leader, he suspected, who glared back at Framingham with a look of displeasure. As he moved back toward the center of the room to purvey the various teams and their competitors, he noticed that the Barony corporal was the only one who accompanied this disputed Pro ... and wondered about that for an instant. Unlike the Barony to not fully support a system champion, he thought and moved over for a closer look at their competitor.

He was surprised once he was able to take a good look at this man, this supposed Pro Jumper, very surprised.

The man had what could only be called an elongated, misshapen head, with a large forehead much, much bigger than normal. His face, however, was pretty plain and almost childlike in its stolid stare. He nodded to the man and wondered if this could have been the results of jumping into a vacuum ... then his science training took over and he knew that wasn't the case. This man ... oddly dressed he suddenly realized in a stylization of caliphate dress, carried anatomical baggage from something that had nothing to do with the results of being in a vacuum for a time ... this was something else. He moved around the two who sat on their benches and back toward the observation point he liked near the center of the room. Time now until the Amateurs were over was brief, and that'd mean a large influx of entrants from the arena and that would be noisy. He sighed. All losers except one who'd be crowing while around him others would be wailing. Such is the life of a contest ... any contest. He nodded to himself and moved back to oversee the lounge to watch over all.

#####

"Celebrants, welcome to the Rim Vacuum Jump Games Open Professional Class finals," said the speaker system over Tanner's head as he peered out the side port of the launch module. Being in charge, he realized had its perks, and this was surely one of them, as he and his XO were positioned directly to the left of the jump field where the Pros would launch themselves into the vacuum arena. Beside him with monitors aimed at them sat the judges, all off-worlders, he noted, from many Confederacy planets. There were Eonians and Altos, UrPoPoians and DenKoss natives, Ducal and Baronial types, and Leudies and Junoites too. All together, the twelve Judges were a cross section of the Confederacy, as it should be, Tanner realized and hoped this would mean that there would be no problems at all. In fact, he thought, the Judges really didn't do much other than police the entrants' bona fides before the competition even began. Once the entrants had jumped, the force-fields monitored the time spent out in the arena, and that meant that the time spans of each jump were measured down to the nano-second, hence, he knew, there would be no room for argument or interpretation— as the clock could not lie!

Within the launch pad to his left, the Pros were gathered with their teams around each of them, nodding and listening to both advice and counsel. Surrounded by the plain Station walls, on three sides and the force-field green sheen on the fourth, there was a hubbub of voices and comments all around. Some of the competitors were stretching, while others had trainers massaging their legs or backs. A few were seated in straight-backed chairs, listening to their handlers, while a couple more were lying supine on the gray Station decking, gathering themselves, it appeared. He wondered for a moment what became of a competitor who didn't win today, and where they'd end up, if anything would happen to them? With ten competitors, nine competitors from other worlds would be also-rans ... but where to, he pondered as the milling around seemed to slow over in the launch pad area. In fact, things seemed to stop. And then he saw why.

A double brace of Caliphate guards, khaki brown and blue booted, marched into the area, making much ceremony for only four of them. Behind them came a string of trainers, a couple of medical aides, and then yes, there was the Caliphate Champion, this Jocko.

He looked small in size and heft, but having seen vids of the long standing jumps this man had made, Tanner knew he could jump. His skin still looked so much like green tea leaves did, dark but rusty somehow and leathery near the eyes and temples. He wore the mandatory simple stress jump suit, but his was in the Caliphate khaki brown with their traditional indigo blue exit-pod belt cinched around his waist. His bearing was like he was already the winner, Tanner thought, but that remains to be seen, and shortly.

Jocko, however, appeared pretty unimpressed with what was going on around him as he strode along behind his entourage and took over a small spot close to the force-field. He began some stretching exercises as he got ready for the Class Jump finals. Having earned his spot over the past months via winning at least once, he and the other nine champions from worlds across the Confederacy, all were getting—wait, Tanner thought as he watched a final competitors enter the launch pad area.

A single Barony officer—no, it was a mere corporal, Tanner could see now accompanied in a very odd-looking competitor with his arm around the larger man's waist. This jump-suited man, lad actually, as he looked younger than all the rest of the competitors by a large factor, had a very odd ... very different looking head, and Tanner thought that "larger than life" about covered it. His forehead is as large as my ready room console monitor, Tanner thought, and his hair clumped out of his scalp in tufts and wisps. He was large, about a full six and a half feet in height but wouldn't weigh more than 150 lbs, and he wore, like Jocko did, the colors of the Caliphate competitor's jump suit. Odd, Tanner thought, and he reached for the monitor screen at his station and quickly fingered for a competitor's listing ... and yes, there were two Caliphate competitors, Jocko and this one, a Caliphate intern, named of all things, Junior Doering.

Intern, Tanner knew, meant he had applied to join both the religion and the worlds therein and was awaiting final review of his application. Winning today would help his case, Tanner thought suddenly, but against Jocko, most of these competitors' personal best times were at least thirty seconds short. Tough crowd,

and the competition was about to begin as the
launching pad coordinators stepped up to
announce the rules formally and to arrange the
line up of worlds to be applied. Most were
listening, Tanner noted, but this Junior was off
in his own world, nodding his head to a distant
drummer while Jocko too appeared to be
ignoring the launch configurations around him.

Once done, the competitors all drew
starting positions via lots, which seemed to take
more time than was needed, echoed with the
encouragement of their retinues and cheering
and catcalls from those in the competitor's
guest's area. Beside the competitors' deck lay
that small bleacher area, holding competitors'
family and friends, investors and backers too.
Within that group, from across the RIM, were
almost an entire pageant of the various races
and citizens, all cheering for their own world's
champions. While no one waved a flag or sang
an anthem, they just about could have, Tanner
saw.

Jocko, Tanner noted, earned the number
three spot from the starboard line while the
Junior lad was at the end in the number ten
spot, as far to port on the force-field as one
could be. And now it was time to get ready for
the call to the line and the competitors last
chance for oxygen. The launch pad quieted, and
Tanner watched as all did these final moments

before the launch.

The ten competitors all moved forward ahead of the yellow line on the deck and awaited the masks to drop from above. Moments later in front of each of them, a mask appeared from above connected via a clear tube to the Station's infrastructure, each hissing from the supply lines. All of the competitors reached for one and held the masks over their nose and mouth to inhale, to take in the gas that would help them last longer, hopefully, than their competitors. At least that's what each of them thought, Tanner surmised as he, among all the rest, watched the ten competitors breathe in ... then out ... then in ... then out ... slow methodical breaths that were to bank the oxygen for use in less than a minute. Some competitors stopped before others, and Tanner noted that Junior stopped well before all the others, his taking of O2 being less than half of all the rest. Others stopped soon after, and then a buzzer sounded, the ten-second warning, as they all moved ahead of that yellow line to the green line only ten feet short of the force-field. Some dropped into a crouch, while others used a set of starting blocks like Jocko did, to launch themselves into the arena a short ten yards away. Quiet ensued, and all awaited the klaxon to begin the championship round.

Hearing the loud horn, all launched into

the vacuum like they were one, exhaling all breath at once as Tanner turned to the monitor above him, while he kept an eye on his monitor that showed each of the ten competitors in a separate individual security window. Propelled by their own strength, some moved out and into the illuminated arena with a degree of speed and some not so fast. One's speed, Tanner knew, would propel you toward the exit force-field a full 100 yards distant, or at a lesser speed, you moved slower than others. Using an exit-pod made you able, of course, to slow or speed your progress through the arena toward the timed exit force-field, all the while watching your opponents and trying to manage the lack of oxygen and the absolute cold at the same time. Being a living breathing organism, trying to survive in negative 454 degree Fahrenheit temperature was surely a challenge, but the real part of being a vacuum jumper was not the competitors, but as Tanner understood it, the challenge of being in a vacuum. That was the true test of being a vacuum jumper ... and not so much beating your competitors. At least, that's what all the news vids said, and how far wrong could they be, Tanner wondered cynically.

Out in the arena, he saw that Jocko had taken a spot under the bright LED lights at almost dead center of the 100-by-100-by-100-yard space. He had jumped quickly to the center and floated, not yet shivering, all noted, and watching around him for those who tended to congregate in the same general area. Except, Tanner noted, for Junior, who stayed closer, much closer to the launch force-field, almost a full eighty yards from the exit field. Surely, Tanner thought, a mistake that only new-to-competition entrants made, as he crossed off this Caliphate intern mentally. Not a chance from that far away.

Above the arena on a large LED sign ran the time, now at twenty-seven seconds, Tanner noted, as the sign counted off the total time out in the vacuum. Space, of course, transmitted no sound at all, so out there he knew it was as silent as a tomb, but in here, the cheering, the catcalling, and the prompting for more stamina was a growing factor all around the launching pad. He could imagine what it would be like over in the major big Station malls and wings where thousands of fans would be cheering and jeering their choices. Here, instead of those thousands, there were only dozens, yet it still was louder, Tanner thought, than he'd ever imagined, as the clock now hit forty-one seconds.

At almost fifty seconds, the DenKoss competitor moved away from the small grouping near the arena center toward the exit force-field and was swallowed into the landing area and out of the competition. One down and nine more to go. But as Tanner and others noticed, the Eonian and the competitor from the Duchy of d'Avigdor had moved closer to the exit force-field as the LED clock now counted off a full sixty seconds. Yet Jocko still maintained the center of the arena, rotating slowly as he stared out at the multitudes that watched both here and all across the Rim via vid feeds.

At seventy seconds, the Alto's competitor and both the Leudi and Nerian unfolded from their semi-fetal positions and moved toward the exit field slowly ... looking at the remaining four competitors who still maintained their spots near the center. The Leudi looked bloated, like vacuum ebullism had begun, as his body had swelled almost by thirty percent, his abdomen footballing in the middle and his eyes almost breaching his face. All noted that he jetted quickly into the exit force-field suddenly, and Tanner hoped that he'd get the best care possible and as quickly as possible too. Bad news, he thought, for all the Leudies out there.

Now with only four competitors left, Tanner watched at eighty seconds as the vacuum began to take its toll. All of them were swelling, body-shape-wise, as they attempted to outlast each other, the chilling of absolute zero beginning to now warm the blood enough to boil though that was fought by the tightly fitting pressure stress jump suits. Only the UrPoPo humanoid looked really bad, as he now moved quickly away from the center of the arena, and all watched as he now slid through the exit force-field and out of sight. Three left, and we're at a full ninety seconds, one and a half minutes of life in an absolute vacuum at absolute zero temperature. Time now was the deciding factor, and the winner was out there right now, one of the last three left, swelling and now beginning to show visual discomfort.

The Conclusion competitor who'd swelled now and whose face had begun to show the telltale frost that accrued around his mouth was now like the rime that gathered around a winter window, snaking out and around the man's nose and climbing to his eyes. While he took in the same oxygen that the other competitors had, or at least he'd had the same opportunity, he was hurting more it appeared as he moved now quickly toward the exit force-field. Behind him followed the six-armed Elbonian, who appeared to also be at an end of his time too, as they both moved through the field and out. And now there were only two, Tanner realized, at 110 seconds.

Jocko, who maintained his still center of the arena holding spot, looked for all to see, in some troubles. He was swollen it looked but because he was such a smaller man, the swelling made him look huskier than normal, but not quite yet as swollen as others had.

Tanner had to look to find Junior though — and where was he ... oh there still hanging back near the launching force-field. He looked too worse for wear, now having a rimed frozen face, and even that clumpy hair looked frozen and snow covered. His eyes, however, never left Jocko, and as Tanner watched, he only now used his exit-pod to move only now closer to Jocko and the middle of the arena.

Jocko, however, was appearing to suffer some distress at a full 125 seconds; he moved slowly now away from Junior, who trailed him by a dozen feet or so, toward the exit force-field. He spun slowly as he manipulated the exit-pod spray and faced away from his movement vector, now staring at what would soon be the only competitor left ... and then he sped up to motor through the exit force-field and out of the arena, leaving the winner, Junior, out there all alone, as he stopped then only a few feet short of that exit and he spun back toward the arena center. He floated there, holding his position, and he looked like the Champion that he appeared to be, Tanner imagined. He held that position, stopped in front of the exit field, for a full ten more seconds as the crowds all over the station roared with delight at his winning jump.

Then, as Junior went through the exit force-field and out of the arena as the new Open Pro Class Jump Champion, the competition ended with a new champion...

Chapter Ten

The bull ensign spoke with a clear emphasis on what he'd just learned from the screen in front of him.

"Sir, permission to page the captain, incoming from Juno marked EYES ONLY, Sir," Lieutenant Whiteside said with a curt interruption to the conversation on the Bridge of the *Marwick*.

"Permission granted, Lieutenant, go ahead," said Lieutenant Rizzo, as he turned to face the lieutenant JG. "Any ideas on that one?" he asked with a raised eyebrow.

"Not a glimmer, Sir," the bull said, "but it's gotta be important." He swept a ship-wide survey and found the captain in the gym down on Deck Twenty-three. He spoke quickly to him using his throat mic and nodded back even though the captain couldn't see him.

"Says he's on his way up to his ready room chop-chop, Sir." He turned back to face the Bridge officer of the day, and Lieutenant Rizzo smiled back at him.

"Doesn't happen often, Lieutenant. Not a big deal though ... last one I remember was about three years ago on the *Henderson* under Captain Farias. Seems the DenKoss merchants had some issues with a string of Leudi trades and were planning on getting their revenge via what could only be called a dust-up of the first order." He shook his head and then chuckled.

"Interestingly enough, the one trade that they were most upset about they couldn't get rescinded, even though we tried to work on their behalf. Seems someone pulled a fast one with those industrial diamonds they discovered over on Eons, you know the ones that the Issians make all their credits on? Anyways, the Leudies got screwed on that one big time ... and the DenKoss made out just fine!"

Lieutenant Rizzo filled his mug once more with what was called coffee, even though he suspected that term was not as appropriate as it could have been and returned to the captain's chair. Working his rear end into the chair, he half-turned to place his mug on the arm of the chair and was interrupted by the captain who walked onto the Bridge quickly.

"Captain on the Bridge," he announced in a loud voice and rose as did the rest of the crew on duty. His hand was rock steady though as he held that full mug firmly and didn't spill a drop.

"At ease, Lieutenant," Tanner said as he strode through the Bridge on his way to the ready room doors on the port side of the Bridge.

"Back to your duties, crew ... Lieutenant

Whiteside, please plug that EYES ONLY into the console and seal off the room," he said as he left the Bridge.

Within his ready room, small as it was, there was a console on the desk and it faced the Bridge wall while the outer wall was all windows pointing out at the Rim. Within a short jaunt of only a couple of light-years away, Tillion lay just to starboard, and while he couldn't see the capital, Mancerat, he knew it was as many race homes, totally un-visitable to humans. No one he'd ever met could say that they'd been allowed off the landing site there, and rumors were that there was an issue with Tillion women—no one had ever seen one, met one, or talked to one even on Ansible he'd learned. Of all the RIM Confederacy members, the Tillion were the most closed-off society except for the Issians though for all purposes that was a cult really not so much a whole race.

On the desk, the console suddenly lit up—the splash screen for the RIM Navy came on followed by the notice that EYES ONLY meant just that ... and Tanner sat very still as the console aperture suddenly went red as the beam shot into his right eye to verify his retinal pattern.

Two seconds later, the screen showed AUTHORIZED and went dark for a further moment and then on screen came Admiral

McQueen's face.

"Captain, we have some—uh—well some interesting news. Off Roor, an Academy ship, the *CS Valiant*, was taken over by what appears to be a group of cadets. Mutiny, is what I'm talking about here ..."

The admiral stopped, shook his head, and sighed.

"Wait, I know, never been a mutiny ever on any RIM Navy ship nor for that matter on any RIM member ship either. Unheard of. And the Academy officers were all simply stunned, loaded into a shuttle, and then auto-programmed to go to the Roor station. Were all fine after medicals and they all to a man report that there was NO issues on board before the mutiny. No arguments, no confrontations ... nothing, Captain. Any ideas?" the admiral said, his head cocked to one side.

Tanner sat for a moment ... mutiny on an Academy training ship? No reason for same? What might be the best way to handle this ... and thank God, he'd thought this through earlier.

"I've no idea, Admiral, as you said this is unheard of. Not a single clue as to the reason for this? No affairs? No poor marks? No slights or religious issues?" Tanner knew the answers to the questions but held out hope the admiral would have an inkling that the mutiny could at least be attributed to something ...

The admiral shook his head.

"Not as far as we can determine. The officers were tried and true, and the students were all at or near the best we've got in this year's graduating cohort! Not a hint of a rationale."

The admiral looked off screen for a moment and then returned his attention to the console at his offices on Juno.

"We have tracked them though ... and they're right now scurrying through the Free Channel if we can believe our scans. They know we can see them, and they know we're coming—the reason I'm EYES ONLY with you today."

The admiral squared his shoulders, faced Tanner, and nodded his head up and down as he now spoke.

"Orders to follow by regular channels, Tanner ... but I want you to follow them through the Free Channel or wherever the hell they're aiming at, and take them into custody. We want to know why more than anything else, I'd think ... though the RIM Council will probably want as much info as you can find out. No one is to be hurt if possible, Captain, but a reminder that mutiny out here on the RIM is the same as everywhere else ... a crime punishable by military court action and yes, death."

He shook his head then, and his epaulets

fluttered on his shoulders, the four gold stars shimmering in the console light.

"Tanner ... take them and bring them in, try to not hurt a soul ... but your judgment in this matter is most important. They need to be tried for this, but to do that, you need to bring them in ... alive. Follow me here?"

Tanner knew he was being charged with the job of finding the mutineers, taking them into custody, and then returning them to face charges on Juno. He also knew that the whole mutiny was a made-up event, aimed only at getting him the ability to land on ITO to find the Pirates as per the Issian plan. But he also knew that the admiral knew nothing about the plan ... and felt badly that the strength of the plan relied on his keeping the plan a secret. From the man to whom he really owed his life.

He nodded back to the admiral and ended with what he hoped was the right way to accept just such an EYES ONLY order, and moments later, the screen went black.

Right, he thought, if they're in the Free Channel, then they'd made good time from Roor and were aiming at getting to ITO in about six more days ... time to tell the crew and to make some plans. He looked out the view-port and watched as the hard stars out there seemed to be etched in black steel. Most were older G stars of yellow and orange, and there were a couple of red dwarfs he could find if he looked hard enough, but most were main sequence stars ... not a single blue giant out here on the RIM. He stood and moved closer, wondering why the mutineers hadn't even come up with a "plausible raison d'être" for their taking over the ship. It didn't matter, he knew, as all would be forthcoming to the admiral when it was over ... yet still it would have been just a bit more solid. Beyond the view-port, the stars still shone and he turned to give the new orders to his crew. Only Bram his Adept would get the true story, but that was as needed, he realized as he left his ready room and returned to the Bridge.

In the mines near Emmanuel on ITO, the miners worked later than usual as the days were growing seasonally longer. Below ground near the second level tunnel, the cage was hoisting up the latest goats filled with ore, and as it moved up vertically in the main shaft, it scraped as usual against the shaft barrel.

In the cage holding the goat, Roison searched the faces in the facing tunnel. She found her aunt, half-smiled, and received a jolting channeled thought in response. Her smile dissolved and she looked up and up at the head-frame and the light from above and waited for them to hit the surface. She swallowed and swallowed again and counted the hours left before the day was over. And she waited.

Once the cage hit the surface and the shaft collar, the cage stopped and the crew on board manhandled the three goats out on the collar floor and maneuvered them to line up the wheels beneath onto the tracks and pushed them down to the trolley cart.

Turning as the surface crew took over the goats and their precious cargo of ore, they moved over laterally to again manhandle three empty carts, or goats, back onto the cage and take the trip down again to the fourth level where the ore vein was especially thick. There, the room and pillar mining was going full tilt as there were over 490 hostage miners who were working the face cut that sloped so very gently down, and the ore was coming out easily. Pained by the underground heat and humidity, the miners were not the best at doing the various tasks but knew that should anyone not follow directions, the mine guards were quick to point out their mistakes with a needler to the leg. Falling on the rough uneven tunnel floor was tough enough, and almost every single miner had scrapes and lacerations from their own clumsiness. But adding a leg that suddenly gave out meant that many fell harder and even against the tunnel walls that were much rougher. Most had scrapes along their temples and a shift without a bloody scrape was a good one!

But hard as the work was, they knew, as did their captors, that every day ore must come out of the ground and their lives depended upon it. Few had resisted and they had simply disappeared from the miners' dorms. Still others had become sick, no one knowing why or how, and they too had disappeared. No one had ever gotten any type of answer to any queries about the missing miners from the captor guards. No one ever would, Roison knew ... and as one of the dozen or so Adepts in the group of hostages, she knew why. Not a single consciousness of any of the missing had she ever seen with her mind's eye after they disappeared, which she knew could mean only one thing.

Throwing off that memory, Roison pulled and tugged the final goat off the cage and somehow misaligned the goat wheels on the tracks and it jammed solid. Like an anchor, it held up the string of goats from being moved forward to connect with the trolley cart, and the rolling cart train stopped cold.

The guard was quickly on her and cursed as he reached for the needler at his hip, and Roison clenched both eyes shut as she froze and dove into his consciousness. A mess of thoughts and half-made wants drifted by, and she still moved down and within ... trying to interrupt the draw of his weapon ... trying to interrupt his instinct.

The guard shuddered and then kicked the goat. He slid his hand off the needler to put his back into trying to move the goat ahead on the tracks as Roison kept drilling down and down pushing the phrase "jammed wheels ... jammed wheels ... jammed wheels" over and over into the mind mess below. The guard heaved and heaved once more as the congested wheels began to turn, and the string of goats suddenly sprung into movement and chugged off toward the refinery.

Roison stood still, opening her eyes to peer at the guard.

He shook his head at her and just said, "Damn wheels must 'a jammed in the track ..." and smoothed his palms against his thighs as he slowly moved back to the edge of the shaft screen fence.

Roison exhaled slowly as she trailed the rest of the goat crew off the collar floor and over to the exit, knowing she'd just dodged a painful needling. She smiled a bit under her hand as she wiped the sweat off her nose. She knew that all the Adepts she had ever met would have been needled as they could see ... but not do what she had just done. She knew that she was different, and she wondered about what would happen to her when puberty came ...

She nodded at the guard who then checked off something on his wrist PDA, and she joined the lineup of other hostages while the cage returned below to gather more hostage miners at the end of the day. She waited and thought of the message her aunt, one of the only other Adepts who were held here in the same dorm barracks, had sent her in those few moments only hours ago.

Turning back into her barracks twenty minutes later, she mounted the stairs to the ground floor and moved down the narrow corridor to her room that she shared with her aunt ... who followed her in ten minutes later.

Roison's aunt held up a finger to her lips signaling silence, took up her meager toilet articles, and pointed down the hall to the communal washroom. Roison followed carrying her towel and toilet items. They were almost alone in the washroom's outer room and washed in side-by-side sinks scratching off as much dirt first with just hot water and then applying the soap and scrubbing the grime of the deep soot and even more mud down the drain.

Roison looked at the woman beside her and thought that she was—or at least had been once—a very pretty woman. Adepts who were always Issians, were generally shorter than most but Aunt Michelle stood almost six feet tall with wavy ash blonde hair and had a way of cocking her head to the side when she listened that made you feel that you were the most important thing in her life.

Roison tried hard to copy that head tilt, and since she was only eleven years old, she knew she had a way to go. If her mom were still alive, she knew she'd agree with her that Aunt Michelle was still pretty, but yes, the past few months here had taken a toll on her, as well as on Roison. Work was hard, mining much harder, and yet there was still something that she felt was more important than all of this.

Michelle turned to her and said only one word, "showers" and moved into the inner area of the washrooms. Stripping off the clothes to be dumped into the dirty bin followed by picking up a new jumpsuit, Roison moved into the shower stalls as quickly as she could. Therein, she felt the warming waters slowly knead her tired small body as the caked in sweat and dirt slowly dissolved and ran down the drain.

The quiet notice that her aunt had entered her consciousness was a start, but she continued to let the water drift down over her body.

She felt no sense of worry in her aunt's message and the resulting knowledge that

Michelle would be attempting to get some of the
hostage miners to stage a minor revolt on an
upcoming day. Roison would be expected to
help as much as she could by getting pre-
selected guards to wallow instead of reacting
with those needlers to get compliance from the
miners. Michelle would be approaching the
others and getting all of the Adept hostages to
help, but Roison would have the major job
when it was time to forge a way out. She would
need to help deflect the Adept who was the head
of the captor guards. This she knew would be no
easy task, and she hoped she could at least
provide enough of an inconvenience to the
Adept to allow the balance of the revolt to work.
She hoped. And she hoped again as the water
continued to wash away the sweat and stains of
the day's work...

#####

As the *Avalon* yawed to port, the Free
Channel nebula was still thick with its red and
orange dust clouds. The nebula, like most, was
simply a huge almost light-year thick wispy yet
sometimes thick fog of colored dust and haze.
While this was a supernova remnant, for a
reason unknown to man or alien, it seemed to
have extended two arms ... one out toward the
Duchy of d'Avigdor on one side and almost
opposite a second arm that pointed directly at

ITO.

And as usual, it was this ITO arm that the *Avalon* now turned into to use as an aid to staying hidden on its final leg down to the planet.

Rhys said, "True and slow, Helm," and received an "aye-aye" in response.

In less than an hour at the *Avalon's* TachyonDrive speed plus the extra overdrive, they were entering the atmosphere and moving down toward the surface.

At the top of the landing glide pillar, Rhys watched his helmsman carefully, not so much as the Bridge crewman was new at this, but that it was always a difficult task landing at the mine tarmac totally unassisted. It was extremely touchy due to having no port administration, landing controls, or beacons, and it required moving around the peaks of the tor that hung over the tarmac.

Hidden in the mountains outside of the capital Emmanuel, it was as if the mine was cloaked by the rock and scree of what nature put both around it and above it. One had to start almost half a mile off the vertical drop and then move laterally using the thrusters as the ship dropped and then spun under the highest tor in the range.

"Helm, we good?" Rhys queried, his voice betraying no emotion whatsoever.

"Aye, Captain, the spin is in 3 ... 2 ... 1 ... and we're laterally dropping now, Sir," the Helm lieutenant said. His hand holding the stick moved slowly to the right as his left hand danced over the throttle sliders. He nodded once ... then again ... and one more time finally.

"Sir, we're under and will be on the ground ... we're down, Sir," he said quietly, as his hands moved over the Helm console, shutting down sliders and toggles and buttons too.

"Acknowledged, Helm," Rhys said and slowly rose from the comm chair and made his way to the lift.

Minutes later, he strode down the boarding ramp to the tarmac that lay beside the mine and its accompanying barracks camp. Around him within the compound that held the mine, no other ships ever touched down here— this was a highly secure landing pad for one single ship only, the Avalon, the Pirate cruiser. A large watchtower stood at the gate into the mine areas of the compound, the guards within studying their landing.

Watching the off-loading of the shuffling line of new hostages just taken from a small passenger ship off Duos, the twin star system closest to the edge of the Barony, Rhys studied them carefully too. All appeared to be healthy and there were very few youngsters, he noted, as most were couples though there were a couple of groups too. They were herded and with the aftereffects of the stunners they'd just experienced, they were all quiet and reserved to a degree. He knew they were all still in shock, and he knew that orientation and learning how to mine would be even more of a shock.

"Needed though," he said to himself and moved away from the bottom of the ramp to the gate leading to the barracks camps.

"Sir," said the gate sentry, "this area is closed off—"

One of the Navy provost guards from the *Avalon* moved ahead to confront the sentry, his hand on the blaster at his side.

Rhys put his hand on the provost's forearm preventing him from drawing the deadly weapon.

"Sentry, I am here on the orders of the ... the person in charge—herself! I am here to check on one single hostage and this is to be on the QT as we do not want to alarm the hostages, which is why I'm here during their working shift."

The sentry fidgeted with his Sam Browne belt and began to answer.

"I would guess that I'd need your name, sentry, so that when I report back to the person in charge, I know who to blame for this stoppage of her desires," Rhys said softly.

"Come on, come on," the provost guard said, "you're holding up our business, sentry!" he whispered forcefully.

The sentry was already nodding before the dressing down by the provost.

"Sir, yes, Sir!" he cried out as he pressed the keys that opened up the gate and stepped aside.

"It's just without uniforms, Sir, I have no idea whom is who, and your ship is unmarked, and we learned that it's not even in the RIM dBase either so ... my apologies, Sir!" he said with some frustration.

"Corporal," he barked out, "accompany this detail and clear their way for whatever they want to do or wherever they want to go. No hindrances or obstructions, complete access to anything within the compound," he finished off.

"Sir, yes, Sir," the corporal said and fell in behind Rhys who had just walked through the gate and strode ahead to barracks number seven.

As they walked down the graveled pathway, their boots crunched the stones in unison, and that sound resonated then echoed back when they passed the alleys that lay between the barracks. Above them the sun glinted off the side of the tor that shadowed the mine compound, rock crystals reflected back at almost every ledge or rock face, shiningly bright today. They marched slowly but made good time as they came up on the barracks with the big number seven on the sign above the door.

"Wait here," Rhys said as he mounted the steps up toward the barracks front door.

"Sir, I was ordered to accompany you—" the corporal said but was cut off by the provost guard.

"Ten-Shun!"

The corporal stiffened quickly and stood ramrod straight as Rhys moved through the door and down the main floor corridor. He looked into a few rooms and saw evidence that they were being lived in, messy bed clothes with few meager toilet articles on the single shelf on the wall. Room after room was taken. Rhys noted the numbering system and climbed the stairs at the far end of the corridor.

Moving directly to room number 211, he stopped at the open door and then stepped inside.

The thin mattress was doubled over on both beds, and the shelf was empty of anything at all. The tiny window had no towel draped over it either. The room as Rhys could see was un-occupied. No one lived in 211. That was pretty obvious, he realized as his shoulders slumped.

Coming down the front stairs, Rhys moved around the still frozen corporal and back toward the barracks gate.

"Dismissed, Corporal" he mumbled, and followed by his provost guard, he made his way over to the compound offices to enter his recent mission report.

No one, he thought, not a sign of anyone at all...

#####

Aboard the *CS Valiant*, the mutineers had made their way in the past day through the Free Channel nebula by following the standard protocols for traversing the nebula. While none on board had ever been through a nebula before, they allowed the ship's computer to aid them with navigation, and the TachyonDrive powered them through, including the turn hard-a-starboard to move toward ITO.

Moving out of the screen that was this cloud of gas and dust, so orange colored for the past few hours, Cadet Ensign Radisson felt the pressure of such a blind trek as a part of their movement toward ITO with calm elation.

"Nicely done, Helm," he congratulated Jorgenson, his Helm officer and smiled.

Jorgenson smiled back and moments later he replied.

"Sir, nav computer says we're spot-on for the course. We're already hours away from bypassing Landers Station and will approach

the mine within about five hours, Nick—er, Sir,
I mean."

Radisson ignored the lapse into
familiarity and nodded.

"Aye, Helm ... stay on course but lay in
that avoidance algo so we can avoid trouble if
possible."

"Ansible, if and when Landers Station
hails us, I want to know soonest— copy that?"
he said and half-turned to his left and the
Ansible officer.

"Aye, Sir, roger that," Ensign Smith
replied and looked over at Jorgenson with a bit
of a pooh-pooh look. Jorgenson just shook his
head and continued to monitor their course.

Ahead on the bridge view-screen, the
planet ITO was dead center, and while still only
a bright dot, it was their target.

Hours passed with normal to and fro that
happens on any starship, except due to the
limited crew, there were no replacements for
the Bridge crew. They labored on, and as ITO
grew, they watched the sidebar up on the view-
screen for any indication that Landers Station
was on this side of the planet.

After peering at the view-screen for over
an hour, the soft gong of the mass detector rang
the three times it was supposed to as the station
hit their sensors.

"Action, Helm ... engage the algo,"

Radisson said harshly and the Helm officer's hands flew on his console.

While it wasn't really there, the Bridge crew slightly appeared to lean to the left as the view-screen suddenly swung hard-a-port as the ship veered off and away from the station.

Almost all eyes were on the view-screen and sidebar, but Radisson was watching his Ansible officer ... waiting to hear that they'd been detected by the station and the Barony.

All was quiet for more than an hour as the Valiant veered off and back out of sensor range ... then veered again to sneak by the station well to port. They all studied that sidebar but it failed to show any indication that they'd been detected. They had slipped by and all breathed a sigh of relief.

"Right, Helm ... candle out and let's see where we are," Radisson said, as they were now close enough to kill the TachyonDrive and go to impulse power to land.

The slide back out of light-speed was quick, and the planet lay below, as the Helm acknowledged same.

"Helm, enter those co-ords, and let's see where we're going," Radisson said, as ITO now filled a major portion of the view-screen. One could hardly see the blue of their seas and the huge landmass of the major continent. It was unlucky that they'd found that side of the world well after nightfall, though the terminator could be seen slowly moving across the globe below with dawn a few hours away.

The squawking of the Helm console sounded, and Radisson awaited the course information from the Helm.

"Sir, it appears that we're about 1800 miles off, but it's nighttime, so we may be landing before dawn ... or just after," Jorgenson said.

That quieted the Bridge as each of them realized they'd not as yet done that kind of a landing before, especially down to a tarmac they'd never even seen. Swallows happened in more than a few of the throats on the Bridge, but they all knew they were committed to landing here.

"Right, Helm ... move us then down to the mine compound, and let's do that at regular impulse, shall we?" Radisson said, figuring that if they could just get the *Valiant* down soonest that'd be the best for all. Best bet, he thought as the ship moved off laterally to starboard and down, down, down to the surface.

Less than an hour later, they were only a few thousand feet above a range of twisted and bent mountains with huge passes, cols, tors, and shelves that stretched for what appeared to be miles.

"More contrast on screen please,

Tactical," Radisson said, and as Frasier complied, the view-screen view got a little clearer. Higher up there were wisps of clouds, but as they watched below, the wisps were gathering into fog and it grew thicker quickly, obscuring vision even more.

These were new mountains, and as such they were as raw as raw could be ... and it was here that the Helm nav console directed them until it gonged three times to signify the co-ords had been reached.

Radisson studied the view-screen.

"Okay ... anyone see anything down there?" he queried quietly.

All eyes once continued to study the screen and a few heads shook from side to side..

"Negative, Sir, plus visibility is now down to less than a few hundred yards," said Frasier over on Tactical to the right of the Comm.

"I see nothing but scree and valley, not a single bit of civilization. But I do see that dusk is about upon us, and that fog is getting thicker too ..." he said.

"Right, Helm, lock her for landing protocols, and let's set her down," Radisson commanded and watched Jorgenson's hands fly over his console.

"Permission to land, Sir?" he said.

"Granted, Helm—take her straight down spot-on those co-ords ..."

As the ship rotated into vertical and began to drop down, the view-screen showed below that there was just a darkening fog ... there was nothing else.

The *Valiant* moved down, directly on the co-ords, as the Bridge grew anxious as less could be seen by anyone. They slammed into the tor that hid the mine compound, and the ship listed hard to starboard.

Klaxons rang wildly as the Bridge crew struggled to recover. Frasier had to re-take his seat as he'd been thrown against the starboard Bridge wall. The view-screen showed only fog as they continued to speed up as they fell, the sidebar roiling with red scrolling warnings, repair bulletins, and hull impact messages. The ship listed off to starboard by about thirty degrees and slowly continued to move even more off vertical.

"Klaxons," screamed Radisson, "Helm, move her back to true vertical, stat!" He punched up the infrared filters on the view-screen, thinking he was late with this tactic.

"Ansible, EYES ONLY report to Captain Scott with co-ords and damage reports now!" he yelled as the view-screen suddenly popped with a solarized scene of the land below.

There was nothing but scree and more scree, and if they hit that even at gravitational speed, there'd be casualties, Radisson knew.

"Helm, move her out off the target below by at least a half-mile, and kill impulse and go to full thrusters," he added as the klaxons died off.

Jorgenson worked feverishly to right the ship and Smith pounded on his keyboard sending off that full EYES ONLY to Captain Scott. Radisson worked the view-screen controls to run an exterior view of the port side of the Valiant. There, he noted, was the issue as the now bent and twisted landing vane came into view. More than forty feet long, its butt end meant to sit directly on the tarmac at landing, it now jutted away from being straight by about twenty degrees, he figured.

"What the hell is with those co-ords?" he said to no one in particular but was answered by a yell from the Helm.

"Sir, look there ... over to port," Jorgenson cried, his hands still dancing on his console as the ship slowly began to work back to true vertical.

Below and off to the way they'd just moved away from was a dull red almost circular area that under infrared showed itself as a heat source or civilization with a single ship on the tarmac.

"Yup, hidden by the Goddamn shelf off that tor that we just hit ... bloody hell!" Radisson swore and shook his head.

"Right, Helm ... soon as you've got us upright, use thrusters to get us back up and over the top of it, and let's see if we can find a spot to set down," Radisson said as the ship came more and more vertically upright. Soon, they were moving horizontally toward the tarmac that lay off to the side but was swinging more under the Valiant as they watched. Fog here was thinner, Radisson noted, but he kept the view-screen on full infrared to stay in charge of their movements. In the eastern sky, a band of lighter coloration was creeping up of the distant mountain range.

Minutes later, they were still vertical but slowly moving horizontally above the flat tarmac that glowed slightly red from the infused sunlight it had sat under all day. That ship was slightly redder than that, but as it was sealed off, there were no hot-spots that they could see.

Still brighter red camp buildings lay off to one side as did the glowing red of the mine, its headstock hot with the huge generators and motors controlling the elevators and air circulation machinery too.

"Anyone see anyone down there?" Radisson said.

"There appear to be guards in those watchtowers, a small group of guards around that ship, and isn't that a patrolling vehicle out there too," Frasier answered.

310

Everyone seemed to nod.

"Right, so with that landing vane now out of true, we're gonna be ditching her right here. Agreed? Or ...?" Radisson noted.

Again all the heads nodded.

"Right then, Helm set her down on her belly, bridge up, and let's see who is home."

Jorgenson's hands flew again on his console as the ship moved to full horizontal from vertical, ensuring that the Bridge was on the top side. He moved gently now on the stick with his hand dancing on the sliders, and the *Valiant* slowly moved on thrusters and did a single loop of the small tarmac and settled down with a thunderous clang, that landing vane beneath the ship.

Moments later as the shutdown protocols were being followed, Radisson had the Ansible officer send one more EYES ONLY off to let them know what had happened. More moments later, the Bridge was shut down, and they sat and waited for whatever would come next. Something would, they knew, and soon as dawn began to break on ITO.

In the ship that was already down sitting on the tarmac before the *Valiant* arrived, Lady St. August leaned over to her Ansible officer on the Bridge and said simply, "send it now," and she leaned back in her chair to wait again.

The message arrived up at Landers Station in moments and was not read but immediately sent to the administration console marked EYES ONLY. Station Commander Cooper read it at once and, he cursed and leapt to the Ansible himself, pushing the officer who had been sitting there aside. His head bobbed as he spoke forcefully into his throat mic, and his stubby fingers stabbed the keyboard with regular rhythm and energy. He quit the Ansible station and moved back to his administration area but couldn't sit. There'd be hell to pay if they couldn't solve this before news traveled back to the Baroness. That's for sure, he thought as he hit SEND with finality.

Staring at the screen for less than a minute, he nodded as the RECEIVED button lit up. Done.

Chapter Eleven

Marching down the green corridor of Landers Station toward the commander's office, Tanner was purposely loudly clanging his boots on the steel floor. Behind him were his XO and Lieutenant Sander who seemed to be glancing side to side at the bare walls but didn't miss a cadenced step.

Ahead at the corner where the corridor veered off to the right, they spun in perfect drill order and moved the last few feet to the Barony guard who was at the administrator's office door.

"Sir?" the guard stated, "your business here?"

He stared straight ahead, Tanner noted, not looking anyone in the eye.

"Captain Scott, RIM Navy to see the station commander, stat!" his XO barked out. He leaned forward to show just how much time was an issue to the guard.

"Sir, yes, Sir" the guard said, "but the station commander is in quarters. Shall I call him, Sir?"

"That'd be a nice thing, Sergeant. Do that for us, would you?" Tanner said dryly. "We'll just wait ..."

313

The guard saluted and whirled to march down the corridor going somewhere, but not apparently willing to divulge that information. The three Navy officers stood and waited. And waited some more.

Tanner wished for drink. Any drink. Just a single shot to help him over the next few minutes. He was still thinking on whether or not a single one would do and wishing he'd had more than that double before leaving his ready room just moments ago when Station Commander Cooper rounded the near corridor and came ambling down the hall.

"Come in, Captain" he said as he palmed the lock-plate screen and waited as the door to the offices slid open.

"Early a bit, is it not, Captain?" he said as he reached for the pot of coffee and poured himself a cup, while the three Navy officers pulled up chairs to sit in front of the desk.

Tanner nodded.

"Yes, we're early but we're on Navy business, Commander. We are here to advise you under the RIM Navy Regs, Section 43 (G) that we're going down to ITO as we are in pursuit of the *CS Valiant* and its mutineers. This is a mere formality but we were ordered to do this in person."

The station commander stared at them one by one and then turned to the captain in front of him.

"You realize that the Natrium Flu is still rampant below, and as such, no one is allowed to break quarantine, Captain? And these RIM health statutes surpass any Section (G) Reg, acknowledged?" the commander said as he sipped his coffee.

Tanner shook his head.

"Under most circumstances, but not this one, as we are in hot pursuit of these mutineers, and RIM law is quite clear on that," Tanner said, his voice low. He watched the commander carefully as the man leaned back and sipped again.

"Docking here at Landers Station, shuttling over, and then waiting for me to get into work is hardly what anyone would call 'hot pursuit,'" he answered.

"Do you even know where these mutineers are, Captain?" the commander asked, his coffee halfway to his mouth but now frozen in mid-movement to his face.

Tanner shook his head.

"Not a clue, but we do know the Ansible registration on the *Valiant*, so we'll begin with that and search grid-wise for that signature."

Over on the bookshelf that stood near the desk, an old-fashioned clock chimed for a few times. There was no other noise within the office for a full minute or more. The surroundings were, if one even cared to notice, what one might call "retro" though to Tanner's eyes, plain out-of-date would be a bit more accurate.

"Right, you've been notified," Tanner said, rose quickly, and flashed a salute to the commander still seated behind his desk.

"I will file a Notice of Objection on this, Captain, and it will be on the Baroness's desk before you leave the dock."

"Of course you will, Commander, and yet we're still going down to get those mutineers— that's what the RIM Navy is all about."

They turned and strode out of the offices and moved toward the lift back to the dock where the Marwick lay.

"Did anyone else think it odd," the XO said, "that that coffee was hot and freshly made before we arrived?"

Tanner nodded.

"Not that we were offered any," he commented as they continued down on the lift.

Moments later, the EYES ONLY went out from the station Ansible to Neres and another to the *Avalon* and Rhys, who was less than a half-day out and who Cooper knew would return with a vengeance.

Hot pursuit indeed ...

#####

As they lined up to go to the mess hall, the hostages were haphazardly leaving their barracks in twos and threes. The sky was just lit by the new dawn, and there were still bars of reddish and pink sky immediately to the east behind the mountain range. With more than 500 hostages, it usually took a while to get organized and then have them trooped off to eat their skimpy breakfast.

Not that it's really even good for building up the needed strength, Roison thought as she filled the spot in line directly behind her aunt. She peered about for a second and then used her Adept sweep to see that she was not being watched all that closely and sent a familiar sentiment and smile to Michelle. Her aunt pushed a hand behind her back and crossed her fingers. Today they had roles to play ...

Marching, or what might be called that, was not a skill that many of the hostages had—after all they were far from military personnel in their other life. It was more of a walk in semi-straight lines toward the large hall at the end of the row of barracks. Beneath their feet, the gravel pathway crunched under foot as they moved slowly forward to enter the hall up the few front steps.

Inside, the leading hostages picked up their trays and cutlery and moved toward the cafeteria-styled service line. The food they were served was generally tasteless, bland, and in small portions as it was dished out by the staff in their white uniforms, and today was no different.

Finding a seat as usual beside her aunt, Roison moved over the bench and sat down. Her porridge and Garnuthian fruit were quickly devoured as she knew she had to eat as there was no guarantee that they'd eat this evening. Her glances around the hall showed not a thing out of the ordinary, all were eating and the couple of guards were chatting over against the far wall. Not a thing was out of place.

At the head-frame on the collar, they waited to go down last as usual in the cage to level two. The hostages who were the miners all went down first and began to hack away at the ore, and it was tossed and shoveled and thrown into a nearby goat that the level goat crews moved back to the main shaft, leaving a full one and taking an empty goat face-down the tunnel to the ore face.

Moving slowly, the cage took Roison and her crew of three others down to the bottom level where the miners had been at work the longest. Moving the full goats onto the cage was hard work; she sweated even now in the cool morning breezes. The four goats filled up the cage with the crew of four and they were moving back up the shaft passing other tunnels and up to the surface.

Unloading meant manhandling those goats off the cage and into the tracks leading to the cart hookup to the powered engine that would pull the line of goats to the far refinery.

Roison winced as her finger got pinched when a block of ore slid down the inner edge of the goat and the resulting blood blister swelled immediately. She nursed it with her lips and sucked on the finger as it began to sting. Shaking her head, she reminded herself for the hundredth time since she'd been moving goats around to never ever stick her fingers over the top edge where the ore lay. And once more she returned to the cage to take the trip down to the next tunnel. Down, then up, down, and then up, again and again.

By almost midday with the ITO sun now almost directly overhead, Roison was tired, and sweat slid down her back as she again pushed the goat, worrying it back and forth to get the wheels to engage with the rails just below. The guard who usually worked the top of the shaft on the collar stood and watched. Roison never asked for help as she knew that'd get her a needle blast to her leg. Finally the goat wheels engaged the rails, and she was able to easily push it along at the end of the lineup.

The mental blast from her aunt caught her by surprise, but she knew not to react to the simple phrase "next trip up," and she sent back a plain head nod. So it begins, she thought.

This trip was down only to tunnel number three, so the cage was loaded and up it began to move until it reached an area just a few hundred feet above tunnel number two. When they hit that spot, Roison concentrated and put all her mind to making a fuse way, way up in the head-frame mechanical room blow—and blow it did with a huge bang.

The cage shuddered and then fell about fifteen feet until the fail-safes kicked in and locked the cage to the I-beam frames that surrounded the shaft. An alarm bell began to clang and from above came some shouting, but as the cage was down at least 500 feet from the surface, Roison could not make out anything that was yelled.

She moved to a near corner of the cage and sat with her back wedged into the V behind her. Nursing her now broken, seeping blood blister with her mouth, she knew that her job was done for now.

She knew that someone would eventually think of the bank of fuses in the mechanical room way above and replace the one she'd just blown.

One of the other crew members, the one named Pamela, walked over to her and said, "So ... any ideas on what happened?" and then smiled at her.

"Not a clue," Roison said.

"You sure you didn't maybe do this? 'Cause if you did and they find out ... remember, there's four of us on this crew," Pamela said with a note of derision in her voice.

"All I can say is that if I were you, I'd find a safe spot to sit and hang on," Roison said.

"Uh ... thanks, I think," Pamela said with a hint of mockery in her voice. But she moved away from Roison and parked herself in the farthest away corner. The other two crew members were new to Roison, but after watching that exchange, they said nothing and soon each of the four cage corners had a hostage wedged in and holding on for what only one of them knew was coming.

Must be a lack of techies around, Roison thought as she waited like the rest of the hostages. They would need to do a diagnostic, she figured, and then think about fuses. How long that should take she didn't know, but the timing was pretty important and the cage did not move a bit.

But more importantly, as she and her aunt had learned via the Master Adept just days earlier, the hostages were now safe. They were locked in the mines away from guards and harm could not befall them. The mine was a prison but one that would keep them safe until help came. Roison hoped that'd be soon ... but as long as she could hold the cage right there, they'd all be safe.

#####

Aboard the *Avalon*, Rhys sat in his darkened ready room, reading the EYES ONLY that the Landers Station commander had just sent. The orange type on the black background was made to be read easily, yet he read it over and then again. The solid block of orange marked the cursor down at the bottom, and it flashed over and over awaiting input.

He slammed his knotted fist down on the desktop, and the keyboard jumped and came down with a clatter.

"Hot pursuit is not even close," he swore and the keyboard jumped again.

He reread the short message as he leaned back, and while he stared out the view-port on his left, his forefinger stabbed the BACK key and the previous EYES ONLY replaced the station commander's message.

She had been blunt and the tone was an order that she expected him to simply follow. No questions. No equivocation. No thinking— just follow her orders.

He watched as the upcoming edge of an arm of the Free Channel nebula appeared as they were moving back to ITO which was now less than two hours away. They soon were passing through this orange and pink cloud and then only a single hour more to reach the planet. Then drop down to the mine. And do her bidding.

A sharp rap on his ready room door broke his reverie.

"Enter," he said.

His Adept Lieutenant Coriander entered and came to attention, saluting her captain, and he saluted her back.

"Sir, thought you should know stat—that the mine is currently closed down due to equipment malfunction—we just got a message up from the admin there—seems something is affecting the cage, and the mine is full of our hostage miners until repairs can be made to bring them all up, Sir," she spit out in one long sentence, standing at attention.

"Fine, Lieutenant. Noted. Keep her at max impulse as usual and go to light-speed when we clear the arm," he said flatly.

"Aye, Captain," she said.

He nodded and dismissed her and watched as she spun on her heels and filed out of the room and back to the Bridge.

It was over and tomorrow the *Avalon* and the crew would be back to being Barony Navy regulars.

It was the end of the Pirates, and of

course, by default, the end of the need for the mine.

This meant that it was also the end of the need for hostages, and that was the cleanup duty that he was ordered to handle.

At least it appeared that a simple mine cave-in would be easy to arrange and not only end the problem of what to do with the hostages now that the Pirates were finished. Buried in the mine was the best way. Simplest. And with the plasma cannon on the Avalon as the weapon of choice, this whole Pirate sojourn could be forgotten.

The orange cursor block still pulsed on the screen, and he stabbed the Acknowledge key. He knew the Baroness would receive his compliance with her orders in minutes.

Rhys stood to stand in front of the viewport and watched as the swirls of ocher and red flitted by, sometimes opening up to show an occasional star or two. For a few moments, the port would be solid dusty colors of pink or orange and that would thin as this arm was right on the edge of the nebula.

He stood and watched as the port slowly cleared and dead ahead lay ITO. And the end of the hostages.

#####
Uh ... Ma'am, can I help you?"

The Barony guard at the mine's compound gate was nervous. He had never even seen a Royal before in real life and in front of him stood Lady St. August.

"Open up, Guard," she said and waved her arm up to show that she wished the gate to be raised.

Behind her stood one of those Adepts, the corporal could see, and a phalanx of about fifty dozen Elite Guards, their blue boots now dirty from the soil covering the edge of the landing tarmac. They had all just marched over from those two frigates that sat on the landing field a hundred yards away.

"Uh ... Ma'am, I am sorry, but no one is allowed within the compound. Orders are no one, Ma'am," he said, his voice cracking just a bit.

"But Guard, you know who I am. I am a member of the Royal family—no rules apply to me or anyone with me, correct? Is that not a part of your training?" she said quietly.

He nodded. He could do no more than that.

"Should I call the guard captain, Ma'am?" he said.

She simply moved her arm up again and waited.

You could see the mental anguish in the young guard's mind and the churning of his training versus his orders. And the training must have won out as he stabbed the buttons in front of him and the gate began to swing up to allow the visitors into the compound.

Moving ahead of the Lady and her Adept, the squad of Elite Guards broke into a trot and moved out sharply into the compound. Some peeled off toward the administration building, but the rest continued on to the top of the mining shaft. There, two climbed the headstock tower of the mining cage and quickly replaced the blown fuse, and the cage began to climb the shaft once more.

Another squad of Elite Guards left the *Sterling* and trotted over to help round up the hostages and manage the movement of the hostages back to the *Sterling* and the Valiant. Together, they'd be transporting the newly freed hostages over to Juno and their freedom.

"Barony Guards, Ma'am?" the Elite Guard asked.

She shrugged.

"They work for the Baroness. They can stay here for all I care, as I don't think they knew much more than to guard the hostages. She can look after them. It's not my job."

She looked at Gillian, her Adept, and raised an eyebrow and got a simple nod in response. She nodded back.

"Have Cadet Radisson Ansible back to

Juno that we're on our way within the hour. And have our Ansible officer radio Eons with the same message."

A scant fifty minutes later, the *Valiant* and the *Sterling* lifted off of ITO and went to FTL within a few minutes more, the rescue of the hostages complete.

#####

Lieutenant JG Whiteside poured a coffee for the captain and softly walked it over to the Comm chair.

"Sir ..." he half-whispered, "Sir, here's that coffee."

Tanner nodded and tilted his head to the arm of the chair for his bull ensign to simply set it down, acknowledging the kindness, but his eyes never left the Bridge view-screen and the edge of the lateral arm of the Free Channel nebula.

The *Marwick* lay in wait, at almost the very edge of the nebula arm that pointed to ITO, hidden in a large swirling cloud of dust here that was especially thick.

They had been here, on station, for over two hours waiting for the Pirates to appear and as such were at battle stations but also in quiet mode—everything was shut down but life support and sensors.

"Helm, confirm the candle is ready,"

Tanner asked his Helm officer, Lieutenant Framingham, and received an "aye" in return.

"Ansible, confirm we're monitoring any registrations within our range," he asked his Ansible officer Lieutenant Bates and received another "aye" reply.

"XO, we good on tactical?" he asked as he spun slightly to his right.

Commander Templeton, the XO, nodded back as he checked his console.

"All weapons up and fully charged, Captain. Pulse cannons fore and aft set; lateral lasers set and plasma on standby," he rhymed off and Tanner nodded back.

"We're ready but where are they?" the bull ensign said with a note of exasperation almost.

A minute passed and then some minutes more.

Tanner sipped his coffee wishing that he could take the mug into his ready room for a bit of sprucing up. *If this takes much longer, I'll need that for sure. Just a double maybe—*

Klaxons screamed and it broke the tension. Just moving through the off-side end of the nebula arm, the *Avalon* appeared less than 20,000 miles away.

Roaring to the Helm to get on the intercept vector, Tanner punched in the captain's code into his Comm console, and the ship's shields jumped to life with their blue glow tinging the view-screen.

The *Marwick* jumped out of the orange cloud and into free space at max impulse, the engines pulsing with a huge surge of power.

"Ansible reporting, Sir—they know we're here, and they're going to light-speed ..." Bates said, his eyes closed as he tuned out the chaos around him to listen to the communications traffic.

"Helm, go to light-speed," Tanner bellowed as the Avalon disappeared and seconds later they disappeared too.

"Ansible—messages?" Tanner queried.

"Moments ago, we got the confirmations from both the *Valiant* and the Lady St. August's frigate, the *Sterling* ... their cargo loaded and on their way back to Juno—they just went to FTL!"

The view-screen showed the mass of the planet just ahead, but of course, there was no sign of the Avalon as the TachyonDrive hid all ships. The next few minutes were chaotic. At least we're on their trail, Tanner thought ... as ITO grew and grew.

"Helm ... douse the candle at the last possible moment," Tanner said.

As ITO filled the view-screen, they all watched as Lieutenant Framingham held his finger directly over the button, and then he punched it and they dropped out of light-speed.

Ahead at the edge of the atmosphere, the *Avalon* was pitching to start its descent.

"Tactical, fire both forward pulse cannons," Tanner yelled, and his XO stabbed the trigger buttons and the *Marwick* rocked to port.

Before them as the *Avalon* continued to pitch to vertical, the twin balls of pulse energy caught the Pirate ship partway through that turn. Her shields held so no damage was apparent, but the shock waves of the double hit pushed her to pitch more wildly than what they had planned.

Waiting for answering fire made the Bridge go quiet. But there was none. The *Avalon* was running not fighting, it appeared.

The *Avalon* fell almost under full gravity pull, the shields glowing as she dropped at thousands of feet per second, with the Marwick right on her tail.

As the land mass below came into focus on the view-screen, Tanner could see mountains and small valleys only … a mass of rock and green.

"Infrared," he barked at Tactical, and the view-screen showed heat signatures from those same mountains but still no sign of any mine.

"Stay on her tail," Tanner barked, hoping that there was no reason for the Pirates to run instead of turning to fight. He thought on that for a full second.

"Sir, the *Avalon* is charging her forward pulse cannons—both, Sir," his XO said quietly. While that did take a full thirty seconds, what it meant was that the Pirates had a target ahead of them—not behind them like where the *Marwick* was still chasing them.

Tanner knew it wouldn't be the *Valiant*, as that was a target the Pirates could care less about. He doubted too that they would aim at the *Sterling* as the Lady St. August was nothing more than a bureaucrat—no, those pulse cannon blasts were meant for the mine and the hostages within.

"Helm, on my mark, light the candle but just enough to go past them and interrupt that coming pulse—"

"Sir," the XO interrupted the interruption coming from the helm, "we can't do that—we're in the upper atmosphere ..."

At the Helm, Lieutenant Framingham's fingers punched in the co-ordinates into the ship's computer, and then that left hand danced over sliders and toggles, and he looked at the captain, smiling.

He nodded to his captain.

"Sir," the XO still protested, "we're plainly too close so the timing would need to be on the order of three or so microseconds of candle—I don't think the TachyonDrive can be that precise."

Tanner nodded to the Helm.

"Helm—now!" he yelled, and in the front view-screen, the world below suddenly jumped as they warped past the *Avalon*. The pulse cannon blasts hit the *Marwick* in the stern, and while the shields held, the klaxons started to scream again. She lurched sideways by half her beam and shuddered as the TachyonDrive quit so suddenly.

"XO, damn those klaxons—fire!" Tanner shouted above the chaos.

The resulting blast to their rear, directly into the path of the *Avalon*, caught her without the forward shields being on as all her power was still holding her rear shields as powered as possible since that was where the enemy was— or rather had been.

The cannon blasts carved into the decks around the top tier of decks where the Bridge and most command and Bridge crew were.

Somehow, one of the blasts had caught the logistic bio-cables that connected the Bridge to engineering, it appeared, and the *Avalon* and the ship yawed hard to port. Even badly damaged, they returned fire immediately, and the rear shields of the *Marwick* dropped again by more than forty percent, and one more such blast would disable their rear shields and make them vulnerable to another pulse cannon blast.

"Helm, altitude?" Tanner asked quickly.

"Uh ... Sir, we're up at about 40,000 feet, Sir—say eight miles, but why?" Framingham asked back, wondering what the hell the altitude would have to do with anything.

Tanner smiled; he'd been in somewhat similar circumstances once before in the atmosphere of a planet in the Earldom ... it might be worth a try.

"Tactical, right after the next pulse cannon foray, lay a barrage of our magnetic mines into the course to port and starboard—but set the closing distance to full extension; turn on our forward shields and push them out to max, and Helm—a burst of max impulse but stay right above those co-ordinates!"

The XO looked at his captain with a look that said, "pardon?"

Tanner just shook his head as their rear shields took another pulse cannon blast, and the sidebar up front on the view-screen abruptly went full red on the rear icon of the ship.

"Sir," Framingham said from the Helm, "shields are down, and they'll fire again in twenty-eight seconds."

As the two ships dropped in tandem, the *Marwick* in the lead pulled slightly ahead to lead by a mile or so. Behind them, the *Avalon* was charging her forward pulse cannon to finish off the *Marwick* as they both flew toward the surface.

At less than seven miles, the atmosphere around the diving ships thickened, and then by five miles, it was noticeable as a whine that sounded like it was tearing apart the various arrays and ship's fins and weapons ports.

But the atmosphere did something else too, especially to falling unpowered objects like mines. Pushing through the full spread of those mines that were smaller than a few yards across was easy for the *Marwick* as she was the first ship in the lineup of two and under power. But that passage, the movement itself through the thickening atmosphere, meant that the motion first pushed the mines aside, but then the mines drifted in behind the *Marwick*.

As they were unpowered, they followed and floated and congealed in the exact path of the *Marwick* whose engines pushed them further back and then back directly into the path of the *Avalon*.

The mines attached themselves to the Avalon hull by the dozens, and they started their countdown.

"Sir," the XO said, "contact in T-minus five seconds."

"Helm," Tanner bellowed, "hard port, full impulse burst, and get us the hell out of here."

Every Bridge crew member swayed in

their seats as the *Marwick* went left hard, and they cursed as the Helm powered up to full impulse.

Behind them the *Avalon* continued still down toward the surface for a few seconds, and then the flash and shock-waves that carried through the atmosphere pushed the *Marwick* to port even more.

The fireball that started to flare off the *Avalon*'s port side appeared first and then blossomed to include what looked like the Bridge ignited too.

Turning away from straight down, the *Avalon* rode a course that drifted a mile or so to starboard of the tor that lay below, flaming now from many hull breach holes that the mines had blown and then drifted back again. Obviously not under Helm control, the *Avalon* drifted back toward the tarmac and compound below ... and then struck the area with vengeance.

As the ship exploded, the *Marwick* was moved hard to port as the shock-wave took her and shook her. The Perseus engine on the *Avalon* blew less than a second later, and the cloud that arose was a huge, black, roiling, thunderous mass of flame-driven gasses. That sent another shock-wave out across the valley and again up the few thousand feet to the *Marwick*.

"Helm," Tanner said, "let's get down

there and set-up rescue duty. XO, shut down Tactical and take charge of the first responders, and if there's any way, get any survivors into Sick Bay."

Tanner continued to watch the fire that now seemed to be a thousand feet tall, black smoke billowing over the valley reaching up and up toward the peaks and tors above. He knew the compound area that he'd barely seen of barracks and buildings and the shafts of the mine were all gone as the crater would surely be almost a full mile across. The area shook almost like a wave on the ocean as the *Avalon* armory first imploded and then exploded at the same time. The ship was a loss, it appeared. While the hope was that someone in charge, someone from the Bridge, would be found alive and could stand trial for the crime of piracy, Tanner doubted anyone could survive that kind of a crash.

"Did you hear back, Ansible, from the *Valiant* or the *Sterling*?" Tanner asked, turning to the port side of the Bridge.

"Aye, Captain, both fully underway to Juno. Cadet Radisson reports that they're crowded but fine, and the hostages on board the *Valiant* seem to be mostly malnourished and dehydrated. Minor injuries and sprains mostly. Numbers on board are 274 men, women, and children."

"And the *Sterling* report?" Tanner asked.

"Sir, the *Sterling*—the Lady St. August's cruiser? She went to FTL and sent only that there are 492 hostages total and they're all under care. Uh ... in case you were interested, Sir—she didn't 'report' at all. This was relayed to us via the *Valiant*," Lieutenant Bates offered, his voice a bit hesitant.

"Whatever, Lieutenant, whatever. Royalty is as royalty does, son," Tanner answered. If he cared at all, he showed nothing to his Bridge crew as they put down as close as they dared to the still burning *Avalon*, klaxons screaming again as the ship's first responders got ready to help search for any surviving Pirates.

Chapter Twelve

The Lady St. August nursed her power drink in her gym aboard the *Sterling*, her trainer still shaking his head.

"Ma'am, a real part of any routine is just that—you need, as you know, to follow the same repetitions to gain muscle mass and lose caloric intake." He shook his head again as she just sat on the bench beside the incline track machine.

"While I understand the issues we've just faced, Ma'am, surely getting back into shape would be at the top of anyone's list. Ma'am. I mean, please, Ma'am," His muscular arms stretched out to her like a persuasive gesture.

This one, she thought, really is a single minded type-A trainer that even though they were only a day or two past the fireball on ITO, he wanted just for her to get back on the machines.

She took another large swig of the gingko and taurine salty mixture and swallowed noisily.

"Enough, Adam," she said, "Be back on the incline in a minute."

She swigged again and then sighed, got up, stepped into the foot mounts, and then pressed the monitoring button on the console to start this set of timed efforts.

The machine began to pulse and time her response to the walking steps up and then down and then up once more. She slowly got into the rhythm and ramped up her output to get into what the trainer was chanting was "her beat ... get the beat," and she did try.

Behind her she knew lay death and the loss of her step-mother's attempt to ... well ... to do whatever she wanted to do to gain some kind of advantage over the RIM and even its Council.

Down in the decks holding the cargo bays, the Sick Bay, and the extra crew bunk decks, the hostages were being treated, fed, cared for, and yes, each of them debriefed and made whole again. At least as good as we can for now, she thought.

The incline machine beeped now that she was hitting her maximum step and lifted her to the plus ten percent to test her resolve.

She bitched at the machine now ... sweat just beginning to course down the swell between her breasts. Her breathing got tougher, and she pushed out the exhales with abandon. Her blonde hair was already sweaty as it now fell in strands that clung to her neck, and she remembered how much she hated to stay trim.

Damn this Captain Scott, she repeated over and over to herself using the repetition to power her push downs on the machine. She felt happy—no satisfied—well, appreciative. She thought that Scott had come through for the best thing for the RIM. Perhaps not for the Barony as her step-mother still was in charge of the Barony and its nine worlds and billions of inhabitants.

But not the hostages anymore. And judging by the reports of the Pirate ship crashing into the mine compound and the death all around, no one would know. No one but her and this Captain Scott. And her step-mother.

All knelt to her, she thought, but not I.

She knew that even though the *Avalon* was gone, the crew as well as the truth must be held in close check for now, but not for long.

Her breathing came more and more spotty as her lungs clasped for air; she was hitting her all-out expenditure of energy, and the sweat now ran down her back and into her gym shorts. Right down in her shoes, the sweat was pooling in the toes, and her steps felt both wet and yet grippy.

"Scott," she said to herself, "we will meet again. This is not over, and with the power of the Barony, I will see that you heel. You will be mine." She nodded as the sweat still poured down her breasts.

"At ease, Captain," the admiral said with

an unexpected degree of force.

Tanner changed his stance from attention to at ease and half-smiled to himself; surely this can't be a bad post mortem. After all, things had changed dramatically in the past month or so with the end of the Pirate threats and the return of all the hostages.

"Sir, if you please, could we discuss the Pirates up front?" he asked, his voice only slightly off point.

McQueen nodded back.

"Yes, Captain, let's go through the list one by one."

Tanner nodded and waited for the admiral to begin.

"First, the Pirates. Destroyed, ship and every single crew member by yourself and the *Marwick*—but did I detect a note of a Kinross Navy upper atmosphere tactic?"

The Admiral almost smiled, Tanner assumed.

"Yes, Sir—the battle of Quaxo—in the upper atmosphere when the Franauts attacked those Kinross floating cities. At least that's what we faced back on ITO. Seemed like the use of those mines in the atmosphere might work again. And yes, they did. I was a bit surprised that atmospherical adherence worked so well on ITO."

Tanner swallowed once and then again.

The admiral knew that tactic well and had made sure all of the Kinross Navy captains knew about it too, even though it was a minor tactic this following of mines behind a powering body through the air.

The admiral sighed.

"Sit, Captain. First, I doubt if I were to ask why I was kept 'out' of the loop on this pseudo-mutiny that I'd get an answer that I would believe. Or think I needed. Or think it's rational. You have let me down, Captain, I would have thought that you would have taken me into your confidence," McQueen said, his voice dry as he simply stared at Tanner. "So, you should know that this is not a dressing down or at least it should not be considered as such," he said again, dryly.

Tanner knew that the admiral was upset but he also knew that there were almost 500 hostages that he'd managed to help liberate.

"So a new mission, Captain. As you may not know—in fact I only learned of this a few months back—the RIM Confederacy is bordered by other inward systems and the Pentyaan Republic among others. To police that border, we use our own boundary buoys, and yes, once every twenty or so years, they all need to be serviced, replaced, or repaired. That's your task, Captain, to do just that to half the buoys."

The admiral almost smiled.

"Report to Operations down a floor and get the mission specs and load parts and buoys over at the dry dock stores. Dismissed, Captain ..."

Tanner said nothing. There was nothing to say, so he just nodded to his admiral....

Epilogue...

Leaving Navy Hall, Tanner went directly to his favorite local bar for a few more of those Randi ales.

And the knowledge that a set of boundary buoys needed no immediate attention.

"'Nother one?" the bartender said.

"Yup, maybe even a double," Tanner said ... as the Scotch slid into his glass...

And maybe another one right after he thought as he hoisted the glass to his lips...

Book Two of the RIM Confederacy is due out in the fall of 2015...

Prologue...

At the very southern border of the RIM Confederacy the space ship *Keshowse* moved ahead and at its slow cruising speed, it could have been mis-identified as a comet. It expelled no exhaust or plasma or anti-matter shower of protons, it simply coasted along at its maximum speed as it unhurriedly went by the boundary buoy and began to enter the RIM Confederacy.

It was of a shape and design that one could see would never ever touch-down on a planet – it was meant for interstellar travel only. Arrays hung off the front of the ship and pods that held unknown equipment jutted out all along some of the sides in seemingly haphazard random fashion.

There were none of the usual armament ports or arrays that one would normally see for plasma cannons or laser weapon barrels or energy pulse lenses. The bridge was plain to see, set back from the front of the huge craft as it jutted up and spread out on the forward decking, its rounded view-ports facing ahead and abeam to port and starboard.

It was amidships that the strangeness of the ship was most apparent where there was a huge four-sided shell-like box that circled the ship's axis and ran for almost 1500 feet, populated with ports and lights that had no apparent purpose. Each of the sides had ports strung in 6 rows all across the length of the box and each was bright from interior lighting.

And the whole ship was huge at more than a half a mile long; it was truly a colossal ship bigger than any other that had ever entered the RIM.

At its speed of slightly more than 30,000

miles per second it was certainly the slowest of
intruders into RIM space as it flew too slow to
make any kind of a beep on any ships display
and that was a part of what was required by the
ships builders.

Still the RIM boundary buoy noted it
passing, and as its automatic plotting algorithm
mapped the course this RIM trespasser would
take. At its current speed and heading, it would
clear the RIM space with no collision issues in
240+ years, hardly worth worrying about, the
AI judged, as it was simply a fast moving comet
as its algorithm drew its own conclusions.

The AI then made that entry in its logs; it
then transcribed the message to be sent to the
RIM capital world Juno and the RIM Navy
network, and parked it in the buoys Ansible
queue where it waited to be sent.

It would wait forever though as the
Ansible arrays had been sheared off more than
a month earlier during a rogue meteor shower
that had come through the RIM space and the
few messages the buoy wanted to send,
continued to be all stacked up and never sent.

So Juno never learned of the incoming
alien ship that had just entered its space and
the intruder's entry year passed and then
another and another...the alien ship crawled
into RIM space until now four years later, it
neared Novertag, the planet in the system

sitting almost on that southern RIM boundary...

Find out more at
www.jimrudnick.ca and sign up
for notice of the launch date too!

www.ingramcontent.com/pod-product-compliance
Lightning Source LLC
Chambersburg PA
CBHW071044250626
47159CB00002B/364